After Jessica

&

Hitman Sam

two British crime novellas

Morgen Bailey

Dear Sally
lovely to meet you
Morge

After Jessica & Hitman Sam

two British crime novellas
by Morgen Bailey

After Jessica is a crime mystery novella
Hitman Sam is a crime lad lit novella

Total Word Count: c.85,000

These two novellas were written in:
2009 (After Jessica) and
2008 (Hitman Sam) but left to marinate
in a file, and brought out every couple of years
for an edit. They were finally edited and
sent to beta readers in 2016 when they were re-
edited and finally submitted for publication.

The stories are not connected other than being
novellas, similar genres, and by the same author.

Discover other titles by Morgen Bailey at
https://morgenbailey.wordpress.com/books-mine

including her chick lit Northampton novel
'The Serial Dater's Shopping List'.
Forthcoming novels will likely be crime too. She
just loves killing her characters too much!

***

Thank you for purchasing this book. If you enjoy it,
please encourage your friends to purchase their
own copy. Thank you for your support.

Contents

'After Jessica', a crime mystery novella   page 7
(c. 37,000 words)

Jessica is an ordinary girl who comes across extraordinary circumstances and pays for them with her life. As well as identifying her body, her brother Simon then has to wind up her affairs but gets more than he bargains for. Who is Alexis, and why are Veronica and Daniel searching for her? Why is there a roll of cash in Jessica's house, and what's the connection between Simon's sister and Alexis?

'Hitman Sam' a crime lad lit novella   page 179
(c. 47,000 words)

Having been made redundant as a photocopier software designer, Sam Simpson is lured by a cryptic advert. As he learns it is for a trainee hitman, will he be tough enough to see the job through? Even James Bond had to start somewhere and Sam, as his alias Josh Bradley, looks forward to enjoying James' lifestyle, although soon embroiled in a love triangle, Sam hadn't expected things to get so complicated so quickly.

About the Author   page 365

Note from the Author   page 366

After Jessica

a British crime

mystery novella

This book is dedicated to Moira,

the inspiration behind the story.

Table of Contents

Prologue: Andy   13
Chapter 1: Alexis   15
Chapter 2: Nate   17
Chapter 3: Daniel   19
Chapter 4: Jessica   21
Chapter 5: Andy   23
Chapter 6: Simon and the Police   25
Chapter 7: Simon and Marion   29
Chapter 8: Emily and Frank   33
Chapter 9: Simon and the Press   35
Chapter 10: Simon   37
Chapter 11: Simon and Marion   41
Chapter 12: Simon and the Police   43
Chapter 13: Beth and Nate   47
Chapter 14: Simon and Marion   53
Chapter 15: Marion   55
Chapter 16: Simon   59
Chapter 17: Beth and Nate   65
Chapter 18: Simon   69
Chapter 19: Simon and the Bank Manager   73
Chapter 20: Simon   77
Chapter 21: Beth and Nate   83
Chapter 22: Simon   89
Chapter 23: Simon and Veronica   91
Chapter 24: Beth and the Phone Calls   95
Chapter 25: Beth and the Neighbours   99
Chapter 26: Simon and Marion   105

Chapter 27: Simon and Marion   107

Chapter 28: Beth, Frank and Emily   111

Chapter 29: Daniel and Rick   117

Chapter 30: Andy   119

Chapter 31: Frank and Emily   121

Chapter 32: Veronica   123

Chapter 33: Rick   125

Chapter 34: Daniel and his Wife   127

Chapter 35: Tania and Rick   129

Chapter 36: Beth and Nate   131

Chapter 37: Marion and the Funeral   133

Chapter 38: The Funeral   137

Chapter 39: Rick   143

Chapter 40: Rick   147

Chapter 41: Simon   151

Chapter 42: Rick   153

Chapter 43: Simon and the Bank Manager   155

Chapter 44: Simon and Veronica   161

Chapter 45: Veronica and Rick   163

Chapter 46: Rick and Daniel   165

Chapter 47: Daniel and his Wife   167

Chapter 48: Beth and Nate   169

Chapter 49: Simon and Marion   171

Chapter 50: Simon and Marion   173

Chapter 51: Simon and Andy   175

Chapter 52: At the Solicitor's   177

Prologue: Andy

Andy slammed both hands on the emergency brake and the train jolted, slowing nowhere near as quickly as he was pleading it to do. He could hear shouting from the carriage behind him, but was too busy concentrating on what, or who, was in front of him to pay any attention. His first thought was another clueless animal, but as he got nearer, he realised it was a car and something inside it was moving.

As the two machines drew nearer, he could smell burning rubber and saw the smoke as the car's tyres made contact with the edges of the track. As he stared at the inevitable, he knew nothing he or the car driver did would be enough to avoid the impact.

He stared at the driver facing him. He could see her hands gripping the steering wheel. She'd screwed her eyes shut, seemingly knowing her fate, but he guessed by her right shoulder dancing forwards and backwards that she was still trying the pedals.

Then to his surprise, she stilled and opened her eyes, staring straight at him. When they were just a few feet apart, she mouthed something like "sorry" but he couldn't be sure. Sorry? Had she done this on purpose? But it wasn't quite sorry. Too quick. Andy shook his head. He didn't know what she'd said, and now he'd never know.

As metal hit metal, it was the highest pitch noise he had ever heard. Expecting the inevitable grinding sound, he remembered afterwards being shocked that it sounded like a beautiful violin. Of course, there was nothing beautiful about what had happened, but instead of being afraid, he was calm. As calm as the woman he'd been face-to-face with, the woman with green eyes.

He wasn't sure why he'd smiled and she'd done the same, before mouthing that one final word.

###

13

Chapter 1: Alexis

Swinging her legs slowly from under the pale Egyptian cotton sheets, Alexis turned to the man in the bed beside her and sighed. He was snoring as loudly as he had been within seconds of the end of their lovemaking. This wasn't how she'd planned her life, but she couldn't complain.

She slipped on her pink silk underwear then stepped into her simple black evening dress, running her right index finger under the straps to smooth them in place.

Turning back to the bed, she gazed at the still-sleeping figure. He gave a loud snort then rolled over to face the other side of the room. Although it was obvious that even a hurricane wouldn't wake him, she crept round the bed on the balls of her feet to his bedside table and picked up his wallet. It was loaded with cash and credit cards as well as a picture of his beautiful brunette wife and their two young children; a handsome trio.

Another trusting wife, Alexis thought before pulling out a bundle of fifty pound notes, leaving a solitary twenty. He'd paid her the night before; upfront as always, but she'd neglected to tell him he was to be her last, that she was retiring, sticking to her day job. It paid well enough to keep her afloat and thanks to the escort work, she'd put enough money by to cover more than one rainy day; a few hurricanes in fact.

She felt a pang of guilt as she put the cash in her purse, but he could afford it. He was a soft touch and would probably have given her the money if she'd asked, especially if he'd known it was to be the last time, but this way it was kept business-like. No emotions. She'd never been good at goodbyes and he'd have no doubt begged her to change her mind. This way, he'd be too angry, no, hurt, to want to deal with her again and she could draw a line under it. With her evenings free, she'd catch up on her sleep, maybe take an evening class… learn salsa or write the novel that kept knocking against the side of her brain, begging to be let out.

Grabbing her cashmere coat, she closed the door quietly and headed for the lift. Tapping the 'down' button with her immaculately painted, but false, red nails she hummed as she waited for the lift. Apart from an abandoned cleaner's trolley there was no sign of life on the top floor.

As the lift came to a smooth stop, a sophisticated lady's voice announced 'ground floor' and a single F-sharp ping indicated the opening of the heavy steel doors. Not looking towards the reception or in anyone's direction, Alexis strode to the chrome and glass revolving entrance doors and left the Cheshire Hotel.

Spotting a small round bin a few yards away, she dropped her mobile into the heap of sweet wrappers, drink cans and day-old newspapers, whispering, "No more hotels, no more tricks. This part of my life is over."

###

Chapter 2: Nate

As she walked away, baby-faced petty criminal Nate Morrison was pocketing his 'winnings' outside the pawnbrokers, and was in need of a new phone.

###

Chapter 3: Daniel

Daniel Goldstein yawned and stretched out his left arm half-
expecting to touch flesh, but felt only Egyptian cotton.
Sometimes, the girls would stay 'til morning but Alexis rarely
had and it looked like she'd not done so on this occasion
either.

After a quick shower and shave, he dressed, put on the
watch that had been lying on the bedside table, and stuffed
his Gucci wallet into the inside pocket of his Armani pinstripe
jacket. Packing his belongings, he took the lift from the
penthouse and carrying his small overnight case and suit bag,
headed to reception to settle his account.

Reading the receptionist's lapel badge, he bade Tania a
good morning and told her his room number to enable her to
bring up his details on her sliver-thin computer monitor.
Reading out the bill for dinner for two, mini-bar and suite
charges, Daniel pulled out his wallet, only then realising how
thin it felt. He pulled the back section open and found only a
single note.

"Shit!... Shit!"

"Is everything all right, sir?" Tania asked.

"Erm, yes, fine." Daniel said half-heartedly. He'd booked
Alexis numerous times and there'd never been any trouble
before. He stared at the row of credit cards and the solitary
twenty, frowning as he handed over the company platinum
card. He'd always paid cash; untraceable transactions, but
using this card was at least still keeping it away from home.
He'd need to be more careful next time.

Tania slotted the card into the payment handset and
Daniel typed in his four-digit code; his youngest child's
birthday, before pressing the green 'enter' key. The computer
beeped and Tania smiled at Daniel. "Thank you, Mr Goldstein,
that's gone through for you. I hope you enjoyed your stay, and
we do look forward to seeing you again."

As Daniel negotiated his two bags through the revolving
doors with his left hand, he selected the 'contacts' option on
his BlackBerry with his right, scrolling down three names until
Alexis' appeared, disguised as Alex Cheshire. Pressing the

green receiver symbol, he put the phone to his right ear and listened to it ring.

"Yes?" a man growled.

"Who's this?" Daniel asked.

"Who the fuck's this?" the other voice asked.

Ignoring the question, Daniel said coolly, "I need to speak to Alexis."

"You can't." And before Daniel could reply, the man continued, "Now fuck off." And the line went dead.

###

Chapter 4: Jessica

Pulling her front door shut, Jessica Price walked towards her car. Although still early morning, it had so far seemed like any other weekday.

Pressing the remote control button to unlock the blue Kia Picanto, she cursed as her feet slid on the late-January ice. She wanted to go back into the house and swap her kitten heels for something more sensible but didn't have time. Her bosses at Andrews, Patchett & Raven wouldn't have minded her being a few minutes late but she thought of the stack of legal files, and accompanying audiotapes, that she'd left behind on the Friday afternoon. Besides, it would take her a few minutes to defrost the car. She picked a stray hair from her red wool jacket. The colours clashed with each other but she didn't care. Everyone said red suited her and she agreed. Scratching her left ankle for the umpteenth time, she pulled up her trouser leg and wrinkled her nose up at the patch of skin that matched both hair and jacket, but then smiled at the new paw-print tattoo almost purring back at her.

As she started the engine, she clipped in the car radio's anti-theft plate and pushed in a classical CD. She normally preferred chart music but a powerful overture was the thing to wake her up. On the way home she'd listen to Radio One, which would remind her she was a trendy thirty-something who could like Franz Liszt as well as Franz Ferdinand.

With the windscreen and windows cleared, she headed out the cul-de-sac and to the main road. The traffic was heavy which was sod's law given Jessica's already tight schedule but the first three sets of lights were all green, making up some time.

As she approached the turn to Eversley, still ten minutes from work, she indicated, then slowed down the car by lightly tapping her foot on the brakes. As she did so, she felt the car slide into the middle of the road. The movement was slow, but enough to clip the corner of a white Renault Trafic van, sending Jessica's car spinning off the road.

Had Jessica been nearer to Eversley, she may have careered towards a brick wall, garden or pavement but still being on the outskirts, her car headed towards the railway line and onto a level crossing.

Had Jessica left her house at the usual time and not had to de-ice her car, she may still have skidded on the ice and clipped a different vehicle, but the level crossing barriers may have been down and may have resisted the impact of her car. Being just those few minutes late, and in the wrong place during those vital seconds, left her stranded when the barriers lowered, the left grazing her rear bumper as it rested on to its white metal supports.

Unlike Jessica, the 08:17 train from Rugby to Milton Keynes was two minutes ahead of schedule. Due at Eversley at 08:47, it approached Jessica's level crossing at 08:42 instead of 08:44.

Jessica saw the train bearing down on her. It was like she'd seen in films, where everything turned to slow motion. Her life didn't flash before her, there wasn't enough time, but she knew she had a choice. Get out the car and run like hell, letting the train crash into it, no doubt killing numerous passengers or stay in the car and try and drive it out of the way.

No choice, she thought as she slammed her foot on the accelerator. The wheels spun but nothing happened. Her heart thundered in her ears as she stabbed at the accelerator and tugged at the wheel; to no avail. She could smell rubber from the tyres' friction and as she looked to her right she could see people jumping out of their cars, others shouting at her.

"Come on!" she yelled at her car as if by doing so, she could scare it into life. She bounced in her seat as if the motion would jump the car itself. "Shit!" Her right foot jabbed repeatedly at the accelerator. "Just once. Do it, please, for me! Please!"

When she knew there was no hope, she relaxed to her fate, and uttered her final word, the word that meant everything to her, the name, the person who had meant everything to her, still did, always would.

###

Chapter 5: Andy

Andy Baker clocked in at the Euston Station staff room at 07:38 and to him, it was just another day, the beginning of another working week. He'd drive the new Pendolino Tilting Passenger Train from Euston to Glasgow and back, with a short break in between. He'd celebrated his fifth anniversary with the company and was feeling good about work. The train was almost full, with 'suits' going up to Scotland on business, 'London weekenders' returning home and a few holidaymakers planning some sightseeing or even skiing if the conditions were right.

With the train settled into a straight stretch of track, Andy switched the control to automatic and unscrewed the top off his vacuum flask. He poured himself a steaming cup of white coffee with three sugars and screwed the lid back on. Retaking the wheel, but leaving the control on auto, he looked at the world outside. The trees either side of the line were crisp with frost and the railway track ahead of him reflected the early morning sun. All the picture needed was some tweeting cartoon birds and he'd have himself a Disney landscape. He smiled. A beautiful day. He loved January, the start of a new year. Spring to look forward to, a new relationship perhaps. He'd needed it after Tom. Ten months was long enough to be alone. Andy was ready. Yes, a fresh start.

He yawned and leant his head to his left shoulder, paused, then leant to his right and opened the nearest window. He sighed and imagined another uneventful journey, broken up only by the stops and occasional announcements. Sometimes he'd play tour guide and slip in extra details during longer stretches or as they approached stations. As he announced the opening of the doors, he'd wish his passengers a pleasant day and look forward to seeing them again. To some other drivers it was a robotic speech but to Andy if it made one person's day a little brighter then it was worth doing.

He drained the last of his coffee and screwed the lid back before leaning over to his bag and dropping the flask into it, all the time keeping his eye on the view ahead of him.

He'd had the odd incident in his time with Patriarch Railways; a cow trying to cross but thankfully being too slow, the wrong type of leaves, the occasional cancellation because of heavy snow. Today was cold but fine. As a favourite song played on the radio, Andy whistled in time and tapped his foot. The train was two minutes early and no one complained about being early.

As the train came out of a sharp right curve, Andy spotted a dark shape in the distance. He couldn't make out what it was to begin with, but instinct told him it wasn't good.

###

Chapter 6: Simon and the Police

Simon swore when his doorbell rang. Having poured milk on his cereal, he dropped the spoon into the bowl and returning the carton to the fridge, headed to the door. Two cold-caller business suits stood before him; a tall man and slightly shorter woman.

Great, he thought, *better not be Jehovah's Witnesses.*
"Mr Price?"

"Yes, but I'm heading out to work." *Shit*, Simon thought, *that was stupid. They'll watch me leave then rob the place. No, too smart for burglars, plus they knocked. Confidence tricksters then, except they knew his name. Easy enough to get…*

The man flipped open an ID badge. "I'm Sergeant Lewis."

Simon laughed as Sergeant Lewis said his name. Inspector Morse had been one of Jess' favourite programmes and she'd almost called her cat Lewis until she found out he was discovered at the back of the local theatre during panto season, so named him Buttons instead.

The officer continued serious faced. "And this is my colleague DS Taylor. May we come in?"

"What's this about?" Simon wasn't the promptest of bill payers but he was sure there wasn't anything outstanding.

"I'm afraid we have some bad news and we'd rather not discuss it on your doorstep."

"Er, sure. Come in. Go through to the lounge."

The officers headed in that direction as Simon shut the front door, his heart thumping as he followed them.

"Mr Price?" the Sergeant asked a clearly vacant Simon.

"We suggest you sit down, Mr Price," DS Taylor said.

Simon immediately thought of his mother.

"I'm afraid there was an accident this morning near Eversley involving…" She didn't need to say any more.

"Jess!" Simon blurted.

"I'm afraid so, Mr Price."

"Is she…?"

DS Taylor nodded. "I'm sorry."

"No… How?"

"Black ice, sir. We have you listed as the next of kin."

"Shit! Sorry. Shit!" Simon repeated as he sank into a chair. He sat there stone-faced as she told him the details. It was like watching TV and doing something else at the same time; you know someone's speaking but it's not sinking in. You snatch bits letting your sub-conscious soak up the rest.

"Mr Price?" Sergeant Lewis said when he'd finished talking but had no reaction.

Was that what they wanted? Simon thought. *A reaction? For him to break down, to scream hysterically? Of course men didn't do hysterics. Only mothers did hysterics. Their mother. Oh God. How was he going to tell her? She'd fall to pieces.* Simon had heard over and over, parents being interviewed on TV saying how they'd never imagined they'd have to bury their child before them and here they were. His mum would be another interviewee saying exactly the same thing. Jess' life would be the clichéd "such a waste of a young life", "snatched away too soon" and so on.

"Simon?"

"Sorry. I am listening."

"It was quick. She wouldn't have known much about it." It wasn't strictly true but it softened the blow.

"That's what we all want, isn't it," Simon replied numbly, "to not feel anything."

"There is something we need to ask you," DS Taylor said. "Your sister had a donor card in her bag. The hospital would like your permission to…"

"If that's what she wanted."

"Thank you. I know it's a difficult decision but time…"

"Of course. Just… sure."

"Thank you. Excuse me then please, I'll need to make a call."

Simon watched the woman leave the room, tapping digits on her mobile.

"Is there anything we can do?" Sergeant Lewis asked when his colleague had left the room. "We'll keep in touch as the investigation progresses but at the moment it looks like a tragic accident. A freak of nature."

Simon laughed. "I'm sorry. It's not funny, obviously, but that's Jessica. Mum said she was a freak of nature, in the nicest possible sense. Mum had been told she couldn't have any more children after me, then along came Jess."

"She'll take it hard then."

"More than you know."

DS Taylor re-entered the room as the Sergeant continued. "Would you like us to break the news to her?"

"Thanks, but I think it would be better coming from me. You turning up on her doorstep would be bad enough, no offence, but with the news you've got, it would finish her off."

The two officers looked at each other then back at Simon. "That's quite all right. Is there anything else you need to know?"

"Just… what happens now?"

"We need you to make a formal identification."

"Oh right. Where?"

"She's been taken to Moorcroft Hospital. We can recommend companies to help you with the funeral arrangements. Unless…"

"We know someone – my dad died a couple of years ago. A heart attack, as sudden but not…" Simon lowered his head, "…the same."

"I'm sorry. Can you come with us?" DS Taylor smiled weakly as Simon nodded.

As they left the house, Simon grabbed his jacket from a hook in the hall.

Pulling his keys out of his trouser pocket, he locked the front door before following the officers to the patrol car. He couldn't help feeling like a criminal as he got in the back and imagined his neighbours' curtains twitching. *Let them think what they want.* Word would get round soon enough.

The twenty-mile journey to Moorcroft Hospital was the longest of his life. He dreaded seeing Jess on a 'slab'. He'd seen many a crime programme, fact and fiction and knew what to expect, although he'd never seen a body in real life, not even his father. He knew seeing one in the form of a friend or family member though would seem real, yet unreal. Memories stick and although he wanted the last memory to be of his sister alive, he had to save this from his mother. She had to remember her daughter as she was; full of life, fun and smiling.

As the patrol car arrived at the hospital, Simon stared at the patients and staff coming and going, all seeming to have the weight of the world on their shoulders. Sergeant Lewis drove towards the 'emergency vehicles only' area and Simon spotted two nurses, standing under what looked like a small transparent bus shelter, smoking. Simon shook his head and thought they, of all people, should know how bad it was. He recalled an article some years earlier about every cigarette 'losing' eleven minutes off a life. To take his mind off his situation, he did some calculations in his head based on a packet a day; almost six eleven minutes per hour, twenty cigarettes in a packet… so they'd lose an average of four hours a day. Simon was still trying to comprehend the craziness of the whole issue, when he realised DS Taylor was towering over him.

   As she opened his door, Simon's mind raced back to a family holiday on a Devon farm when he'd put the child lock on his door despite being told not to, and was terrified of what his dad would say. Now it was another kind of terror. He wanted them to be wrong but the feeling in the bottom of his stomach told him they weren't.

   They walked to the reception desk in single file and were then escorted through the maze of corridors towards the rear of the building. When they reached the mortuary, the hospital worker stepped back and bowed his head. DS Taylor turned to Simon. "Please brace yourself. Your sister sustained significant injuries."

   Simon gulped then nodded as the DS opened the door.

###

Chapter 7: Simon and Marion

Sliding the key into the lock, Simon turned the key 180 degrees to the right, pulled down the white PVC handle and opened the door.

"Mum?" he whispered.

No reply.

"Mum?" Simon repeated a little louder, walking to the kitchen / diner.

Marion Price dropped the spoon she'd been holding into the cereal bowl. "Hello, dear… shouldn't you be at work?"

"Yes, only… I have something to tell you. Something bad."

"Is it work? Have they let you go? You know, it'll be fine. You'll find something else. You're a bright–"

"No, Mum," Simon interrupted, "it's Jessica."

"Is she all right? Where is she?"

"There was an accident. This morning, on her way to work."

"Where is she?" Marion repeated.

"At the hospital. At Moorcroft."

"Then she's going to be all right."

"No. I'm so sorry."

"No!" Marion groaned and sunk to her knees. "No, it's not true. Who told you? They've got it wrong."

"Sorry, Mum, it is true. I've seen her."

"Where?"

"At the hospital."

"You've… you've been to see her? She's… it's definitely her?"

Simon nodded.

Marion, sitting on her knees, said, "but why didn't anyone tell me? Why didn't you tell me?"

"The police came to see me before I went to work. They only just caught me, I was running late." Remembering her question, he continued. "Jess had me as next of kin."

At the use of the 'had', Marion winced. She couldn't think of her daughter in the past tense. "I want to see her."

"I don't think you should. She's…" Tears welled up in his eyes. "It was a bad accident."

"How? Did she…?"

Simon helped his mother onto the nearest chair and sitting opposite her at the table, recounted the morning's events, though suitably toned down. She grasped a tissue from a box he'd moved from a nearby sideboard. As he spoke, she pulled it to pieces.

As Marion stared at the tablecloth trying to take it all in, Simon walked over to the kettle and flicked the on switch, taking two blue-shaded mugs off a tree of six.

"So it was quick?" Marion said finally, as Simon put her tea in front of her.

Simon nodded again.

"What happens now?"

"It's quite straightforward, they said. I've made the formal identification…"

"Oh, Simon."

Simon's eyes filled with tears. "It wasn't her."

"What?"

"No, I mean, it was her but she looked so cold; so pale. Not as we know her. So full of life and…" He gulped at his tea.

"I can't take it in."

"I know. They said it was an accident, black ice. Nothing she could have done. She'd tried to move her car, drive it out of the way of the train."

Marion yelped.

"She did it to save the passengers," Simon continued. "She'd always put herself last."

"Was anyone else…?"

"No. No one badly injured, a few bumps and scrapes apparently. The train had slowed down but not…" Then he remembered Jessica's cat. "Mum, can you take Buttons?"

"Of course."

"I could but I work long hours and… I think he'd rather be with you."

Marion resumed staring at the tablecloth. "We'll use the same company as with your father."

"Bennett's? Leave it with me. And I'll sort out her house. I've phoned work to say I won't be in today but I'll say I need more time. I'll get her numbers and contact people."

Marion nodded and tried a smile, which was reluctantly forthcoming.

"It'll be on the local news and in the papers. You may get people phoning you. May be best to leave the answerphone on and I'll deal with it when I come back. I'll stay for a while if that's OK."

"That would be lovely," Marion whispered.

"If you speak to anyone, give them my number and I'll handle everything."

"Thanks, dear." Marion replied, not listening, eyes fixed on an embroidered bee hovering over a delicately sewn red rose.

###

Chapter 8: Emily and Frank

"Em! Phone's ringing. Do you want me to get it?"

"Thanks, love. Up to my armpits in soapy suds." Emily heard her husband stomp along the landing from the bathroom to the bedroom and the phone stopped.

A few seconds later, he thundered down the stairs and into the kitchen where Emily was drying the lunch dishes.

"There's been an accident."

"Andy!"

"He's fine. He was driving though, so he's understandably upset. They've given him some time off. He'll ring later to have a chat with you. I said we'd go over and see him but he says he's fine. I'm not convinced so I think we should give him time then… Here, sit down. You look awful."

Frank put the kettle on and made his wife a cup of tea, then held her hand while he explained what had happened.

###

Chapter 9: Simon and the Press

"I'm off to collect Buttons." Simon was heading for the hall when the phone rang. "Shall I?"

"No. Let it go to the answerphone."

"That's a good idea."

The answerphone clicked in. "*Hello. This is Marion Price. I can't take your call, so please leave a message after the beep. Thank you for calling. Is that it? That button? Oh, yes.*"

"*Hello, Mrs Price. This is the Eversley Echo. We've heard about your daughter and extend our condolences to you and your family. We were wondering whether you wouldn't mind giving us a short statement. You can ring any of the features team on… 01632 821821. Thanks very much, Mrs Price, and again, we're sorry for your loss.*"

Marion stared at the phone. "How did they find out so quickly?"

"I think the police tell them. In a way I'm surprised they've not been in touch sooner. I'm so glad I beat them to it. Imagine if you found out from them first."

Marion shuddered.

"Are you warm enough? Shall I put the heating up?"

"No. I'm not cold."

"Do you want me to stay here?"

"It's fine. You go."

"I'll ring the paper later? It's too soon for you to deal with it."

Marion nodded, mouthed a 'thank you' and returned to the kitchen.

As Simon opened Marion's front door, a barrage of flashbulbs blinded him. He put his right arm to shield his eyes and the lights stopped. Several microphones were thrust towards his face with numerous reporters speaking at once.

"I'm sorry, I can't understand you," Simon said, squinting.

The nearest reporter to him repeated her question. "Mr Price? Can you tell us what happened."

"You don't know?"

"We'd like to hear it from you."

"My sister died this morning, that's what happened."

"We understand."

"And how are you feeling?" another reporter asked.

"Are you serious?" Simon snapped. "How do you think we're feeling?"

"We're sorry. Of course. It must be a difficult time."

"Have you ever lost a sibling? A daughter?"

"Well…"

"Please, we're trying to deal with this."

"Certainly, Mr Price. We just…"

"If I talk to you, will you leave my mum alone?"

The reporter looked at the group. "We will."

"What do you want to know?"

"We'd like your reflections on what's happened and tell us something about your sister."

Simon shook his head and sighed. "I'm told by the police that Jessica was travelling to work and her car skidded on some ice, it clipped a van and ended up on the railway line."

"With they be pressing any charges?"

"Against who?"

"Er… anyone, sir?"

"I don't know. For Christ's sake, I've only just told my mother she's lost her only daughter."

"We're sorry…"

"So you keep saying."

"A few words on your sister, please, Mr Price," another reporter shouted out.

"Jessica… was fun-loving, had a great sense of humour and someone who would do anything for anyone. She'll be sorely missed and we ask that you respect our privacy."

A couple of the reporters nodded.

"Can I go now?" Simon asked, breaking the silence.

"Thanks very much, Mr Price."

"Will you go too, please."

The group reluctantly disbanded and Simon waited until they'd driven off before leaving his mother's house.

###

Chapter 10: Simon

The white PVC door slammed against the hall's wooden
meter cupboard, the echo reverberating through the empty
1930s semi. Simon removed his key from the lock and
switched on the hall light. Bending down and picking up half a
dozen pieces of post, he closed the door behind him, locked it
and walked towards the kitchen. He felt along the side wall
and switched on the light. On the floor on the far side of the
room was a fresh litter tray and by the fridge / freezer near him
were two bowls, one almost to the top with water, the other
contained remnants of dried cat food.

"Buttons?" Simon called loudly but there was no reply.
He called again but no sign of the cat. He looked around the
room for the back door key and saw a bunch hanging on the
side of a chest-height cupboard. Ignoring a small window lock
key, he selected the next three smallest and tried each one in
turn. The second worked and he went out into the garden,
calling the cat's name.

A few seconds later, a squeak emerged from a nearby bush
and Jessica's black and white cat ran into the light streaming
from the kitchen window and towards Simon, purring and
weaving its body around Simon's legs. Simon wasn't
particularly a cat lover but Buttons was Jessica's and she'd
adored him so he picked him up and made a fuss as if he
were a long-lost child.

As they returned inside the house, Simon lowered
Buttons gently on to the kitchen floor and watched him run
towards his food bowl. Simon then noticed a series of beeps
coming from the direction of the lounge. A red flashing
number eight greeted him as he walked over to the
answerphone and pressed the green 'play' button.

The machine dutifully beeped and said robotically,
'*Message one, received today at 9.21am. The caller withheld
their number.*' "Alexis, it's Veronica. Where are you? I'm
getting irate phone calls from Daniel and he says a bloke's
answering your mobile. I'm at the office. Give me a call, will
you, as soon as you get this."

Simon stared at the machine, "Sorry Veronica. Think you've got the wrong number."

The machine beeped again: '*message two, received today 9.46am*'. "Alexis, I've tried your mobile a couple of times but some guy keeps answering it and telling me… he's not very nice. Please ring me. You're probably asleep but I need to speak to you."

Simon frowned and muttered "her, again."

The machine continued: '*message three, received today 11.53am*'. Another withheld call. "Alexis, it's Veronica. Daniel's giving me earache. Says you left in a hurry and you have something of his? You've got my mobile number, ring me on that. I've got a lunch appointment so I'm leaving the office. Ring me today, will you, so I can sort this out."

Simon shook his head. "My, Veronica, you are persistent, and you're persistently getting the wrong number."

'*Message four, received today 1.37pm.*' read: "Jess, it's Elliot. You've not arrived at work yet. Hope you're OK. I wanted to ask you where the Contini papers are but I'll see if I can find them on your desk. Will you give me a call anyway please. Thanks. Talk to you later."

Simon wrote down Elliot's name making a mental note to look up his number when he collected Jessica's mobile the next day. Failing that, he'd Google the company.

The machine had already beeped again and Simon caught '*…five, received today 4.51pm*'. "Jess, it's Daph. Elliot's doing his nut. Says he's found the Contini case paperwork but needs them typing a-sap. Are you sick? I'll do Contini before I leave tonight but can you ring me if you're not going to be in tomorrow. If you're not, we'll get a temp but need to know either way. Thanks, hon." Simon added Daph's name to Elliot's.

'*Message six, received today 7.15pm*' read: "Alexis, it's Veronica."

Simon shook his head.

The machine continued, "I need to know whether you're free tomorrow night. Daniel says he needs someone to accompany him on a business meeting and he's willing to overlook last night, whatever that means. Maybe he just wants his stuff back. He's a regular and asked for you so I don't want to let him down. Sindy may be free but I know he prefers you. Oh, and can you give me your new mobile number. I don't want to get that jerk again. So, what happened last night, with Daniel? Oh, and another thing... shit, I've got to go. Ring me, will you. Thanks. It's Veronica. You've got my number."

"Yes, Veronica, I think we know it's you." Simon said, then with his face close to the machine, "Veronica, stop calling here. You've... got... the... wrong... number!" Simon didn't do shouting at people but shouting at machines he did do, and today of all days, it made him feel better. Actually, he didn't know how he felt. *Too early. Baby steps*, he thought.

The machine beeped. Message seven was received about an hour later but consisted of a few seconds of mixed silence and background noise before the caller hung up and the machine went on to the final message.

'*Message eight, received today 9.16pm*'. Simon looked at the clock on the mantelpiece. He'd only just missed the call. The machine continued. "Alexis, it's Veronica. I'm not going to ring again."

"Thank God!" Simon said, during a brief pause.

"I need to know what's going on. You know I can't get you on your mobile, can't get on your landline. If you don't ring me back tonight I'm going to have to call Sindy. I can't mess Daniel around like this. I'll give you until ten."

"Call Sindy then, Veronica. I dare you!" Simon threatened, sticking his tongue out at the small black box. He wanted to press the 'delete all messages' button but he needed Jess' work number so resisted the urge. He could delete them one by one, he was sure, but it would mean playing the messages again and that wasn't something he wanted to do. It was getting late and he couldn't face Veronica another five times.

Simon dialled 1471. The recorded operator's voice said, '*Last call received today 9.18pm. The caller withheld their number*'.

"Of course you did, Veronica. Didn't want anyone but Alexis to get hold of you, but she's not ringing you, is she?"

Knowing he was to go to Eversley police station the following day to collect his sister's belongings, he took the piece of paper with the two names he'd written and, in the absence of Buttons' carry basket or a cardboard box, Simon took the throw.

Keeping the cat in the house, Simon laid the throw on to the back seat of his silver VW Polo, and returned to the house. Switching out the kitchen and lounge lights, he picked up Buttons, who'd been sitting at the bottom of the stairs watching Simon come and go. The cat made a slight whimper but didn't struggle as Simon had expected. Simon switched off the hall light, shut and locked the front door and put the house keys into his jeans pocket.

"There we go, mate," Simon whispered and lowered Buttons gently on to the back seat.

The cat was quiet and stared back with big brown eyes.

"It's going to be fine. You'll love being with granny, she'll spoil you rotten."

At the word 'granny', the cat purred and Simon smiled. "Yes, you'll be fine."

He did a quick tour of the house. Nothing untoward; nothing except for the three thousand pounds sitting innocently in the lounge pine chest of drawers.

###

Chapter 11: Simon and Marion

A knock on his bedroom door woke Simon from a troubled sleep. His mother stood in the doorway wearing a baby blue towelling dressing gown, her eyes red and puffy.

"Hi, Mum, are you OK?"

Marion nodded and entered the room carrying a tray holding a steaming mug and plate of buttered toast.

"Four slices? I'm not hungry."

"You need something. You didn't eat last night."

Simon watched his mother put the tray down on the top of a chest of drawers. "What's the time?"

"Ten thirty."

"Did you sleep?"

"Not really. I still can't take it in. Your dad, now… this."

"I know. I can stay here for as long as you like."

"Thanks Simon, but you have your home, a job. Have you rung work since yesterday?"

"No. I'd better do it. Explain everything and… I'm sure they'll be fine. There's a lot to sort out. The funeral, her house… where's Buttons?"

"On Jessica's bed." She looked at the wall to the room next door. "He isn't hungry either."

"Poor thing. Are you OK with him living here?"

"Of course, it'll be company for me. The arrangements… it's too much for you to do alone. Tell me what I can do."

"It's fine. I can manage." He paused. "There was something I forgot to tell you yesterday."

"Yes?"

"Jess carried a donor card. Did you know?"

"We chatted about it once. She said she wanted to. I didn't know she had."

"I gave my permission, was that all right?"

"Of course. It's fine. I'm… pleased she'll be helping someone else."

"Have you spoken to Gran or Aunt Helen yet?"

Marion shook her head. "Your gran wouldn't understand and... I'll go and see Helen and Graham at lunchtime. I do anyway on a Tuesday…" Her voice trailed off and she looked down at her faded red slippers.

"I can go with you… or on my own…" Simon offered.

"Thank Simon but it's fine," she replied rubbing the underside of her nose with the back of her curved index finger, "your uncle will be there. Helen said he's working from home this week so…"

"I'd better ring work and get down to the police station."

Marion looked up suddenly. "They have some news?"

Simon shook his head. "No, I have to go and collect… collect Jess' things."

Tears brimmed Marion's eyes. "Of course. Simon… thank you, you're being so brave."

Simon smiled wanly. "On the outside, Mum, just on the outside. It's hard."

As Simon entered the kitchen, Marion was cleaning the oven. It was a job that was always dreaded yet this seemed perfect. The vigorous action appeared to melt the anguish, not completely of course but enough to have her humming to the radio in the background. Simon wasn't fooled. She'd probably break down again while he was out.

"I'm off then. Won't be long." Picking up his car keys from a bowl by the kitchen door, he walked into the hall before turning back and saying, "I phoned the office, they're fine. One of my colleagues will cover my work until I get back."

"OK, love." Marion looked at the buffed-to-within-an-inch-of-its-life oven shelf.

"Shall I get some shopping on the way back? Do we need anything?"

"Oh, yes. Milk… bread… and… and cat food… erm…"

"Sure. I'll get the basics. No harm in having spares. You sure you don't want me to go to Aunt Helen's with you? I can be quick."

"No, love. I'll be fine. As you say, Graham's going to be there. You go."

"Right then, see you later."

###

Chapter 12: Simon and the Police

Simon pulled into Eversley police station car park, his stomach lurching as he saw a large white van with a dented front wing being towed into a large wire compound. Simon was certain it had to be the one involved in Jess' accident; the one responsible. Apart from the dent there looked to be nothing wrong with it and therefore probably nothing wrong with the driver. Simon knew it was a 'tragic accident' but at the same time he couldn't help but feel angry. Maybe the driver was going too fast or wasn't paying attention. Accident or not, Simon wanted... no, needed, someone to be responsible.

He got out of his car and slammed the door. A couple of uniformed officers walking by stared at him then continued chatting before turning into the station. Simon looked over at the compound, at the van was parked with the recovery truck driver unhooking it. Simon's gaze then rested on the small car next to it. "Oh no!" he said as he recognised the last three letters of what was left of the number plate. JES. He remembered the day his sister had bought the car. She'd been delighted that it was accidentally personalised. She wasn't one for spending money on such luxuries but to have it free was a bonus.

The blue Kia Picanto was almost unrecognisable as a car let alone the make and model; as well as being less than half the size, the whole of the roof had been sheared off, Simon hoped courtesy of the fire brigade. He wanted to turn away, stop looking at it, but his legs had rooted him to the spot. 'It was like watching a train wreck' – was that the saying? Simon shook his head as he thought of the phrase and how he'd never seen anything as tragic in his life. He and Jess had talked about how they'd wanted to 'go'; one of many morbid conversations they had while sharing a bottle of wine and a DVD. He'd said in his sleep but Jess said she wanted to go out with a bang, more of a statement; to finally be a headline and she'd cruelly got her wish, though far sooner than anticipated.

"Can I help you, son?" a low voice mumbled near his ear.

Simon jerked round and saw one of the officers he'd earlier seen walking into the station. There was no sign of the colleague.

"Sorry. I'm here to see Sergeant Lewis or DS Taylor. I've come to... to collect some belongings."

It was evident from the officer's expression that he knew who Simon was; that Jessica's death was the lead subject at the station. Simon guessed unexpected deaths were still far and few between. The local rag recounted crimes almost daily but thankfully more small-time stuff.

"Sir?" the officer said gently as Simon's gaze drifted.

"Sorry. Yes, I'm here to see... sorry, I've said that already."

"Don't worry sir, I'll take you to them. I'm so sorry for your loss. We're doing our best to find out what happened."

"Are you on the case?"

"Yes, sir, a lot of us are. I'm PC Thompson. David Thompson. It's looking like an accident but we need to investigate thoroughly. I'm sure you can appreciate..."

"I do, thank you. Her mum and I are... we're grateful for everything you're doing. Sergeant Lewis and DS Taylor have been very..." Simon tailed off.

"Come this way, sir. This won't take long; some forms to sign and you can be on your way. I'm sure you have a lot to take care of."

As they walked side-by-side into the station, the officer said, "Were you given a Victim Support pack, Mr Price?"

Simon nodded as a female officer behind the counter buzzed them through. He followed PC Thompson to a side office where he recognised DS Taylor.

"Hi there, Mr Price. How are you doing?"

Simon shrugged. "You know..."

"Sure. I can imagine. Sergeant Lewis has gone back to the scene to do final checks at that end. The train track's reopened but it's loose ends. We've taken statements, and forensics have done their bit so it's just testing your sister's car."

"It's here, isn't it? And the white van."

"Yes. Both here. We've interviewed the driver and his passenger and they've confirmed that it was an accident.

Black ice. That's the way the investigation is going, if that helps. No one to blame."

"No. I mean, yes, it helps. That… that there's no one at fault."

"So you've come to collect your sister's things."

"Yes please."

"Certainly." DS Taylor got up from her desk, scraping back her chair, and walked over to a neighbouring desk. She picked up an archive-type box and walked towards Simon. As she approached him, she said, "I need you to sign a release form please."

Simon signed the form, took the box, which was lighter than he'd expected, thanked the officers and left the room. As PC Thompson escorted him back down the corridor, Simon couldn't help but look in the box. On the left was a bright red jacket, which he lifted, expecting to see her shoes. The right half of the box contained a handbag, book and mobile phone. Simon had bought the phone for her for Christmas and remembered how excited she'd been when she'd taken it out of its packaging. It was the same model as his so he'd been able to show her how it worked and they'd spent Boxing Day morning Bluetoothing information to each other.

As they reached the front door of the police station, PC Thompson opened the door. "Do take care, sir. If you think of anything that you'd like to ask, please do let us know. We'll of course keep you informed of progress."

"But it looks clear cut, doesn't it?"

"Yes, sir, it does."

"Will there be an inquest?"

"There will, yes. Should be straightforward though; plenty of witnesses."

"Thank you for everything. You've been so kind."

PC Thompson smiled faintly and shut the door. Simon walked down the steps and towards the vehicle impound, to Jessica's shell of a car and the almost-perfect white van. He chewed the inside of his mouth as he imagined the scene, tears welling up. He closed his eyes and let a solitary tear run down his right cheek.

As he reached his car, he leant the box of Jessica's things against the boot, holding it in place with his hip and left hand. He wiped his right cheek dry with his index finger then wiped his finger against his jeans. It produced a dark blue line along the material for a moment then was gone. Simon pressed the unlock button on the remote twice and lifted up the boot, carefully placing the box on to the dark grey carpet lining. He stared at the contents, unsure as to what he should do with them, or the things in her house. The cat had been an easy problem but her worldly goods were another matter. She liked car boot sales so maybe she'd want him to have a stall, or several stalls until everything had gone, or give it all to charity. He'd take each day as it came and deal with whatever threw itself at him.

###

Chapter 13: Beth and Nate

"Do you mind?" Beth Morrison snapped at her husband as he clenched one hand around the other and cracked his fingers. "You know it's my favourite."

"CrimeTime? Are you trying to be funny?" Nate said, his face straight as a backbone.

"No, Nate. Why?" she paused to glare at him. "You said you were past all that."

Nate stayed silent.

"Nate?"

"I am… honest," he said, not convincing either of them.

Beth shook her head and turned back to the TV as a gallery of reprobates appeared on the screen. She laughed as one of them looked similar to her husband. Gritting her teeth and insisting on getting the last word, she said, "You'd better be."

They sat in silence for the rest of the programme then Beth left the room to put on the kettle. Whilst she preferred to go to bed early, Nate was a night owl so their last-thing routine consisted of her making him a strong black coffee and herself a cocoa and hot water bottle, before heading upstairs to continue the latest crime or thriller novel. She'd grown up on humour and chick-lit but her tastes had become darker in her twenties, probably influenced by a string of associations with even shadier men.

It was a routine they had. If she wasn't asleep by the time he came to bed, she'd go through to the bathroom and brush her teeth while he got changed into his prison-striped pyjamas, a running joke she'd not found so funny recently. She put some of her feelings down to the proverbial seven year itch, but their relationship had been unravelling for some time. She yearned for some excitement and while he got his kicks from breaking the law, she was fed up with not knowing where he was all the time and the appearance of new things in the house.

As Beth heard Nate's footsteps up the stairs, she slotted the bookmark into the core of the book and closed it. She stared at the dark figure on the front, the graveyard and the handprint of blood and sighed. Maybe she should go back to

47

reading lighter stuff. She stretched up her arms behind her head and pulling her hair back into an imaginary bunch, she pressed her palms against either side of her head and yawned. She needed an early night. That would help; and to be more of a sound sleeper. If Nate insisted on watching TV too loudly, Beth stomping down the stairs, and belt with a cushion usually did the trick.

Frank Lambert, a retired policeman-turned-security guard, had his eye on his neighbour. Frank and Emily, his wife of twenty-three years, had moved into the 1980s semi-detached from new and their then next-door neighbours, a young couple, had been delightful. For the first few years at least. Cups of sugar and recipes had exchanged hands over the dividing fence but the Lamberts heard arguing and the occasional crash as something solid, possibly the sugar cups, had rebounded heavily against the Everest-air-thin shared walls.

Soon after, the wife left and the house was put on the market. It then changed hands a couple of times before another young couple moved in the year before. Whilst Frank vaguely recognised the man, he couldn't put a name to the face and had never warmed to him. The woman on the other hand was charming and bonded quickly with Emily, as her predecessors had. Both Emily and Frank wondered why the young woman stuck around but they guessed it was financial or emotional but said nothing.

They'd hear the odd clattering and heavy footsteps but being quieter than the original owners, weren't any trouble.

Beth had been calling round more often, to Emily's delight, as she was a born entertainer and usually had a batch of brownies or sponge cake on the go.

The two women were deep in conversation in the lounge when Frank walked in.

"Morning ladies, don't mind me. I'm looking for my glasses."

"Morning, Frank," Beth said, looking around the room to see if she could spot the elusive specs.

Emily, on the other hand, looked at her husband. "Try the kitchen table. I saw them there this morning."

"OK, thanks, love. Morning, Beth."

"Frank," Emily said. "There's still tea in the pot. Would you make one for Beth?"

Frank looked at Beth who smiled and nodded.

"Sure. Then I'll leave you two in peace. Are you all right, Beth? You look a little peaky."

Before Beth could reply, Emily said, "You were going to leave us in peace?"

"Oh, yes, sorry Em. Won't interrupt. I know what you women are like when you get together. Bye, Beth."

"Bye, Frank. Nice to see you."

Frank nodded and left the room.

Emily lowered her voice. "Think he was after some gossip. He's got some idea in his head about your Nathan. Thinks he knows him from somewhere but then he's been like that about almost everyone since he retired. You can take the man out of the security business… Gets under my feet if I'm honest."

"I know what you mean. I can't wait for Nate to go out to work, not that he does very often but he's trying."

Emily grinned. "Yes, so is Frank. Now, about your baby… does your Nathan know yet?"

"Not yet. I'm picking a good moment to tell him but there aren't many of those these days."

"Won't he take it well?"

"I'm not sure. He's always been good at dodging the subject of children. If he thought it was going to be a boy he might be happy."

"And money?"

"Bit tight at the moment. I'm only working part-time and Nate's sort of… in between. Which reminds me, what did you mean when you said that Frank had an idea about Nathan. What sort of idea?"

"Beth… He likes you but he's not sure about your husband. Frank, he's on the lookout for you."

"That's kind of him but he needn't worry. Nate's not a bad person, just easily led. Had some trouble in his past but he swears it's all behind him."

"And you believe him?"

"I guess."

"That's a 'not really' then."

"Erm…"

"I'm sorry, Beth. I shouldn't pry. It's your business. It's just that… we wouldn't want any harm to come to you, now you've got a little one on the way."

Beth smiled unconvincingly. She'd received the news a week earlier but it still hadn't sunk in.

"Is it mine?" Nate snapped.

"Of course it's yours. Who else's do you think it would be?"

"How far gone are you?"

"Nate, you've got such a way with words."

"Sorry, how long…?"

"About six weeks."

"You've known for over a month and you choose now to tell me?"

"I've known for a week and yes, I had to choose my moment. You've not been easy to talk to recently."

Nate seemed to recognise her vulnerability. He stepped towards her, putting his arms around her and kissed her cheek. A tear met his lips. He looked up at Beth and whispered, "It's great news. A little shocked, that's all. A family; three of us. A fresh start."

Beth sniffed. "Really? But you… you're not cross?"

"Cross? Why would I be? I did have something to do with this."

"I know, but I didn't think… I wasn't sure, only sometimes you say…"

"Hot and cold, that's… you know me, Beth. You know I love kids."

"When you can hand them back."

"It's a big responsibility but it might be just the thing."

"And when it gets too much?"

"Then we'll talk about it. I've not been here for you but that's going to change. I'm going to change. I'll get a proper job and…"

"You will?"

"Sure. We're only getting by on your wages and it's not fair." He led her to the sofa and pulled over a footstool, propping her ankles on top of it. "Can I get you anything? A nice cup of tea?"

"What's happened to the Nate that I know and sometimes love?"

Nate laughed. "I'm still here, just buried under mush."

Beth smiled. If this was what pregnancy did to her man then she'd have a football team. Money was another matter and she'd not believed him when he said he'd get a job, that he'd go straight, but miracles did happen; just not usually to her.

###

Chapter 14: Simon and Marion

There was no sign of Marion when Simon got back to her house. He figured she'd gone to break the news to his aunt and uncle. He didn't expect her back any time soon so was surprised when she arrived shortly after him.

"You told them?"

Marion nodded.

"Is it a stupid question to ask how they took it?"

"Not well. Helen's in pieces. I couldn't stay. Graham couldn't take it in. They'd heard something about the accident on the news but hadn't realised…"

"You don't think something like that could happen to someone you know."

"No, you don't."

"I was going to go over to Jess' house, see if I can do some phoning around, and get some of her numbers. Which reminds me, Mum…"

"Yes?"

"Do you know someone call Alexis? Jess didn't have a lodger, did she?"

"Not as far as I know. She's had a couple in the past but no one recently, I don't think. Why do you ask?"

"There were messages on her machine to Alexis from someone called Veronica. I thought after the first time that it was a wrong number but she kept phoning so she must think she's got the right number."

"Maybe there's an address book."

"I've got her mobile but there's no Veronica or Alexis on it."

"Jess' mobile?"

"Yes, in amongst the things I collected from the police station."

"Where is it now?"

"I brought in the phone but left the box in the boot of my car. I wasn't sure what to do with it."

"Please, Simon, bring it in."

"Are you sure?"

Marion nodded so Simon retrieved the box and put it gently on to the kitchen table. "Do you want me to stay or shall I go to the house and leave you with…"

"I'll be fine."

Simon nodded and grabbed his car keys off the kitchen worktop.

###

Chapter 15: Marion

With Simon gone, Marion kept busy. The oven was already
spotless so she cleaned the kitchen floor tiles. White with thin
blue edging they showed every speck and whilst she'd not
been particularly bothered before, everything seemed to
matter now. Armed with her blue square plastic bowl and hot
soapy water, she knelt down with a larger scourer and
scrubbed. Like the oven, the furious action felt therapeutic and
the tension in her shoulders eased slightly. For a moment her
thoughts were concentrated on her task in hand but then guilt
took over, Jess came flooding back, and tears dripped into the
bowl, making small dents in the foam. Marion slammed the
scourer into the bowl, ignoring the water soaking her thighs.
She dropped her head into her hands and sobbed.

Buttons appeared and scurried over to Marion. He put
his front two paws onto her damp trousers and nudged his
head against her right arm.

Marion looked up at the table and the box of her
daughter's things. She wondered how long she could put off
looking inside and dealing with them. Torn between finishing
the floor and the box, she compromised and gave the rest of
the tiles their first clean and left them to dry.

Sitting on her chair by the back door, Marion pulled the box to
the edge of the table. She couldn't bring herself to look inside
but took out the items one by one.

"Little by little, Marion... baby steps."

An image then formed in her mind of Jess' first steps, the
floral dress and pink socks. Marion closed her eyes and
breathed deeply.

She looked down at the jacket and picked it up. She held
it by its shoulders and another image appeared; of a few
weekends earlier when they'd been sitting down to dinner and
Jess, wearing the same jacket, had told her and Simon of how
settled in her job she was and that she was planning on taking
up an evening class. Marion tried to remember what she'd
said she was going to do. Ceroc? No. Languages? No, that
wasn't it either. Marion remembered the couple she'd pictured
at the time; Salsa. And there was something else, something

classroom-based. Marion stared at the table. Writing. Biography, no, a novel. Her daughter was going to be a novelist.

Marion held the jacket to her nose and sniffed. There was a faint smell of her daughter's perfume but it was tainted, not her really. Marion folded the jacket like a shop assistant folding an item of stock and carefully laid it on the table, to the left of the box.

Moving her hands to the right side of the box, Marion pulled out a medium-sized black patent handbag. She opened the zip and looked at the contents. Again she felt like an intruder but these were the things her daughter had had with her when she'd died. They were cherished possessions and Marion wanted to cherish them on her behalf, strange though it felt. Marion removed her purse and looked inside. There were three compartments; one for loose change, one for notes and receipts, and a smaller divided segment for cards. Apart from half a dozen coins and a couple of ten pounds, the notes section appeared to be empty until Marion saw a piece of paper from behind the money. As she pulled it out from the back of the purse, Jessica smiled back. Marion slumped down on to her chair. Jessica was surrounded by four other grinning faces; two women and two men, all of a similar age. She didn't recognise any of them but assumed they were friends or work colleagues. Marion was reassured by the fact that her daughter had been happy but it didn't make looking at the photograph any easier, so she tucked it back behind the ten-pound notes.

There were two credit cards in the smaller section, and Marion made a mental note to speak to Simon about cancelling them. She guessed he'd do that while he was at Jessica's house, as he'd have had the statements there, but she wanted to make sure. Marion put the purse on the other side of the box so she wouldn't forget. She seemed to be forgetting a lot recently.

At the bottom of the handbag was the bottle of French perfume, which Marion knew Jessica had worn for years. *A creature of habit*, Marion thought and put it back inside the bag. There didn't appear to be anything else in it so she put it to next to the jacket and looked in the box.

In the corner was an empty leather case for which she assumed was Jess' mobile phone. Marion remembered her opening its box on Christmas Day afternoon and how thrilled she'd been. Technology was rather beyond Marion so when they set up the phones on the kitchen table on Boxing Day morning, she'd left them to it while she made them all a late breakfast then pottered around the house tidying up from the night before, declining their offer of help.

The last item in the box was a book. Marion read the title: 'Blood Ties', written underneath the author's name, and studied the image of a silhouetted figure holding a gun towards what looked like a deserted alleyway. Marion shuddered and wondered how a woman, Kay Hooper in this instance, could write something so dark, and how Jessica could like reading such a grisly thing. Jess wouldn't hurt a fly and yet even when she was younger, she'd always had her nose in something like this. It used to be Stephen King and James Herbert but horror to crime seemed a grown-up process. Still, unconceivable to Marion who favoured humorous biographies, she realised that no one knew anyone else completely and no doubt, there were sides to her daughter she didn't know, and now would never find out.

###

Chapter 16: Simon

Simon pulled up outside his sister's house and switched off the car's engine. He sat for a moment thinking about the enormity of the task ahead of him. First thing was to let Jess' friends know what had happened. The chances were that they'd heard about it but no one had rung him or his mum. He figured that they wouldn't have their numbers and Jess' mobile battery had died since he'd checked it. Although it wasn't funny, he laughed at the irony. He'd meant to use his charger but in the hurry to pack his things he'd forgotten to get it. He'd find Jess' and use that for both. In the meantime there would likely be more messages on the home phone including the delightful 'I won't phone again' Veronica.

Letting himself in, he headed straight for the lounge and sure enough, there were seventeen messages. He skipped through the original eight and let the rest play out. Veronica's dulcet tones asked the machine where its master was. Naturally it hadn't a clue and even if it had it wouldn't have been able to reply.

The next dozen calls were from her work, the gym and friends saying that they'd heard the news, how awful it was and asked whoever was listening to their messages to accept their condolences. Most of the callers were thoughtful enough to leave their numbers. Simon listened to the varied voices on the same theme with muted attention as their words relived the enormity of the situation.

Call fifteen, from an Andy, snapped Simon out of his trance. "*I'm sorry for calling. I got this number from directory enquiries and hope it's the right one. Jessica Price? I know what happened to Jessica, I was there. I'm so sorry but there was nothing I could do. I tried, really I did, but I couldn't stop it. I've driven that train for over five years and nothing... I'm sorry. I don't know what I can do, if I can help or anything but if I can, my number is...*"

Simon wrote down the number, adding it to the list of other names and numbers he'd been writing on the pad beside the phone.

The final two calls were from Claire of Edwards, Wade & Talbot insurance company. They'd been advised of the accident from the police but had some details missing and would be very grateful if Miss Price could call them at her earliest convenience.

"So would I," Simon said to the handset, "as it would mean she was alive."

The second of Claire's calls was an apology realising she'd omitted to leave her direct dial and if she could have a return call today she could process the claim. "Get the wheels in motion," she said and laughed.

Simon wasn't laughing.

After making a cup of tea with a splash of almost-out-of-date milk and two sugars, Simon made the dreaded phone calls. Most had left their landlines so Simon gathered that they were at work when he called, for which he was thankful as face-to-face or rather voice-to-voice would have made the task much harder. They'd be upset, he'd get upset and… he didn't want to think about it. He left the same message on each; that he was grateful for their call and best wishes, and would be in touch again if appropriate. It sounded rather businesslike but Simon needed to be in control.

With four calls left, he made another cup of tea and looked for an address book. Pulling open the right side drawer under the phone in the lounge, he saw only a box of tissues (making a mental note of those in case he needed them later), some freebie DVDs that Jess collected from weekend newspapers and a neat set of glass coasters of edge-to-edge picturesque stones. That was Jess; neat. Not a thing out of place.

Getting a coaster out for his mug, he closed the drawer and opened the left one. He was glad he'd put his mug down when he saw the bundle of rolled-up notes.

"Shit! Jessica! What the hell?"

He wasn't sure whether he should take it out or not. He'd never seen her have so much money before, lying around. He knew she wasn't a criminal but curiosity got the better of him and he removed the bundle and closed the drawer; as if removing the one item out of its hiding place made it less suspicious.

He sat on the sofa and took off the elastic band. The notes were bundled into ten fifty pounds, with one of the notes folded over at right angles like they do at the banks, and there were six bundles.

"Three grand? Jess, what are you doing with three grand?"

Simon replaced the money in the chest of drawers. He'd decide what to do with it later. Looking at the remaining contents – more newspaper discs, some CDs, more notepads and a pile of pens and pencils and her mobile charger and hands-free handset – Simon picked up the charger, pulled out Jess' mobile from his jacket pocket and finding a spare socket on a five-gang extension lead, plugged it in. It beeped briefly and a strip of green lights flickered in sequence. He then rifled through the CDs and selected a Beethoven compilation. Ludwig was one of their mother's favourites and perfect for background music while Simon looked around the house.

"Right, Jess, let's find your paperwork and make some more calls." Train driver Andy and the insurance company would be hardest. Veronica and Alexis would wait.

The bundle of money was still playing on Simon's mind and he hoped that somewhere along the line, one of the phone calls would answer that question but he certainly wasn't going to ask about it. If it was Jessica's fair and square then no one else need be involved. If it wasn't hers then maybe not even their mother should know about it. He'd cross whichever bridge needed crossing and deal with whatever he found on the other side.

With no sign of paperwork downstairs, Simon went to the back bedroom, which he knew Jess had been using as a study the past few months.

On a bookshelf were over a dozen ring binders, each labelled with their relevant contents. Another of Jess' skills was organisation; the advantage of being a secretary, Simon supposed. He chose the 'Utilities' folder first and called the companies involved. As each phone call progressed, Simon got into a better routine of explaining that his sister had passed away and that their services were no longer required. He left the electricity company til last and was asked to give a final meter reading when he was ready to sell the house. He'd been warned that it could take a few weeks to be granted power of attorney but he'd been given a Green Form and Social Security paperwork so he could make the necessary arrangements. Collecting the death certificate was the next step. Like Marion, keeping busy was helping him get through what needed to be done.

The next thing he'd need to look for would be her Will, or at least a solicitor's letter or some confirmation that a Will had been registered. Of course, although the police saying Simon was her next of kin, his mother was legally but he'd honour Jess' wishes if she wanted to leave anything to friends.

He remembered the four phone calls he'd yet to make. Train driver Andy had his voicemail on so Simon left a message in a similar manner to the others but added, "Would you call me back. I'd like to know more about what had happened to my sister. I'm sorry. I realise it'll be hard but I need to speak to someone who was there."

The insurance company was very understanding. Mortified she'd made such a horrendous mistake, Claire said she'd deal with the police and would only call Simon when she needed to.

He then looked down at Jess' mobile which had sprung back into life and was almost at full charge. It only then occurred to him that he could have swapped their batteries over but he'd been busy and neither Veronica nor Alexis had called in the meantime so he couldn't see that matter being particularly urgent. He pressed the 'names' button and tapped the down key a couple of times. He found 'Alexis mobile' and jotted down the number. He scrolled back up to start from the end of the alphabet but there were no Vs. So Jessica knew Alexis but possibly not Veronica. But why had Veronica been calling Jess' house? Alexis must have been staying there or passed the landline number as a secondary contact number for some reason.

Simon dialled Alexis' mobile number from the landline. It rang for ages and Simon expected it to go to answerphone when a woman answered.

"Hello?"

"Oh, hello. Is that Alexis?"

"No, it's not. Who's this?"

"I'm Jessica's brother, Simon."

"I'm sorry, Simon, but I think you've got the wrong number. There's no Alexis or Jessica here."

"So you don't know Jess?"

The woman paused. "I don't think so. No, *I* don't."

"Sorry to have troubled you."

"No problem," the woman said and hung up.

###

Chapter 17: Beth and Nate

"Whose phone is this?" Beth growled at her husband as she disconnected the call.

Nate hesitated before saying, "Mine."

"Why did someone ring asking for two women and why have I never seen it before?"

"It's a replacement. I lost my other one so I got this… cheap… and I guess it's still got an old number." He held his left hand out, palm side up.

"How cheap?" Beth's eyes narrowed, phone still clasped in her right hand.

"From Camden market," he said, hand still outstretched.

"If you're lying to me," she said, reluctantly putting the phone on his palm.

He opened his black leather jacket and slipped the phone into an inside pocket. "Honey. I promised."

"You did and I won't forget it. Any more trouble and you're out of here. You understand? I'm not bringing this baby up with its father in prison."

Nate longed for the other look to return, the vulnerable one. He wasn't so keen on this look. This look implied that it could hurt him at any time. Carrying a sprog obviously didn't mellow her and from what he'd heard of hormones, he thought he'd better lock away the kitchen knives.

Something was niggling at the back of Beth's mind as she went to do the washing up that evening. She'd known Nate for long enough to know when he was telling the truth, which wasn't often. Even a simple question like 'does my bum look big in this?' gave him away. Not that she was overweight. The never-going-to-happen-in-real-life figure of Lara Croft was, Beth knew, how Nate liked his women and Beth's size twelve frame would never match it but somehow they'd been attracted to each other and after three years, had got married. Beth wasn't so sure what she saw in him these days but she was a traditional woman and took her vows very seriously. Sickness, health, richer, poorer it was, and that was how it was going to stay; until prison or another medium separated them.

She couldn't however, get the phone call out of her mind. The chap, Simon, had seemed convinced that either of the women he mentioned… Beth racked her brain… that Alex, no, Alexis, or Jessica had a connection to the phone. He'd been quite desperate so it had clearly been important. She knew there was more to it than her husband was letting on and she was determined to get to the bottom of it.

"You're up late, Beth."

Beth nodded.

"Aren't you tired?"

She shook her head.

"And you don't normally like Top Gear."

She shrugged.

Nate wasn't thrilled by the silent treatment but at least she was spending time with him. They usually did their own things when a programme was on that one favoured more than the other. He'd go down the pub during her soaps and she'd read her book when he had blokes' shows on.

Beth, on the other hand, had one thing in mind. To get to the leather jacket that was slumped over the end of the sofa. Nate's end. The jacket went everywhere with him; everywhere except bed and she was going to get that mobile phone if it killed her. Or him. *You've been reading too much*, she thought, *letting your thoughts get away from you. It was a wrong number and Nate's right, he got it from someone who buys and sells and the last person wasn't careful enough. She hoped that was it was but she had to know for sure.*

She finally broke her silence. "Cuppa?"

He looked at her sincerely. "Mmm, please. Thank you." He then returned his gaze to Jeremy Clarkson and 'The Hamster'.

Beth figured that if he wasn't going to go to bed then she'd make him something that would encourage him.

She returned a few minutes later with two cups of steaming hot chocolate. Whenever she was feeling amorous, which was less often than him, it always did the trick. He'd drink, feel sleepy and relaxed and lead her upstairs.

She'd waited until a few minutes before the end of the programme knowing he'd not be interested in the documentary that followed. And true to form, he'd not even needed to let the credits roll when he was rubbing his eyes, stretching his arms and yawning.

"Are you coming up, Beth?"

"Sure, in a minute. Let me do the washing up and I'll be with you."

"OK." Then, with a wink, he said, "See you up there."

Beth wasn't in the mood but maybe by the time she'd done the washing up, after checking the phone of course, he might have fallen asleep.

As he got up off the sofa, he went to grab his jacket.

"You're taking that to bed?" she asked a little too quickly.

Nate laughed. "You're right, wasn't thinking. I'll hang it up in the hall so you don't tell me off for cluttering the place."

Beth smiled half-heartedly and followed him out to the hall, pausing a little too long, while he put his jacket on the hook.

"Beth?"

"Mmm?"

"Are you following me?"

"No, sorry. Just, er, going to the kitchen. But was… was waiting for a kiss."

Nate grinned. "Come 'ere."

Beth did as she was told and felt his tongue dart into her mouth. As she backed off to go to the kitchen, he kept hold of her with his right hand and rubbed her stomach with his left. "I'm pleased, you know. It was a shock. I can't wait for another Nate."

Heaven help us, Beth thought as she turned and walked slowly to the kitchen.

As she stood by the sink, she waited until she heard the bathroom sink taps run before going back into the hall. She slowly pulled back the left side of Nate's jacket and pulled out the mobile.

Walking back into the kitchen, she shut the door and pressed buttons, grateful that whoever the phone had belonged to hadn't been security-conscious enough to put a code on it.

Once she'd worked out how to take off the key lock, she pressed the 'menu' button, the phone not too dissimilar to her own, then went into the call history. She knew that the last person to ring was Simon when the caller ID had come up as 'Home'. So Nate had to be lying and had no rights to the phone. The least she could do was to return it to its rightful owner but she didn't recognise the area code. With the phone in her hand, she returned to the lounge and pulled open a drawer that contained the phone directory. The first section after the index and introduction was a numerical listing. 01632 came up as Eversley. She didn't even know where that was.

Returning to the kitchen, she saved the phone number into her own mobile's contacts list and went further back into the call history on Nate's mobile. There were seven in a row from someone called Veronica.

Beth came out of the history listing and went into 'names'. She scrolled down to see if Simon was in there but was surprised to see that there were only five names in the entire list: Cherry, Daniel, Home, Sindy and Veronica. Daniel had to be the boyfriend, so the three women must be girlfriends; the only three that Alexis had presumably. Not even Jessica had made the list.

Beth looked at the clock on the top right of the screen. 10.45. It was too late to ring Veronica or Simon and certainly too late to ring the other names. She didn't bother writing down their numbers as there were no recent calls from them, missed or otherwise.

The toilet overhead flushed so she quickly put the keypad back on 'lock' mode and crept back to the jacket before the bathroom door opened. She did the washing up then joined her husband upstairs.

Beth thought of more than England in the next few minutes and when Nate was snoring away next to her, she turned to face the wall and went to sleep, a frown planted on her face.

###

Chapter 18: Simon

Phoning the bank proved to be more of a tricky order for Simon. They'd been, naturally, reluctant to give him any details over the phone but had made an appointment to see the bank manager the next day to discuss her affairs.

Simon had just put down the phone handset from speaking to the bank when it rang. "Hello?"

"Hello. Can I speak to Simon?"

"Speaking." He paused to let the caller continue.

"Hello, Simon. My name is Andy Baker. You phoned and left a message. About your sister. I'm the train driver."

"Yes. Thank you for calling back. I'm so sorry for what happened."

"Shit, so am I. If I could have stopped the train, I would have. Please understand that."

"Oh, I do. The police say it was an accident, that my sister's car clipped a van on the ice and got stuck on the track. Do you remember what happened? Were you hurt?"

"Cuts and bruises. We all escaped with cuts and bruises. Thanks to your sister. She was so brave, so calm. She tried to drive the car off the track but it wouldn't budge. Did you know that? I slammed on the brakes as soon as I saw her, of course.

The two guys from the van ran…"

"You saw the van drivers? Have you spoken to them?"

"Yes, at the scene. They're shaken up as you can imagine. They tried to help but couldn't get to her in time. Neither of them was injured and no real damage to the van. I think the police took it for tests."

"They have. I've seen it, in the police impound. Dented wing, that's all."

"And the mess that your sister's car… I'm sorry. You don't want to hear that."

"I've seen it. She didn't stand a chance."

"What would you like to know?"

"I'm sorry. I don't know. Your side of events."

Andy recalled the morning as best he could, as Simon sat on the sofa taking it all in. It was much as the police had described it and Simon was reassured that it had been quick and Andy agreed that it appeared to be a freak of nature, bad timing.

"Thanks so much for ringing, Andy. It can't have been easy."

"Of course, I wanted to. I feel for you, mate. If there's anything else you want to know. You have my number."

Simon thanked him again and hung up.

With the Veronica and Alexis matter still up in the air but looking like being unsolvable, all Simon could do was continue going through the paperwork. He'd deal with the other people in Jessica's mobile's phone list another time.

He looked at her bank statements in preparation for the meeting for the following day. He'd assumed that the two files had been one recent and one old but each one was a separate account, both with the same bank, both the same type of account so it didn't make sense. It was only when Simon looked at the far right side balance column that it became clear. One was a standard account with a salary going in and utilities, shopping and cash coming out. No lump sum mortgage payments but Simon guessed these were coming out of the other account. The other statement, however, had far more going in than coming out. Simon flicked through the statements until he reached the oldest at the back. The account had been opened just under a year earlier and there were regular deposits of a few hundred pounds at a time; more money than a regular day job could ever pay. It would explain the roll of money downstairs but not how it had come to be there. It also explained why there were no mortgage payments.

No mortgage? Jess, what on earth had you got yourself involved in? Simon thought as he put the latest statement on top of its predecessors. He heard a click downstairs as the CD came to a stop. Poor old Ludwig had been playing his heart out, mostly ignored.

Simon switched on Jess' computer, which lit up an 'apple' logo and waited to be asked for a password. From conversations from behind their respective laptop over their mum's dining table at Christmas, he knew the two possibilities that his sister used and he was greeted with a picture of a leopard after tapping in the first.

Letting the start-up programmes load, Simon went to the box room over the hall, but it contained a bed, ornaments dotted on shelving, TV and a few books; no personal items – a guest bedroom, nothing more.

He then headed into Jessica's bedroom and to a wall of three wardrobes. Opening the left door of the first one, he hadn't known what to expect but he wouldn't have been surprised to see a pole dancer's outfits or whips and chains. He wasn't disappointed. Both sides were packed with designer eveningwear; he was no expert but it smelled of money. He opened the next wardrobe, which was stuffed with enough clothes, shoes and handbags to kit out a small boutique. The third wardrobe contained business suits, jumpers, skirts and a thin raincoat; the Jessica he'd known. The woman who owned, and presumably wore, the contents of wardrobes one and two was for no one he knew. Jessica's life involved another woman; a girlfriend, had to be. "Come out the closet too, Jessica, you're so busted."

All Simon had to do was wait for Alexis to turn up. It was clear she lived there from the clothes she had, more than Jessica's. She'd obviously lost her mobile but she had to come back for her stuff.

Failing that, maybe Veronica would break her word and call.

Simon checked Jessica's emails; a mixture of friends, colleagues, and spam. Having deleted the spam, he replied to the rest, recognising some names from the phone calls. He copied and pasted the text from one to another, personalising as necessary as he went along. He'd heard his sister talk about some of them but he'd never met them and realised that was a side of Jessica's life he knew little about. Having replied to most of them, it occurred to him to ask them about Alexis so contacted them again. As it was unlikely he'd get quick answers, he shut down the computer.

He went into the box room, picked a book at random, a thriller judging by the cover, and headed downstairs. Holding the book in his left hand, he tugged the lounge door handle with his right so that the door was at as near to a forty-five degree angle as he could get it, then lay the book on the hall floor, aligning the spine with the radiator.

He slammed the front door behind him then drove away, singing along to Heart FM.

###

Chapter 19: Simon and the Bank Manager

Simon's appointment with Everlsey Bank was for ten-thirty so he had a light breakfast and left his mother's house just before nine-thirty. Leaving after the rush hour would get him into town in plenty of time to go to the Registry Office to collect the death certificate then on to the bank.

He found a parking space a few doors down. The queue in the Registry Office was short so he was outside in less than twenty minutes.

Wearing smart jeans and a casual shirt, and clutching Jessica's 'bank' files, he walked through the double electronic doors of Eversley Bank and headed for the reception desk. The young lady asked him to take a seat and said that Mr Frizzell wouldn't be long. "Can I get you anything to drink, Mr Price?"

Simon looked at her name badge. "Just some water please, Carol." He felt as if he'd had enough tea recently to the point of sloshing as he walked.

Carol smiled and disappeared into a back room. Simon sat in one of two reception chairs and picked up a 'Banking Times' magazine. He glanced at the contents but wasn't paying attention and before he knew it, a tall figured loomed over him.

"Mr Price?" The man smiled sympathetically.

"Yes."

"I'm John Frizzell. Would you like to follow me."

Simon followed the manager into a side room and was directed to another seat.

The man sat behind the desk and tapped a few keys on the computer keyboard. He stabbed at the enter key with a flourish as if part of an amateur dramatics class. "I'm so sorry to hear about your sister. It was on the local news last night. Terrible, just terrible. I can't imagine what you and your family must be going through."

"Thank you, Mr Frizzell."

"John, please. And you're here to tie up your sister's affairs."

"Sort of. I'm waiting for probate, which I think I'll be dealing with as Jessica listed me as next of kin. My mum's… it's best that I deal with this."

"Of course. There are wheels that we can get in motion until probate comes through."

Simon stared at a certificate on the wall behind John. 'Wheels in motion' seemed to be everyone's favourite phrase in these circumstances.

"Mr Price?"

"Sorry. I wanted to ask you about these two accounts actually."

"I must just ask you, before we proceed, if I can take a copy of the paperwork you will have been given. Data Protection Act and all that."

Simon handed over the Death Certificate and other documents that the police had given him and Mr Frizzell left the room.

He returned a couple of minutes later with the glass of water Carol had gone in search of.

"Thank you," Simon said as the glass was put in front of him.

John passed the original forms back to Simon who put them into one of the 'bank' files. He then pulled out the two latest statements and handed them to the manager.

"Ah yes. Her private and business accounts."

"Business account? I thought she worked for someone else. A solicitor's?"

"She did but the number two account was a business account, for her self-employment status."

"Self-employed? Doing what, do you know?"

"I'm sorry I don't. Because both accounts were registered in her name and her co-signature's on the second, we don't need to know and we didn't ask."

"Co-signature? Do you have the other name?"

"Certainly." John scrolled the screen. "Alexis Starr. Double r."

Both men paused. "You don't look surprised," the bank manager continued.

"I am, but I'm not. I've been hearing the name Alexis a lot over the last few hours but I don't know who she is. Do you have a current address for her?"

"Let me have a look... Here we go. Yes, it's the same as your sister's."

"I thought so."

"But you don't know who she is?"

"No. I never met her at Jess' house. Do you know when she became a co-signature?"

"February last year, when the second account was set up. The first was set up in 1993..."

"When... Jessica started working?"

"That sounds about right, going by her date of birth."

"And was this Alexis a co-signature on her first account?"

"No, just the second."

"The business account."

"Yes."

"So, lodger or friend and business partner but not girlfriend."

"Mr Price?"

"Sorry, thinking out loud. A partner of a few years would normally be on a private account as well as a business account, yes?"

"Not always but quite often, especially if they live together."

"Mmm. Do you recall ever having met Alexis?"

"No, sorry, I don't, but I can ask my colleagues."

"If you don't mind, that would be great."

"Certainly. Leave it with me and I'll see what I can find out for you."

"Thanks very much."

"And you'll let me know when probate comes through then we can have a chat about what you and your parents want to do with the money? What sort of investments we can help them with?"

"There's only my mum and I. My father died..."

"I'm sorry. I should have remembered. They had an account here."

"It's OK. You're not expected to remember everyone."

"No, but I do remember your sister."

"You do?"

"Oh yes, she was the one who deposited most if not all of the money."

"Really?"

"I saw her on numerous occasions. I often oversee large deposits."

"And large withdrawals?"

"Always, except I don't think there ever have been any from your sister's account other than to buy her house. If there were they'll show up on the statements you have there."

Simon nodded and smiled.

"So, thank you again for calling in Mr Price and again, I'm so sorry about your sister. Please pass on our condolences to your mother and if there's anything else we can…"

"Thank you. I'll bear that in mind."

Simon's brain was a swirl as he drove to his sister's. The main objective of the trip was to check the emails but he also wanted to do more digging, find out anything he could on Alexis Starr. Whatever Jess' files, electronic or paper, Google or Yahoo had on her, he wanted to know the connection between them. Whatever it took, he'd find it.

###

Chapter 20: Simon

The house felt cold as Simon opened the front door to number fifty-one Berry Avenue. He wiggled his key out of the lock and pushed open the front door. The book still lay where he'd left it and the lounge door at the same angle, give or take a degree or two. He sighed. So, Alexis hadn't turned up. Granted it had only been a few hours but he had hoped she would have had to return for some of her things even if it wasn't to stay the night. And she would have moved the book, wouldn't she?

Bolting up the stairs, missing every other step, he headed for the main bedroom and looked in the middle and right cupboards first but everything was where it had been the day before. He opened the right wardrobe, hoping that although they were Jessica's clothes, Alexis may have preferred something more... ordinary. But again, nothing had moved.

Heading to the back bedroom, he leant down to the skirting wall sockets and flicked on both switches. After typing in the password, Simon let the computer do its stuff while he switched the heating to constant and returned downstairs to put on the kettle. He looked in the fridge for something to eat and made a mental note to check the sell-by dates. Jess had always been fussier than him, and he'd tease her for chucking stuff out the day after the 'use by' but she was of the 'it's there for a reason' camp and he supposed it made sense.

Adding milk and sugar to his tea, he threw the spoon into the washing up bowl and made another mental note to do the washing up before he left. The kitchen had been spotless when he'd first arrived but the empty cups and plates he'd created from the tea and sandwiches now made an ugly pile in the sink. That was another thing they'd differed on. He'd throw everything in the bowl whereas she'd neatly stack on the right draining board. "What's the point of having two draining boards if you don't use them," she'd said, "and if you shove everything in the bowl you've only then got to take them all out again when you want to fill it with clean water." The directions of toilet rolls were another bone of contention; he was an in-facer, whereas hers had to face out. "You can't get to them properly if they're clung against the wall. If they face out there is plenty of space to grab the end." He couldn't argue with that logic but guessed that some siblings had to be different; like a PC and Mac – they were born that way. She'd stopped short of hotel bedroom-style folding the end corners of the toilet rolls in, but then nothing would have surprised Simon. He'd never been to her office but imagined her impeccably neat desk with drawers of pens and pencils, filed in rows liked soldiers on parade.

He turned on both taps and squirted in some washing up liquid, then topped the bowl up with the remainder of the boiled water and dumped the cups, plates and cutlery in being careful to not let any of the suds spill over the top. As he did this he stared out the window and looked around the back garden. It was the exception to the rule. Whilst Jessica's house was almost spotless, the garden was definitely a work-in-progress. It looked like there had been a plan but it had been done in stages and each stage appeared to have been interrupted. It didn't matter. Simon saw little point in doing anything to it, especially at this time of year, when whoever bought the house would… what was the saying?… put their own stamp on it. The shed would have to be sorted but unless there was anything he or his mum wanted, the new owners could have whatever was in there as far as he was concerned.

With the washing up done and left to drain, Simon returned upstairs. He pulled out the study chair and slumped down. Pulling it forward with his feet until the wheels hit the footrest, he made himself comfortable.

There were five replies; all from friends but none knew of anyone called Alexis. It occurred to Simon that if the two girls lived together then it was likely that they shared the computer. He typed 'Alexis' in the Finder search bar and waited for a moment before '0 items' appeared at the bottom of the screen. That didn't make sense. She must have used the computer for something, called documents or files by her name or written some kind of correspondence from that address. Jess surely would have photos on there of the two of them. Simon flicked over to the 'Mail' system and did the same search but frowned at the same result.

78

He decided that the next route was the internet so double-clicked on the Safari 'compass' and waited for the preset home pages to appear.

He typed 'Alexis Starr' into Google and clicked on the magnifying glass icon. In a mere 0.23 seconds, the screen revealed over twelve million results; the first page showing just ten of them.

The first link was to Alexis' MySpace page. "Yes!" Simon clenched his fist and punched the air. "Unusual name, this must be her." He smiled as he clicked on the first link but then read on.

"Bugger. Female, eighteen years old, Strong Island NY / Peacham, Vermont, United States. There must be others." He clicked the back arrow, returning him to the results page.

"Alexis Starr's professional profile... excellent. We already know she's a business woman. She this must be... oh. Sales Manager, IBM, Stevenage. Mmm... could be. Stevenage isn't that far away. She's a manager for a large international company so she could be working away." That would have explained the fancy clothes thought she couldn't imagine sequins and leather in a client meeting. Simon smiled. Actually, yes, he could imagine... He shook his head. "Get to the point, Simon." There was no photograph on the page but there was a bright orange 'view full profile' button so Simon clicked on that. He was greeted with a log-in screen so decided to go to the other search engine links before going through the process of setting up an account, if he needed to be that thorough.

The third link was for an American actress who again was unlikely but a possibility so Simon clicked on the blue underlined text. "Maybe, maybe not." An American actress, yes, but in porn movies. That would explain the outfits but Simon had a feeling that 'his' Alexis was English. He worked his way down the links and was getting nowhere fast. Despite the unusual name, there were lots of needles in this proverbial haystack and he'd gone from seriously underwhelmed to overloaded so decided he'd give the bank another go. Being the only solid lead on Alexis' connection with his sister, he called the Eversley Bank and asked for John Frizzell. Tucked the cordless handset under his chin, he closed his eyes while serenaded by what sounded like Chopin.

It occurred to him while he was on hold that he'd not told the phone company about the situation, their details hadn't been in the utilities folder, but it saved his mobile bill if he made calls from the landline, plus he'd need to use it for the broadband so he decided to leave them 'til last.

"Hello?" a voice said, interrupting a particularly mellow piano solo. "Mr Price?"

Simon's eyes sprung open and he grabbed the handset.

"Sorry, hi. Is that Mr Frizzell?"

"Yes, Mr Price. What can I help you with?"

"I wondered if you'd found anything out about Jessica's business partner, Alexis Starr."

"Yes and no, Mr Price."

"Simon, please."

"OK, Simon. Our records show that Jessica opened the account in February last year."

"Yes."

"In both the names of herself and Alexis Starr."

"Yes…" Simon frowned, learning nothing new.

"They both had to sign the initial paperwork."

"Yes…" Simon put his right hand out sideways then rotated it as if to hurry the man up. It failed to do the trick.

"Which your sister did."

"OK."

"When she set up the account."

Simon remained silent.

"And Alexis…"

Hoorah! Simon thought.

"…signed a couple of weeks later. The dates are thirteen days apart."

"So someone saw her."

"Y…es."

"So they can tell me what she looks like."

"Erm, no."

"I'm sorry, I don't understand."

"The paperwork was administered by a colleague who left a couple of months later. So I'm afraid that's a dead end."

Dead loss, more like. Simon smiled an air stewardess' grin at the phone and thanked the manager, who offered to be a call away if he needed anything else.

Simon chewed his left thumbnail as he frowned at the screen. He'd been doing a lot of frowning but he guessed it was better than bawling his eyes out. This had almost become a game and he was like a dog with a bone when there were loose ends to be tied and it seemed that in Jessica's life, there were plenty of those.

###

Chapter 21: Beth and Nate

A loud moaning within inches of her left ear greeted Beth as she woke the next morning. Rolling over to face her husband, she normally found him attractive but he'd slobbered in his sleep and had bedding imprints in his cheeks. With a sudden urge to vomit, she threw back the duvet and raced to the bathroom. Unsure as to whether it was the baby or Nate that was making her feel sick, her mind wandered back to the mobile phone in his jacket pocket. Switching off the bathroom light, she looked in at the sleeping figure in the bedroom before heading down the stairs.

The names and numbers of the last two callers were stored in Beth's own mobile so she wasn't sure what else she needed to do until she saw the flashing yellow envelope.

"Of course, text messages." This one had come from Veronica so Beth unlocked the key lock and pressed the 'view' button. *Would whoever now owns this phone, please ring me. I've been trying to get hold of Alexis and am getting worried. It's not like her. If you know her or where she is, please ring.*

Veronica wasn't the only one getting worried. This no longer seemed to be a simple case of a previous owner trading it in for a newer model, not that she'd believed Nate's story anyway. She'd hoped…

She heard a snort from upstairs and froze. Snoring resumed and she went into the phone's inbox. There were as few messages as there were contacts, and all but one were from Veronica. The second one was from Daniel; an irate message asking her what had happened and why had she done what she'd done.

"Did you dump him, Alexis?" Beth smiled. She'd remembered the two names when Simon had rung because of TV characters. Jessica Rabbit and Alexis… 1980s, big shoulder pads, Dynasty. Alexis Carrington. Played by… the blonde, now silver-haired woman who'd been on one of those Celebrity Big Brothers? No, Masterchef. Hell's Kitchen. She shook her head.

"Linda Evans," she whispered under her breath, "married the older chap, Blake. But then who did Joan Collins play? Krystal. Linda Evans was Krystal, Blake's wife. So if Joan Collins was Alexis, which Carrington did she marry? And wasn't she a Colby?" She tapped the back of the mobile against her upper lip. No, the Colbys were after Dynasty so Alexis was a Carrington, but whose?

As Beth tried working out the Carrington / Colby family trees, she heard a creaking floorboard overhead and the slam of the bathroom door.

"Shit." She put both mobiles side by side and typed Daniel's number into her own. She quickly read Veronica's other messages, and returned the phone to its main screen. She heard whistling from overhead: 'Valerie', Nate's favourite song of the moment, especially the Zutons' cover. More versions than Gershwin's Summertime, she'd ribbed him.

She heard the toilet flush, so marched out to the hall and stuffed Nate's mobile back into his jacket pocket. She was still at the bottom of the stairs when the bathroom door opened. She swung round to face the top. "Honey?"

"Yeah?"

"I'm making some tea. Would you like one?"

"Please. That would be lovely."

"And toast?"

"Uh huh."

"One or two slices?"

"Two, please."

Beth was walking to the kitchen when Nate called her name.

She returned to the bottom of the stairs. "Yes?"

"How are you feeling? I heard you being sick earlier. You got morning sickness?"

"I guess so, but better now."

"You'd tell me if there was something wrong, wouldn't you?"

"Of course. Don't worry."

"OK," he said cheerfully, "be down in a sec."

He seemed to be taking this baby seriously after all. *Miracles do happen*, Beth thought as she filled the kettle with enough water for two. She settled it back into its cradle then took some bread out the fridge. Putting two pieces in the toaster, she leant back against the worktop and waited.

She didn't have Nate down as a 'new man' like Richard E Grant was at the beginning of 'Jack & Sarah', one of Beth's favourite films, but he was at least showing an interest. The kettle boiled as she noticed her mobile sitting on the counter. Nate wasn't likely to look through it but she slipped it into her dressing gown pocket, not wanting to take any chances. She was a "safety girl". Beth smiled as she remembered the line from another of her cherished movies, 'Pretty Woman'.

She wasn't sure how long he'd had the phone, the first time she remembered seeing it was yesterday but he was unlikely to have even noticed the names otherwise he would probably have deleted them. Not that the names would have meant anything anyway, but she had a feeling they meant something to Alexis and that she meant something to someone else; to Jessica, Simon, Veronica and possibly still to a man called Daniel.

With a busy day ahead, Beth decided to wait until Nate was firmly out the house to call Veronica, Daniel then Simon.

Heavy footsteps down the stairs snapped her out of her thoughts.

"Morning."

"Mmm?" Nate plodded in scratching his head. "Morning, Beth." He watched her butter his toast and hand him the plate. "Are you sure you're all right?"

"Yes fine. What about you? You look dreadful."

"Mmm, I'm… fine." He said, stealing her word and munching his breakfast. "Just tired. And you sure the baby's OK?"

"Of course, don't worry. It's all quite normal." Beth walked over to the kettle and made the tea.

"You haven't been for a scan yet, have you? I haven't missed anything?"

Beth laughed. "Not yet. Going on Friday, come with me?"

"Of course. I can't believe you're six weeks gone already?"

"Yes, Nate, six weeks 'gone' as you put it," she said, handing him his tea.

"And you've only known a week?"

Beth nodded.

"Didn't you know straight away?"

"Nate, how old are you? It amazes me that you even know how babies are made."

Nate sniggered. "Oh, yes, I know that all right." He looked at the expression on her face but grinned and said, "Sorry, not funny." He put the mug and plate on the worktop then bent down to put his head on her stomach. "Has baby taken mummy's sense of humour away already?"

Beth gave her husband a light tap on the top of his head. He looked up and grinned again.

"You can melt the sternest of women's hearts, Nathan Peter James Morrison."

The only other people he'd ever heard use his full name were his parents and the priest at his and Beth's wedding and that's the way he wanted to keep it. "Thank you, mother."

It then dawned on her. She was going to be a mother; responsible for another human being; two children in the house. Beth smiled and shook her head. She couldn't stay cross for long and maybe she'd got him wrong about the phone. If he was involved with anything she'd know. Wouldn't she?

"Nate, what are you up to today?"

"Oh, the usual; nip out for a paper, come back, make some calls, have some lunch, go down the job centre and…"

"Why don't you go down the job centre this morning?" she said a little too eagerly.

"I'd rather stay here with you." He fluttered his eyelids at her playfully.

She curled her lips into her mouth to suppress a laugh. "I've got chores to do. You'll only get under my feet."

Nate looked wounded. "Don't you want me, Bethy Wethy?"

"Ever since I said I was expecting your baby you've gone all mushy."

Nate hugged her fiercely then pulled back a little, looking at her stomach.

"It's the size of a peanut. You can be as rough as you like."

His cheeky grin re-appeared.

"Anyway," she said, trying to return to the subject, "job centre. This morning?"

"I ought to, given our change in circumstances."

"That would be good. We can't keep going on my wages."

"Speaking of which, will you be gone by the time I get home?"

"Probably, I'm on two 'til ten until Sunday."

"So you don't mind if I..." He paused.

"If you what?"

"Go to the pub at lunchtime with the lads."

Beth normally wouldn't have been particularly thrilled with the thought of him spending time with the reprobates he called friends but if it meant him being out the house longer then it suited her just fine. Of course she could make the phone calls on a break at work, but being home alone meant no prying ears. Besides she wanted to do some digging around the house without him in it. "I'll have a shower then."

"Mmm?"

"I didn't *think* you were listening."

"Sorry."

"I'm going to have a shower."

"OK."

"Do you want anything from town when I go?"

"No, thanks. I work at Tesco, remember?"

"I know but there must be things that even they don't sell."

"That's sweet of you, but we've got a full fridge and I'll bring home some stuff to top up the freezer. Unless you can think of anything?"

"I'll surprise you."

"All the time, Nate, all the time."

87

Chapter 22: Simon

Simon frowned at the computer screen. So much for the internet being the fountain of all knowledge. It was as if Alexis Starr, the fifty-one Berry Avenue Alexis Starr anyway, was a ghost. He needed to get hold of Veronica. Maybe a call to the phone company would help. He'd have to phone them at some stage to say what was going on. He leaned over the desk to pick up the cordless landline when his mobile rang. "Hello?"

"Mr Price?"

"Speaking."

"Mr Price, Sgt Lewis here."

"Hello. Do you have some news?"

"Our investigations are ongoing but we've interviewed everyone on the scene and forensics are still working the vehicles. It shouldn't take much longer."

"Thanks for letting me know."

"What I was phoning about is that your sister's body is being released. Do you need any help with making the arrangements?"

"Do the police do that?"

"We can put you in touch with–"

"Thanks but we have a company in mind. They were very good with my dad."

"Of course. No problem. I'll keep you updated but..." He paused. "You take care, Mr Price, and let me know if you need anything."

"You've been so kind."

"You're welcome, sir. Speak to you again no doubt."

Simon stared at the phone holster and slowly slotted the handset back in it. That was it then. His sister was dead and those arrangements had to be made. He tilted back his head as he felt the tears coming. There was nothing to stop him, no one around but that was what worried him; that he wouldn't be able to stop. He leant over the desk and picked up the landline phone, typed in his mother's number and was about to press the phone icon when 'ICE MUM' appeared on the screen. "ICE hey, Jess? Your 'In Case of Emergency'? How ironic that the thing you programmed in your phone to help you, killed you. The stuff that you loved playing with when you were younger, had in your Southern Comfort and Lemonades, skied down, watched that film on DVD with Sid the Sloth that made you laugh, with his lisp like Granddad's."

Simon pulled back the study curtain to reveal a Christmas card scene. Snow was falling heavily and settling on the grass and shed roof. He shivered. His left hand vibrated. He looked at the screen and 'ICE MUM' stared back.

"Hi, Mum."

"Simon?"

"Yes. Hi."

"Have you seen the weather?"

"Just opened the curtains. Bit heavy isn't it."

"Are you going to be long?"

"I've got a few things to do here."

"Oh, Simon. Please hurry before the roads get bad. I'd hate to think of you…" she paused.

"OK. I'll leave now."

"Would you? Thank you. I know I'm being silly but…"

"No, it's fine. I'll switch off the computer and come back." Without wireless internet connection in his mother's house, it seemed pointless in taking the computer with him.

"I'll see you shortly then."

"OK."

"Thanks, Simon."

###

Chapter 23: Simon and Veronica

Simon hung up and was about to put the phone back in its cradle when it rang again. The screen showed 'Withheld number'.

"Hello?"

"Oh, sorry, I think I've got the wrong number."

"Who are you after?" Simon blurted.

"I think…"

"Were you after Jessica?"

"No. I have. I've got the wrong number. Sorry to…"

"Please." Simon begged. "Don't hang up. Were you after Alexis?"

Silence from the other end.

"Alexis Starr?" Simon repeated.

"Yes."

"Do you know Jessica?"

"No, sorry."

"Is she friends with Alexis?"

"I don't know. I suppose so."

"You suppose so? I'm sorry I don't get it."

"Alexis is… is an… employee of mine but she seems to have gone off the radar."

"Are you Veronica?"

Another pause. "Have you been listening to the messages?"

"Yes."

"Is Alexis there?"

"No. I don't think she's been here for a while. Her clothes and things are still here but…"

"Then she can't have gone far."

"I don't know. I don't know what's missing. You see, it's my sister's house."

"And your sister is Jessica."

"Yes."

"Then can I speak to her?"

"I'm sorry you can't."

"Can you give her a message she can pass on to Alexis?"

"Sorry, I can't."

"Get her to ring me?"

"I'm sorry. I'm not being awkward. It's just that… Jessica died on Monday morning."

"No! How?"

"Road accident."

"That's terrible. And Alexis?"

"I don't know. I think she might be away on business."

"I doubt that."

"Why?"

"Because as far as I know she only works for me and I've not sent her anywhere this week."

"What is it that you and Alexis do?"

"We're in… we're in Human Relations… Resources. I'm her… HR manager. There's little travel in HR."

"Client interfacing, isn't it. Keeping everyone happy."

"You could say that, yes."

"And you have no idea where Alexis is?"

"No. Not since the weekend."

"And you've not heard from her. No, of course you haven't otherwise you'd not be phoning here."

"Have you tried her mobile?"

"Yes. I've been trying it since Monday but there's a guy answering."

"I get a woman."

"You have Alexis' mobile number? Sorry, what did you say your name was?"

"Simon. I listened to your messages and assumed you'd got the wrong number but then I was going through Jess' mobile and Alexis' number was on it. I assumed it was the same Alexis so..."

"So you rang it and got a woman's voice?"

"Yes."

"And you're sure it wasn't Alexis?"

"She said it wasn't; didn't know her or Jessica."

"Then I don't know what we can do next. Just wait for her to call or turn up?"

"Aren't you worried? That she's not turned up to work?"

"A little, especially because she left under a cloud…"

"That Daniel chap?"

"Yes. But she's freelance so she sort of comes and goes as she likes."

"You can get freelance HR?"

"Yes. Anyone can go freelance on just about anything these days."

"So that would explain the account."

"Sorry?"

"Jessica set up a joint account with Alexis and I'm trying to tie up loose ends."

"This is the only other number I had for Alexis other than her mobile so I assumed it was her house. They were living together?"

"I'm not sure. It looks like she was living here but Jessica had never mentioned her. She would have if it were serious enough to have a joint bank account, surely, even if it were a business account."

"Unless she had a reason not to. Are you sure they were only living together?"

"What do you mean?"

"They weren't married… you know civil partnership or life partner or…"

"Oh, no. Jess would have said something. It would have killed my mum if she'd not been to her wedding, civil or otherwise. Our mother's very open-minded and besides, Jess had never said of any feelings towards women, and I'd know. She had a string of men in her life."

Veronica snorted.

"Veronica. Can I ask you a question?"

"You can ask."

"How did you pay Alexis?"

"I can't say."

"It won't go any further. I promise."

"It wasn't regularly like wages. I'd pay her in…" Simon could tell she was trying to weigh him up. Did he sound like a snitch? "It was always cash. Lump sums. Easier that way."

"Thank you, Veronica. That matches the bank statements but I wanted to be sure. So, what do we do now?" Simon continued.

"I guess we wait for Alexis to surface. I've brought her quite a lot of work over the past few months so I don't think she'll be in hiding too long... unless she's moonlighting somewhere else."

"Maybe. I've got plenty of other things to sort out without worrying about Alexis."

"And I'll let you know if I hear anything from her."

"Please. Can I give you my mobile number?"

"Sure, let me grab a pen and paper."

Simon read out his number and thanked her for calling. He hung up and put the phone back in its support. Conscious of his worrying mother, he closed the computer programmes and shut off the machine, waiting for all the lights to disappear before switching off the wall sockets.

"That wasn't a productive afternoon, Simon," he said to himself. At least he'd finally spoken to Veronica and whilst neither of them had got very far, he felt he had an ally, someone else who was trying to find the elusive Alexis, and surely two heads were better than one.

Leaving the book in the hall, and the door at the same angle, he locked up and trudged down the white path back to his car. He switched on the engine, put the heating up full blast and watched the snow fly off the windscreen as he set the wipers going. He used a credit card to clear the side windows and wiped it on his jeans before putting it back in his wallet.

The roads were slushy but he was still rather nervous driving back to his mother's. It was too early in the evening to be icy but he wasn't going to take any chances. He'd not had his tyres checked since the MOT back in the summer and made a mental note to do so next time he was going past a garage. He made another mental note to buy a notepad to write down all the mental notes he'd been making. His head was hurting and he didn't have the best memory in the world. Jess seemed to have been born with the recollective brain cells and he wished he'd asked her how she did it.

###

Chapter 24: Beth and the Phone Calls

With Nate showered and dispensed to the job centre, Beth sat down on the sofa with her mobile and large mug of hot sugary coffee. She took a sip, winced as it burnt her tongue and scrolled to Daniel's name in the phonebook. Making these calls was all she'd thought about since the night before yet she didn't have a clue what she was going to say.

She pressed the 'call' button. It rang twice before being answered.

"Yes!" Daniel barked.

"Is that Daniel?"

"Yes. Alexis?

"Erm…"

"Lexi where the hell have you been?"

"I'm sorry…"

"I bet you are, you little tart."

"Now, hold on…"

"No. You don't run out of me, take my money then expect…"

"Wait."

"What? You're phoning to say sorry? Give it back?"

"No."

"Then what, Alexis?"

"I'm sorry, but you don't understand."

"Hold on. You're not Alexis."

"No, that's what I was trying to say."

"Then who the hell are you? And where's Alexis?"

"I don't know."

"You don't know who you are?"

"Of course I do, but I don't know where Alexis is. I was hoping you'd be able to tell me."

"Who are you and what are you doing with her phone."

"I've come by her mobile and I'm trying to get it back to her."

"Come by… how."

"I'm not sure."

"You've knicked it?"

"No, I haven't."

"Found it then."

"Sort of. So you don't know where she is."

"No and if I did, I'd…"

"Sorry to trouble you," Beth said, and hung up. "One down, two to go. Simon might be complicated, so next is friend Veronica."

Scrolling down, she highlighted Veronica's name and pressed 'call'. It immediately went through to her answerphone.

"Hi. My name is… erm, I've got Alexis' phone and I'm trying to find out… I'm trying to get it back to her. Can you give me a ring on my mobile number. Alexis' is… I haven't got it at the moment but… I know where it is but… oh, will you just ring me." Beth relayed her number and hung up. She'd expected to speak to Veronica so had more of a speech ready. She'd be more prepared when she rang back, and hoped that it would be before she had to go to work.

Next she rang Simon on the 'Home' number. It also went to answerphone. She left a more coherent message and again, asked him to call her on her mobile. She wondered why she was going to so much bother for a missing mobile, especially if it was going to land Nate in trouble but it seemed to be far more complicated than she'd expected and she was more than happy to dabble in a little excitement for a while.

She leaned back against the sink and tapped her right foot on the lino. She wasn't sure what to do next other than clean the kitchen and she wasn't in the mood for that. She switched on the kettle for another cuppa and was just getting the milk from the fridge when her mobile went.

"Hello?"

"It's Veronica. You rang about Alexis."

"Oh, yes. Thanks for calling back."

"Sure. You say you have her mobile…"

"Well, yes."

"And you got it from her?"

"Not exactly."

"How then… exactly?"

"I came by it." Beth then winced as she'd used the same phrase with Daniel and remembered his reaction.

"You found it?"

Beth couldn't, didn't want to, explain. "Er, yes."

"So why are you ringing me?"

"I thought you might be able to tell me where she is. Jessica's brother's been ringing."

"Simon?"

"You know him?"

"Only since this morning. I spoke to him briefly. Where did you find the phone?"

"In the street," Beth lied.

Veronica laughed. "No, I didn't mean specifically."

Beth paused, not an expert at trying to make things up as she went along. "Camden. Can you get a message to her?"

"Alexis? I would if I could."

"You don't know where she is either?"

"No. It appears we're all after her."

"Do you know why Simon is?"

"I don't know. I guess it's to do with Jessica's death."

"Jessica's dead?"

"Yes. Simon didn't tell you?"

"No, but then with conversation with him was also brief. I tried to ring him again but got his answerphone. I'm glad I spoke to you first."

"So what do we do next?"

"I don't know, Veronica. You see I'm just looking to get her phone back to her but Simon seemed worried and you…"

"It's not like her, but then her actions haven't been normal recently."

There was an uncomfortable silence, which Beth finally broke. "Thanks, Veronica. I'll ring you if I hear from her. You know, if she calls her phone. Should I ring the others on her address book?"

"Who else is there?

"Daniel…"

"Shit! You haven't rung him!"

"I have, and he thought I was Alexis and…"

"And I bet he wasn't pleased to hear from you."

"Yeah, you could say that. He said he didn't know…"

"No, he doesn't have a clue. Keen to find her as we are. And the other names?"

"Three: her home line, Cherry and Sindy. I was going to ring–"

"No need," Veronica interrupted, "I've already rung them. They're… colleagues."

"That's strange."

"Why?"

"Because that means that there are no friends listed on the mobile."

"So it's a work phone then."

"Maybe, but you'd have friends on it too though, wouldn't you?"

"I guess so."

"Thanks again, Veronica."

"OK," Veronica said and hung up.

###

Chapter 25: Beth and the Neighbours

Beth looked at her watch. She had an hour and a half until she had to leave for work. Time enough for a shower, quick lunch and some advice.

Grabbing her keys, she headed out the front door and took a left at the gate. She knocked on her neighbour's door.

"Hi, Emily."

"Hello, Beth. How are you?"

"OK, thank you. Is…?"

"Have you told him about the baby?"

"Last night."

"How did it go?"

"Surprisingly well."

"Let's not talk on the doorstep. Come in."

"I have to go to work in an hour. It was actually Frank I wanted to speak to."

"Oh, dear. What's he done?"

"Nothing. I'd like to pick his brain."

"Goodness. He'll be chuffed. I think he's in the shed. Please, come in."

"Thanks."

Beth followed Emily through to the back of the house and across a path dividing the neatly manicured lawn. She then noticed the gardening implements in the older lady's hands.

"Have I interrupted you? I'm sorry."

Emily looked down at the trowel and fork. "I was going to break for lunch anyway. Bit too cold to do any more. Just the basics; weeding and so on."

"Rather you than me. I don't touch the garden once the ground gets too hard. There's always too much to do indoors."

"You wait until you retire. There seems to be more than ever to do."

"Can't wait." Beth said with a smile.

The women reached the shed and Emily tapped on the plastic window. Frank looked up from his bench and nodded. Emily opened the door and smiled at Beth.

"Thanks, Emily."

The shed was an Aladdin's cave. Packed with tools, pieces of wood and camping equipment, Beth looked at the bench. Frank, working on something intricate, was wearing a magnifying glass on an elastic strap around his forehead.

Beth burst out laughing at the Mr Magoo figure in front of her. Frank took off the strap.

"I'm sorry, Frank." Beth said, stifling another laugh.

"It's fine, Beth." Emily butted in. "I think it's hilarious." She turned to her husband. "Frank dear, Beth wants to pick your brain. So doesn't have long, which is just as well." She winked at Beth then returned to the lawn.

Frank patted the seat of a chair next to his.

Beth smiled and sat down. "You've got quite a collection here, Frank."

"Impressive, isn't it?"

"Makes my house look truly minimalistic."

"Thankfully it's not all mine."

"Oh?"

"Emily's son, Andrew, asked me to store some bits and pieces when he moved house and it's still here, despite him living three miles up the road!"

"He moved recently?"

Frank laughed. "Not exactly; five years ago."

"Oh. He's like my brother then with his stuff at my mum's house, except he only left it about six months ago. I still suggested she should car boot it. If he's not used it for six months then he doesn't need it, does he?"

"That's what I keep saying to Em' but she says that it's his stuff and we can't sell it. Of course, having been in our possession for so long, it's legally ours but..."

"Sorry, Frank, to interrupt... it's actually your technical expertise that I want to ask you about."

"OK. I'll try."

"Nate bought a mobile phone from the market and has had a few phone calls on it. I've spoken to the people who rang and there seems to be something odd about the whole thing."

"Odd? How?"

"It seems to have belonged to a woman called Alexis. A colleague of hers has rung a number of times, as has a friend's brother."

"And you're thinking that it's stolen?"

Beth noticed a certain look in Frank's eyes. She knew she had to tread carefully. "Oh, I don't think so, as he said it was from the market, but there's something quite urgent about these people trying to get hold of this woman Alexis."

"In their tone or what they say?"

"The friend's brother, Simon, rang first."

"Looking for Alexis."

"Yes. But then I dug deeper and found messages from a woman called Veronica, also looking for her."

"Has either of them called the police?"

"I don't know. I don't… think so. I didn't think to ask. Another odd thing. The mobile only has five contact numbers stored in it."

"Maybe it's new and she's only got around to…"

"That's what I thought, only it doesn't look particularly new to me."

"Have you got it with you?"

"No. I had to put it back in Nate's pocket in case he came home while I was here. He doesn't know that I've been looking through it. He'd do his nut."

"Doesn't he trust you?"

"Usually, but I quizzed him about it the night before when Simon rang on it and he said he'd bought it fair and square so I had to let it go."

"If it's not new, maybe it's a work phone?"

"That's the conclusion I came to. Veronica said she and two other people on the list were colleagues."

"And you think she's gone AWOL from work?"

"Yes. And another name in the book has also been trying to find Alexis. A guy called Daniel who seems far from pleased. Veronica knows him but wouldn't say the connection. I thought a boyfriend but I got the impression he wasn't."

"Good detective work, Beth," Frank said with a genuine smile. "But what makes you think that something's not quite right?"

"For Alexis to have gone missing and her friend's brother to ask if I know his sister. It just felt odd."

"I see. Maybe she's gone on a last minute holiday and not told anyone. What did the guy's sister have to say?"

"She died recently."

"Alexis?"

"No, his sister, Jessica."

"And that's why Simon's trying to find Alexis, so he can tell her?"

"I suppose so."

"But he seemed concerned he couldn't reach her."

"That does make sense. He would want her to know. But Alexis' colleague didn't know where she was either."

"Have you asked Nate?"

"I didn't see the point. If he bought it from the market he wouldn't know its history."

"If? You don't believe him."

"Oh, I do. It's just… I didn't see how he could help."

"I'm not sure how I can either."

"An expert ear. You must have dealt with missing persons."

"Of course. I'm happy to be a sounding board but…"

Beth looked at her watch. "I'm sorry. I have to go to get ready for work. Can I pop in tomorrow?"

"Of course, any time. It's always lovely to see you. Oh, and congratulations. Emily told me."

Beth blushed. "Thank you."

"When are you due?"

"Mid-September."

"Lovely time of year. Andy was a September baby. It was an Indian summer that year, Em' tells me. He's her son. We met… Anyway, yes, so warm, she said. After the terrible summers we've been having recently, it may well be again."

"I'm not sure that I'd want it that warm when I'm built like a hippopotamus."

Frank laughed. "It's not that bad. Em' only did it the once but she sailed through it, despite the heat."

"I'll have to pick her brain next time I get to chat to her."

Frank laughed. "She'd love that. With the absence of grand kiddies, it'll give her a new lease of life."

"So Andy doesn't want children?"

Frank shook his head. "I think it's unlikely, although there are ways and means these days. And of course he needs to find someone to have children with first."

Beth smiled. "Thanks again, Frank. I'll see you tomorrow."

"Sure. We'll have a cuppa and a good chat. I'll have a think in the meantime and see what I can come up with."

"I've not given you much to go on."

"You'd be surprised. We'd have the tiniest shred of evidence and build a whole case around it."

"And you solve them?"

"Sometimes, Beth. Yes, sometimes."

###

Chapter 26: Simon and Marion

The kettle boiled and Simon made the teas.

He and his mum sat at her kitchen table looking at the box, which Marion had refilled with Jessica's things, all except for the purse, which Marion held in her left hand.

"Simon, have you phoned the credit card companies to cancel her cards?"

"I have, yes. Jess' study is scarily organised. She's got files for just about everyone so it was easy."

"That's so typical; her whole life so structured, everything in its place."

Simon thought about the piles of paperwork stuffed into the drawers in his dining room. "Doesn't take after me, that's for sure."

Marion stared into the hall. "I keep expecting her to walk through the door. Simon?"

"Yes, Mum."

Marion pulled a photograph from the purse and laid both on the table. "Do you know any of the people?"

Simon shrugged. "Colleagues? Friends? Both? One of her colleagues, Daph, left a message on her landline on Monday. I spoke to her Tuesday afternoon by which time she'd heard the news. Sounded in bits."

The mood in the room remained sombre until Simon was distracted by Buttons brushing his feet. "Hello, chap."

Buttons purred then meowed.

Marion smiled weakly.

Simon nodded. He couldn't believe what had happened in the past seventy-two hours and was amazed at how composed his mum was. He wondered when the wall was going to come down, when it was going to sink in that her daughter had gone.

And to him that he no longer had a sister.

###

Chapter 27: Simon and Marion

Bringing the teas to the table, Simon spoke. "There's something I haven't told you, about something I found at Jessica's house."

"Oh?" Marion looked at the serious expression on his face. "Should I be worried?"

"No. A few things aren't adding up."

"Like what?"

"Three thousand pounds in a lounge drawer."

Marion mouthed a 'w'. "Three thousand pounds? What was she doing with that kind of money?"

"I don't know."

"Maybe she was planning a holiday."

"She didn't say anything."

"You know what she's like; going away on a whim. Though hopefully not for a year like when she went to Australia with whatever his name was. What other explanation can you think of?"

"Shaun. That's not the only thing. Did you know she'd paid her mortgage off?"

"What? On her secretary's wages? She can't have done."

"That's what I thought but I found two bank accounts; a standard one with normal incomings and outgoings, like wages and bills, which was ticking over, but the other one had loads of money in it."

"How much?"

"Twenty-seven thousand."

Marion laughed. "Had she won the lottery or something?"

"She would have told us, we're family. Besides it couldn't be anything like that because there were steady lump sums paid in, little going out."

"That doesn't make sense."

"I know. I've been struggling to figure it out. The account was in her name and a woman called Alexis Starr."

"Alexis Starr? Who's that?"

"Not sure. I've spoken to Alexis' boss but she wasn't very helpful."

"Why not?"

"It appears that Alexis has gone missing."

"And Jessica never mentioned any of this to you?"

"No, nothing."

"Then what's the next step? What happens if you can't find Alexis? Can you close the account without her?"

"I'd not thought that far ahead but I doubt it. If it takes two people to open it, it would probably need her approval to close it. Besides, some of the money's bound to be hers."

"Have you told the police any of this?"

"Why?"

"If someone's missing and there's all this money involved."

"Oh, Mum. I don't think it's a police matter. She's probably just away. I don't think it's anything dubious."

"Thirty thousand pounds in just a few years. It doesn't sound right, unless this Alexis was a high-flying executive and most of it's hers."

"The bank manager didn't seem to think there was anything to worry about."

"Could this Alexis be away on business?"

"Her boss said she wasn't."

"Then what are you going to do?"

"I don't know. I really don't."

Simon looked at his mother across the kitchen table. "I've got to make the call, you know."

"I know."

"Have you got the number?"

"It's in the address book by the phone, under F. I wrote it in there yesterday."

"Thanks."

He reached to the windowsill behind him, picked up the phone handset and the address book, flicked to the relevant page and dialled the number.

"Hello. I'd like to arrange a funeral please... thank you. Yes please. Price... Jessica. Next Monday?" Simon looked at Marion. She nodded. "Monday will be fine." Simon then gave the funeral company their contact details. "I see. Of course. No. Thanks but I'll come to you. Yes, tomorrow will be fine. See you then."

"Do you know what Jess wanted?" Marion asked.

"Not really. Do you?"

"Something simple, like her father's, probably."

"Sure. I think she'd go for that. Do you want to come with me tomorrow?"

"I can. I want to help, but…"

"It's OK."

"I'm sorry. I don't think I could talk flowers, caskets and so on. I know it has to be done, it's just that…"

"It's fine, Mum, honestly. You're best keeping busy here. Do you want the wake here?"

"Wake?"

"Or hire a hall or?"

"Here is fine. We'll just have family and friends. A quiet do."

"OK. I'll sort it out. Quiet and simple. Nothing complicated."

Because of course, Jessica wasn't complicated at all, was she?

###

Chapter 28: Beth, Frank and Emily

As promised, Beth returned to see Frank the following day. Although the snow had deterred Emily from her garden, it hadn't put her husband off dabbling in his shed. Beth knew the way so left Emily to put the kettle on.

Beth knocked on the shed door.

"Come in."

"Morning, Frank."

"Oh. Morning, Beth. You don't have to knock you know. I'm not doing anything top secret."

"It's lovely and toasty in here."

"Yes, that electric heater," he said, pointing to the far end corner of the room, "blasts it out. Emily doesn't approve as it sends the meter into overdrive but she likes me being out from under her feet so she can't have it both ways." He smiled cheekily.

"What is it that you are doing out here?"

"Just soldering. Please, take a seat."

"Soldering?"

"It's a thirty-watt Antex Miniature with replaceable plated tips and a thermostatic control." Frank gushed. "It's wonderful. Emily bought it for me for Christmas."

"I take it that it was an asked for present. I wouldn't have a clue."

"I did drop certain hints, like leaving a catalogue on the dining room table with the page marked and item circled."

Beth smiled. "That's the kind of clue I like. And what are you soldering, Frank," she asked hoping that his explanation would decipher the word.

"I repair radios. I'm working on a CB at the moment but usually it's FM / AM ones. Suppose I'll be out of a job when everything goes digital."

"You make a living out of this?"

Frank laughed. "Oh no, pin money. Normally word of mouth."

"And that CB is that the sort that truckers use? Nate loves the film Convoy, always singing it which drives me nuts."

Frank burst into song, "breaker one-nine, this here's the rubber duck..." and they both burst out laughing.

"Frank."

"Yes, my dear."

"Have you thought any more about our chat yesterday?"

"I have, but I don't think there's anything to worry about. If Nate bought the phone from the market, it could have been sold to the dealer by anyone. Mobiles are hard to track unless people register the serial code, which they rarely do, and report the loss to the police, which they don't unless it's stolen, or put a security lock code when switching on, which they never do. And it's too old to have a tracker, so unless this woman, Alex…"

"Alexis."

"Yes. Unless Alexis was one of the few who do what they're supposed to then it's unlikely that Nate's got anything to worry about."

"Oh, no. He doesn't worry."

"No. I don't suppose he does. It's highly likely she did an upgrade and the shop sold it on."

"Wouldn't they get more money selling it as second-hand in the shop?"

"It depends, Beth. Sometimes they have so many that they only keep the special or latest models, and sorry Alexis, but this doesn't look like either. The shops also make so much money out of the new contracts that the cost of the old phone is nothing. If the contract is, say, twenty pounds a month that's two-forty a year, although most decent phones are on a thirty to thirty-five pound so that's three-sixty upwards."

"Gosh."

"That's how they can afford to give away free laptops with broadband packages. Plus with those they sign people in for two years, not just one. Sometimes eighteen months but usually two years."

"Blimey, Frank. You know your stuff."

"Em's son bought me a mobile for my birthday last year, and bought himself a new laptop at Christmas, courtesy of a bonus at work apparently. An anniversary or something. Anyway, before he bought it, we were discussing what tariffs there were out there and I said about the free laptops but he said they were quite basic but he's got Sky and that they do a good broadband package so he bought a better laptop with cheaper broadband. I've hinted at Em that we should do the same but she says the old computer's perfectly fine. It's slow, like me, but I suppose she's right."

"We are sometimes." Beth beamed.

Frank laughed. "And you don't let us forget it."

"About the phone…"

"Do you have it with you now?"

"No. Nate's still got it. I couldn't get it again, and besides I've looked through the call history, address book and texts, so I don't know what else it could tell me."

Frank frowned and scratched his right sideburn. "I don't think there's a whole lot that you can do, Beth. You could ask Nate again where he got the phone from, but unless he knows this Alexis woman, it won't help."

"No, that's what I feared."

"Unless Simon or Veronica ring you with some news."

Beth nodded. "It's been an interesting chat though, thanks Frank. I know a bit more about tariffs, CB radios and soldering."

Frank laughed. "Any time you want to talk technical, pop into my 'office'."

Beth put her right arm on Frank's left shoulder, said "Thank you" and left the shed.

Emily was walking down the garden with two cups of steaming tea when Beth met her halfway.

"Oh dear, are you leaving already?"

"I ought to get back."

"But I've made you your tea."

"Lovely. Thanks Emily."

"Was Frank useful?"

"He was, thank you." Beth said, although she didn't feel any further along in the finding Alexis process.

"Unless you have to go, why don't you take your tea back to the kitchen, let me drop this in to Frank and I'll come and join you. Drinking by yourself is no fun."

"That sounds lovely. And I don't suppose you have any of your delicious brownies?"

113

Emily smiled. "You must have smelled the new batch. You are eating for two after all."

Taking a couple of clean plates from the draining board, Beth put them on the table next to her cup of tea and another which she'd found next to the kettle, assumed to be Emily's.

Beth pulled out Emily's chair as she approached, armed with a plate of brownies.

"Thank you dear. Does Nate do things like that for you?"

"Sorry?"

"Be a gentleman?"

"Sometimes, when he thinks about it."

"But you have to hint?"

Beth laughed and took a brownie from the offered plate. "Yes, usually."

"Like stand next to the chair and cough?"

"I tried it once, in the early days, but he asked me if I wanted a glass of water."

"Which was a chivalrous thing to do."

"I suppose so."

"And he took the news of the baby well?"

"Very, amazingly. He seems keen on the idea. Even talked about getting a job."

"There's a turnaround."

"He goes to the job centre every week, but then he has to or he doesn't get his allowances, but he seemed quite upbeat when I came home from work last night."

"That's good. It looks like things are looking up for you."

"I hope so. I'm just concerned that…"

"Yes?"

"That Nate's not given up his old life."

"What makes you think that?"

"He has a new phone and…"

"You don't think he bought it."

"He says he did, but I'm not sure."

"What makes you think he didn't?"

"Because people keep ringing looking for the owner of it."

"Maybe she lost it and that's the only number they have for her. Could he have found it?"

"He says he bought it from the market."

"And that's not possible?"

"It is but something doesn't feel right."

"And the people who ring, what do they say?"

"It's all rather complicated. One is the woman's boss and she says she's gone AWOL. The other is a friend's brother who's trying to get in touch with her because his sister died."

"And this is what you were talking to Frank about?"

Beth nodded.

"And what did he think?"

"That there was probably a perfectly reasonable explanation for it."

"There then. What else can you do?"

"Nothing. And you're both right. I can't get in contact with someone I don't know, especially if people who know her can't. She might try and ring her mobile, if she has lost it although I think she'd have done that by now and there aren't any missed calls or messages from her."

"Maybe she thought she had no hope of getting it back so didn't bother."

"Of course. I think I'm making a bigger deal of it than it is. Looking for something exciting."

"Having a baby is a big thing."

Beth patted her stomach and beamed. "I know. Actually, that reminds me. Frank said you could give me a few pointers, when you had your son."

Emily smiled. "My dear, that was quite a long time ago but, here, have another brownie and I'll do my best."

###

Chapter 29: Daniel and Rick

Whilst a lesser man in Daniel Goldstein's position might have written off the measly sum of three thousand pounds, and put it down to experience, he was going to have the last word if it killed him.

So, it appeared that not only had Alexis done a runner from him, but also from Veronica, that bottle blonde fifty-something mutton dressed as lamb, who was as useful as wet toilet paper.

Him, bitter? That wasn't Daniel's style. Daniel got even.

He tapped a few numbers on his BlackBerry keypad and hit the green phone icon.

"Speak."

"Rick. It's Daniel. I need you to do something for me."

"Sure."

"I need you to do a background check."

"Name?"

"Alexis Starr."

"Real name?"

"Shouldn't think so."

"Any more details?"

"She works for Veronica Ziebis of the Fraulein Agency in Chelsea."

"Yes, I know who she is."

"Veronica is being less than forthcoming. See what you can find out, will you?"

"Sure. And what does this Alexis look like?"

"About five-ten, auburn hair, awesome figure, you know, the usual kind that I go for."

"Hair colour genuine?"

"Think so."

"Tattoos or birthmarks?"

"Black paw-print on left inside ankle. Done recently, itched like hell, she said."

"OK. Gotcha. Call you back if I find anything."

"I need you to find something, Rick."

"In your bad books is she?"

"Just find her, Rick."

"Sure thing, boss. If she's out there, I'll find her."

"It's the weekend tomorrow so don't ring me on this number. I'll be at home. Call me at the office on Monday. You've got the private line?"

"Got it. I'll ring you then."

"With news, Rick."

"Yeah. I'll have something by then."

"You find her and I'll pay double."

"Right you are."

###

Chapter 30: Andy

"Damn it." Andy slammed down the phone. He was supposed to be on compassionate leave. How could they be short staffed enough to drag him back? The last thing he wanted to do was drive a bloody train, especially at the weekend. Weekends were shitty, full of tourists. Weekdays were a breeze with tunnel-vision business suits and the occasional single mum, but Andy avoided weekends. Thankfully he hadn't been asked to do the long haul again, just the Home Counties run. No stretches of all-the-same countryside, however beautiful it may be, but the thirty-five mile shuttle to Tring and back. Commuter belt Hertfordshire suited him. Or was it Buckinghamshire? He could never remember.

###

Chapter 31: Frank and Emily

A holiday wasn't something on the agenda for Frank and Emily until they walked past the travel agents and a card entitled 'Winter weekend on the Norfolk Broads' caught their attention. They stared at each other and smiled. Frank grabbed hold of the door and pushed.

"Good morning. How may I help you?"

"Morning. We'd like more details on the Norfolk Broads weekend please."

"Certainly. It's a coach trip leaving Victoria coach station tomorrow morning and returning Sunday night. How does that sound?"

"Tomorrow?" Emily said. "Can we do it that quickly, Frank?"

"Sure. Now Andrew's working, we're free to do whatever we like."

Emily loved it when Frank looked like that. His cheeky schoolboy grin and she fell for it every time. "OK love, let's do it."

###

Chapter 32: Veronica

With Alexis planted firmly at the back of her mind and the
working week over, Veronica lay back in her recliner, sipped
her glass of Veuve Clicquot Reserve and clicked the 'play'
button on the DVD remote. The opening credits were rolling
when her mobile rang. Tempted to ignore it, she looked at the
screen and frowned at the 'withheld number'. *Could be a new
client*, she thought, so tapped the answer button.

"Ziebis."

"Is that Veronica Ziebis?"

"Yes. Who's calling?"

"The name's Rick. One of your girls has been
recommended to me."

"Oh, yes? Who recommended the agency?"

"You have a girl 'Alexis'?"

"I do, but she's not available at the moment. Who did you
say...?"

"When will she be free? I'm in no hurry."

"I have a lovely girl called Cherry. Petite and busty."

"Does she have auburn hair?"

"She can be whatever colour you like, Mr..."

"No, has to be natural."

"Then I'm sorry I can't help you."

"You can tell Alexis that I'll make it worth her while."

"I'm sorry, but–"

"So you keep saying. There must be a price. Money isn't
a problem."

"I appreciate that Mr..."

Rick wasn't forthcoming with a surname. "She'll be well
looked after."

"I'm sure she will, sir, but unfortunately there's nothing I
can do. I can take your details and–"

Rick ended the call.

###

Chapter 33: Rick

So Veronica had got Rick nowhere. Next stop the hotels. Daniel's office was in Belsize Park so Rick figured that the hotel he used wouldn't be too far away. He flicked to the Safari's blue compass icon on his laptop and typed 'hotels, belsize park' into the Google search box. The selection appeared in lowest to highest cost order so he scrolled to the bottom and started with the two-hundred pounds a night and over. There were just three in that price range: The Heathdown, The Erste Classe and The Cheshire. Rick liked things in alphabetical order so began with The Cheshire, which was actually quite handy as he knew someone who worked there. He picked up his mobile and dialled the number.

"Good evening. The Cheshire Hotel, Tania speaking, how may I help you?"

"Tan, it's Rick."

Tania immediately lost her Westminster accent. "Hi. How are ya?"

"Good. On a mission. Know a girl called Alexis Starr? Probably a hooker."

"Don't ring any bells. What does she look like?"

"Tall. Five nine or thereabouts, taller in heels. A copper-top."

"Could have been a girl in last weekend. Who she was with?"

"Can't say, Tan, client confidentiality."

"Was it Mr Goldstein?"

"Know him?"

"He's a regular. Think she was too. Don't know her name of course as the girls never pay the bills."

"Sure it was her?"

"Fairly sure. Only this time I think there was some trouble."

"In what way?"

"Don't know for sure but he seemed flustered when he came to pay his bill."

"She took some money?"

"Only thing I can think of. He still had his cards to pay with so I guess it was just cash."

"Any way of tracking this Alexis down?"

"I can chat with the other girls. Not sure how far I'll get but I'll see what I can do."

"You got my number?"

"Etched on my brain."

"Thanks, darling. I owe you one."

"Two."

"Eh?"

"There's last time, remember?"

"The Stravely case. How could I forget?"

###

Chapter 34: Daniel and his Wife

"How many times? I don't know where it came from."

"No one we know has ginger hair and yet, Daniel Samuel Goldstein, I find a ginger hair on your suit jacket. How do you explain it then?"

Daniel hated it when she called him by his full name and she only did so when she was angry. "I don't know, darling." His mind was sprinting. "Ah, we have a new post girl. She's got ginger hair. She's seventeen and very plain. It must be her."

"Seventeen and plain. She's the right age. Maybe you like a plain Jane now, Daniel."

"Her name's Alex," he said then winced.

"I don't care what she's called. If it's hers, how did it get there?"

"She delivers the post."

"She delivers the post to your PA, not you."

"Then I got it from my PA."

"Gail's a brunette, like me."

"No, I mean…"

"I know what you mean, Daniel, but I'm not buying it."

"Someone at the restaurant at lunchtime, then. I don't know."

"You've never been a good liar."

Daniel shrugged as his mobile phone rang. "I've got to take this," he mouthed and walked off.

###

Chapter 35: Tania and Rick

Tania tapped the number into the screen. The dialling tone echoed in her ear.

"Speak."

"Rick, it's Tania."

"Hi. Got anything for me?"

"One of the girls says she met Alexis a few times."

"Yeah. Where?"

"Always here at the Cheshire. In the bar, in between joh… clients."

"What did she say?"

"This girl was quite quiet. Loud-looking but quiet."

"Loud-looking? What the fuck does that mean?"

"Confident. But didn't say much."

"Right. And how does that help me?"

"She let slip."

"Christ, Tania. What did she say?"

"That she lived near Milton Keynes."

"Milton Keynes? Sure?"

"Yeah. Not the city but a village outside apparently."

"It's not a city."

"What?"

"Milton Keynes. It's not a city. It's a borough."

"A borough? Don't you mean a town?"

"No, a borough."

"Borough, as in borough council."

"Kind of."

"You're smarter than…"

Rick growled. "Tania. Alexis?"

"That's all I know. Some village south of Milton Keynes."

"South of. You didn't say that before. Would you know the name if I said it to you?"

"I don't think she knew."

"OK, hon. Thanks. You free next week?"

"Sure."

Dropping his mobile on to the desk, Rick clicked on his internet's 'favourites' menu and selected 'private bank records'. His work allowed him access to almost any kind of information, almost up to the doors of the Houses of

Parliament. He'd tried to cross the threshold of Downing
Street during one search but their security code had been too
tough a nut for even him to crack. Bank records on the other
hand were a doddle. He typed in 'Alexis Starr' and a reel of
details appeared before his eyes. He smiled as he found the
record he was looking for. His Alexis Starr was registered as
holding a joint bank account with a girl called Jessica Price.
He jotted down the address on a scrap of paper and put it in
his jeans pocket.

###

Chapter 36: Beth and Nate

A usual weekend for the Morrisons consisted of housework by
Beth and relaxation and TV by Nate but since the
announcement of the baby, roles had been reversed. He'd
gone out early to the corner shop, brought her breakfast in
bed and while she was in the bathroom, was doing the
previous night's washing up.

As she switched off the shower, Beth heard a noise from
downstairs. "He's hoovering?" she said to herself then opened
the bathroom door, shouting down the stairs. "What have you
done with my husband?" No reply. She walked through,
naked, to the main bedroom and took her robe from the back
of the door. Halfway down the stairs, the hoovering stopped.

As she walked into the kitchen, she laughed. The table
was laid out with fresh cups of tea and a single orange
gerbera in a glass vase she'd bought for their third wedding
anniversary. Nate was reading the local newspaper which
was sprawled on the work surface.

"What have you done with my husband?"

"Good morning, again. How are you both feeling today?"

"We are well, thank you for asking. Anything
interesting?"

"The usual doom and gloom. I think everyone should
have a baby, cheer themselves up."

"Not everyone can afford to, including us."

"Oh, hush. We'll be fine. They were quite positive at the
job centre yesterday. Green shoots and all that."

Beth looked at her husband and smiled. *Yes*, she
thought, *green shoots are appearing everywhere.*

###

131

Chapter 37: Marion and the Wake

Monday morning and Marion was rushing around the kitchen
baking. Almost every inch of the worktops was covered in
Tupperware-boxed cakes, sandwiches wrapped in cling film
and matching white cups and saucers.

"You're going to a lot of effort."

"I want to. Jess liked a party."

"The extra chairs are all set out in the lounge. What do
you want me to do next?"

"Can you get the serviettes out of the drawer under the
glasses cabinet. Oh, and get some glasses out while you're
there. A couple of dozen should be enough but I've got some
spare plastic beakers. I think most people will want something
warm; tea or coffee but just in case. Do you think they'll expect
wine? I'm not sure I've got any?"

"I think they'll be happy with whatever you give them."

"I don't feel prepared."

Simon put an arm round his mother's left shoulder. "You
can feed an army in ten seconds flat. The freezer's always full.
If in doubt, you can always shove something in the
microwave. I don't suppose people will be too hungry
anyway."

"It'll be lunchtime but you're probably right. We always
have food left over. We did with your fa…"

Simon smiled. "Keeping your mind off things though, isn't
it?"

Marion nodded. "Have you put out enough chairs next
door?"

"Yes, Mum. And I'll get the glasses ready."

"Thanks. Don't know what I'd do without you."

"I'm here for as long as you need me." The doorbell rang.
"I'll go."

Marion's sister and brother-in-law stood on the doorstep. The
snow had stopped and was turning to mush as the rain tried to
wash it away.

Simon mustered a smile. "Hi, Auntie Helen, Uncle
Graham."

Graham nodded. Helen stepped into the hallway and gave Simon a hug. "I'm so sorry, Simon. How's your mum?"

"Oh, you know. Keeping busy, making lots of food; what she's good at."

"I'll see if I can give her a hand with anything."

"Hi, Simon," Graham said, offering his hand.

"Hi, Uncle Graham." His uncle looked so soulful that Simon hugged him instead.

"And how are you?" Graham asked as Simon released him.

"You know. Doing the same as Mum; keeping myself occupied. There's so much to do."

"If I can help in any way… I should have said earlier."

"Oh, I think it's OK. It's just sorting Jess' house out, making sure I've let everyone know, tying up all the loose ends. That sort of thing."

"I remember when my mum died. I know it's different, she was so much older, but there was her house and…"

"Sure."

"What have the police said?"

"That it was an accident. Black ice, mother nature, no one else to blame."

Graham gripped Simon's arm and smiled briefly.

"I've got to set out some glasses in the lounge."

"Let me help," Graham said, following his nephew into the kitchen.

The two women were deep in conversation when the men walked in so they collected as many glasses from a side overhead cupboard as they could carry and took them into the lounge. Simon walked in, imagining the room full of people all talking about his sister, nodding sympathetically, saying what a tragic waste of life, and so on.

It still all seemed so remote. There was only he and his mum left. In the space of two years he'd lost his father and sister; half the family. Although his mum wasn't old, she'd already retired and using her bus pass to him indicated the start of a new chapter in her life. Of course to Marion it had been a time to look forward to; more freedom and independence, but if she could swap those for her husband and daughter, she'd do it in a flash.

"Simon?"

"Sorry."

"Do you want the glasses dotted around the room?"

"Yes please. Anywhere you see flat space."

"Do you have coasters?"

"In the kitchen drawer underneath the middle cupboard."

"OK." Graham placed the glasses together on a clear side table and went back to the kitchen, going over to Marion. "I'm so sorry, Marion."

"Thanks, Graham."

"I know this is a stupid question but how are you?"

"Going through the motions but once today is over…"

"I know. Once normality sets back in, it'll hit you but then you'll have time to grieve properly. You have to be strong today for everyone else."

Marion nodded and returned to her sister who was sitting at the kitchen table staring at an embroidered bee.

Graham took the packet of laminated blue and gold-striped coasters out of the drawer and returned to the lounge. Simon had placed the glasses so that wherever anyone was standing or sitting they were likely to reach one. Graham went around the room lifting up each glass placing a coaster underneath it.

Simon stared out the window. "It's snowing again."

"I know. It's not been this bad for years."

"Do you think it'll prevent anyone coming today? It won't stop the service, will it?"

"I shouldn't think so. People will set off early. Have you got anyone coming from any distance?"

"London, I think, is about the farthest."

"That should be fine."

"The train driver wanted to come."

"What?"

"I spoke to him last week. He asked if he could come."

"Do you think that's a good idea?"

"I don't know but he asked. It wasn't his fault, he tried to stop. There was nothing he could have done."

"I'm sure there wasn't but do you think it'll do him any good, or your mum, for him to be here?"

"I don't know. But what could I say? He was the last person to see Jessica alive."

"OK," Graham murmured. "Right, what needs doing next?"

"Not sure. Think Mum's done everything else. The vacuuming… she's cooked every recipe under the sun."

Graham smiled. They all knew Marion would want everyone to be well fed and watered. "It's good she's keeping busy."

The men returned to the kitchen where Marion was icing a cake and Helen was piling plates on to the kitchen table.

"Is there anything we can do?" Graham asked.

"Marion?" Helen looked at her sister.

Marion shook her head, deep in concentration. "I think we're there. I'll do the hot food when we get back from the crematorium."

Graham looked at the mountains of food piled on to serving plates lined up along the work surfaces. "There's more? How many people are you expecting?"

"About a hundred," Marion said, piping edging onto the cake.

"A hundred?" Simon stepped forward. "We know that many people?"

"There's the neighbours, Jessica's friends and work colleagues, other family and… people who want to show their respects."

"And they're all coming back here?"

"I think so."

"Oh, Mum. You should have said immediate family and friends only. They'd have understood."

"But I like having people here. I want it to be crowded, to feel that Jessica was so loved."

"You know she was loved. We loved her."

"I know, but we need people to eat all this food."

Simon frowned but if it made his mum happy. "OK. Are you sure there's nothing else to be done? We've got half an hour before we have to go."

###

136

Chapter 38: The Funeral

The crematorium car park was packed when Simon drove in.

"God. Who are all these people?"

"I told you: friends, family, well-wishers."

Camera flashbulbs bounced off the car windows as they parked up.

"Are the press still interested?" Marion released her seatbelt.

"Have you had any trouble with them?" Graham asked.

"No, not really. They were at Mum's for a while but then they lost interest. Once they realised that it was an accident, they moved on to something more newsworthy. I'm not sure what they expect to get here."

The family got out the car and acknowledged the cameras surrounding them. Once past, the photographers, with just the prospect of back shots, chatted amongst themselves then disbanded, leaving the other mourners to file into the church.

As Simon walked down the central aisle, he recognised the two police officers from the week before. Had it only been a week? In a way it had gone quickly but so much had happened that it also seemed like an eternity. There were still so many questions to be answered but there was time. Let this day be over then he could piece everything together.

Sergeant Lewis and DS Taylor both nodded when Simon walked past their row. He led his mother, aunt and uncle to the front row and Simon slotted in beside them then looked around the congregation. There were so many faces he didn't recognise. There were some family and friends near the front that he knew but the people in the middle and rear rows were strangers. He wondered how many were there out of morbid curiosity.

"Simon."

"Yes, Mum."

"Do you know everyone here?"

"Er, no. Do you?"

"No. I wasn't far off with guessing a hundred, was I?"

"How did you know?"

"A feeling."

"But you don't want everyone back at the house, do you?"

"Why not?"

"Because the majority aren't here because they knew Jess, they want a piece of the event."

"Really? It'll be nice to be surrounded by people."

"Even if for the wrong reasons."

"They made the effort, didn't they?"

"I suppose so but…"

"They're here now. The food's done, it should be eaten and everyone have a good time."

"A good time?"

"She wouldn't want it any other way, and besides…"

The music stopped and the pastor stepped forward. The service was beautifully moving and tributes were paid by those who knew her. Simon went first and celebrated his sister's life rather than mourned their loss. Marion didn't speak but mouthed occasional comments as Jessica's friends and colleagues took their turns.

As the assembly left the chapel, the car park was empty. No hangers on or press, no noise other than the occasional bird or squirrel scurrying around in the snow.

Marion and Simon stood at the chapel entrance as people filed out, clasping or shaking hands as they went. Murmurings of sympathy and offers of food were exchanged and people filed to their cars. Some left immediately but most respectfully waited until Simon, Marion, Helen and Graham pulled out before making a procession like a slow, sombre conga.

As Simon drove Graham's saloon car down the slope to the cemetery entrance, he noticed a line of cars driving in, he presumed for the next ceremony and sighed as he thought of the conveyor belt of mourners paying respect to their deceased. He supposed that it was particularly busy at this time of year; the post-Christmas flu season. Looking at the cars snake up the long drive, he sighed.

"You all right?" his uncle asked from the front passenger seat.

"Yes, fine, just thinking about things."

"The cars coming in as we're driving out, like a shift change."

Simon sighed again and turned left.

Simon drove onto the driveway and the other cars filled both sides of the road. He collected people's coats and hats as they entered the house and made a stockpile of garments in Marion's study. Conversations took shape while Marion and Helen made final touches to the food. Graham was on drink duty and soon everyone had both hands full with glasses and plates and were deep in discussion.

"You must be Andy."

"Simon?"

"Thanks for coming. I know it can't have been easy."

"Of course. Some people may think it's strange but I wanted to."

"We're very grateful. Jessica's mum and I."

"You're both holding up well. I know if it were my sister, not that I have one…"

"I don't think it's sunk in yet."

"No. It's still early days, isn't it?"

"Yes, although it seems like forever, in a way. There's been so much to do and so much has happened in the past week. I can't believe that this time last week I'd only just found out and was going to the hospital."

"It must have been awful. And you had to tell your mum?"

"That was the hardest thing ever. Horrible. Just awful."

Andy put his right hand over Simon's left arm and let it linger. "If there's anything I can do. I know I'm not local but if I can help."

Simon looked down at Andy's hand then into his eyes. "Did you know that only two percent of the world's population have green eyes?"

Andy remained silent but remembered his hand and swiftly removed it. "I'm so sorry, Simon, that was inappropriate."

Simon burst out laughing.

"That's something that we say to our inmates."

"Sorry?"

"How inappropriate something is."

"Sorry."

"Oh, no. It wasn't a criticism."

"You work in a prison?"

"No. Rossythe Rehabilitation Centre. Just the other side of Milton Keynes."

"Oh, OK."

"I work with people with severe learning difficulties and brain injuries. They're residents but we call them inmates. Kind of cruel, and obviously not to their face."

"You have to have some patience for a job like that. What do you do?"

"CBT mainly. Cognitive behavioural therapy. I read to them then we discuss it. We have group sessions and one-to-ones. It varies from patient to patient."

"Wow. Have you always done that?"

"I knew I wanted to be a doctor and the brain appealed to me. I think it's the sponginess of it."

"You're kidding."

"Kind of. It always amazed me how much it can retain and what we can do with it. I thought of going into mainstream psychology but then a friend had a rugby accident and I veered into this."

They stood in silence for a moment then Simon said.

"Have you always wanted to drive trains?"

"Oh, yes. Sad as it may seem. My stepdad had a train set in our loft and we'd play on it for hours, especially at the weekends. Used to drive my mum mad. Now they're both retired so she complains about him being under her feet all the time, although he potters around in his shed for hours instead, so nothing much changes."

"And you do the long distance runs?"

"Usually but I've just come off a short commuter shuttle for the weekend. A few colleagues called in sick so I got last minute notice."

"That's a bummer."

"Time and a half Saturdays and double-time Sundays so I can't complain."

"But you get no weekend."

"True but I do weekday shifts normally so I'm luckier than most."

Marion tapped Simon on his arm. "Simon, your uncle's disappeared. I think he's chatting to someone in the garden. Would you mind taking some drinks round? Maybe this young man can help you." She winked.

"Sure. Mum, this is Andy. He was driving the train last Monday."

"Oh, Andy. I'm so sorry."

"Mrs Price, there's nothing to be sorry about."

"It must have been awful, knowing there was nothing you could do."

"Thank you."

"Thank you so much for coming. We're so grateful."

Andy looked around the lounge. "Jessica knew a lot of people."

"So it seems." Marion lowered her voice. "I don't think everyone knew her but it's nice to have lots of people to look after."

Andy smiled sympathetically and followed Simon to the kitchen for more supplies.

###

Chapter 39: Rick

"After one hundred yards, turn left and you've reached your destination... You've reached your destination."
Pulling up outside the 1930s semi, Rick put the car into neutral, switched off the engine and sat nav. He peered through the passenger window. The house looked ordinary; a dark green metal post box to the right of the front white uPVC door bore white plastic numbers five and one. Rick nodded to himself and flicked open the door handle. He looked around the u-shaped close, and apart from a woman walking her dog on the green, everyone else appeared to be at work. He smiled. It would make snooping easier.

The black wrought iron gate squeaked as he swung it open. He walked to the top of the front garden and peered through the lounge bay window. The colours of lilac and pale blue looked girlie to him and not at all lurid as he'd expected. Maybe she was a different person at home to the one at 'work'.

"Once a tart, always a tart in my experience," he mumbled to himself.

There was an alcove next to the fireplace to the right of the room containing shelves of books, a large flat-screen TV, DVD video combi, and Sky+ box. All were on standby.

Despite the lack of car and other signs of life, he rang the doorbell and waited. Nothing. He rang again but harder and therefore louder. Again no one came to the door. He turned and looked at the neighbouring houses. They were still as quiet and the woman and dog had gone. Rick fished in his jeans pocket for his 'magic gadget'; which opened anything from a beer bottle top and petty cash tins to the trickiest of front doors and lunged it into the lock. With some twisting, the door clicked and he pushed down the handle, skipping over the threshold and closing the door deftly but silently.

Rick frowned as he saw the book on the hallway floor. So maybe she left in a hurry. He loved spooking people so picked the book up and put it in the kitchen sink's empty washing up bowl. She'd probably not remember leaving it in the hallway but certainly wouldn't have left it in the kitchen. He walked through to the lounge and saw a flashing two on the answer machine. He pressed the 'play' button. *Message one, received Sunday 9.43pm.*

"Alexis. *This is getting beyond a joke. It's Veronica again.*"

"Hi, blondie."

"*Daniel's on my back again and he's getting to be a pain in the arse.*"

"He'll be thrilled to know that," Rick chuckled.

"*Think he's got some guy asking for you.*"

"You're sharper than you look, blondie."

"*I don't need this hassle Alexis. I know you've lost my mobile and Simon says that you've not been there since his sister died but you've got to come back at some stage. Damn it, Alexis, put me out of my misery. Are you still on my books or not?*"

"She won't be when Daniel's finished with her, Veronica. He's really pissed."

"*If I don't hear from you by the end of the day Alexis, you're off my books. I'd rather keep you because you're a good worker and popular but I'm not going to be messed about like this. Ring me. Bye, Alexis.*"

"I bet you don't keep your word Veronica. If she's so good, you'd be mad to drop her. Still, I guess a woman scorned and all that."

He wrote down Veronica's name on the back of the scrap of paper from his jeans pocket and pressed the red 'delete' button. The machine beeped again. *Message two, received Monday 10.46am.*

"Mr Price, it's John Frizzell here. Eversley Bank. I'm sorry to ring you like this but we have some news about that account your sister and Ms Starr had. Can you ring me back, please. I think you have our number but if you need it again it's…"

Rick wrote down his number, and pressed the 'delete message' button, grinning like Jack Nicholson's Joker. "Gotcha."

He just needed to work out a plan.

"Hey, Em, it's Andy. Says he's met someone!"

Emily rushed from the lounge into the hall and grabbed the phone receiver from her husband. Although Frank liked technology, he'd not quite got round to upgrading the phone to a cordless. "Would be so useful when we're in the garden," she'd said. "But that's the only time we get peace and quiet," he'd replied so she'd let it go. So far.

"Hey, darling. What's this about a new special someone? Really? Nice. Ah, lovely. I'm so pleased for you. I know. It's been a while. Where did you two meet? Oh dear. That's awful. The two of you could come over for dinner... Oh, not that serious. The invitation's there. What does your new 'friend' look like? Attractive, yes. Tall, yes. What colour eyes? Ah, that's nice, dear. Did you want to speak to Frank again? He's gone off to the shed but I can get him... When do you go back to work? That's not fair. Couldn't someone else do it? Yes, you did tell me before our weekend away. Yes, it was lovely. Quite cold and the coach smelled of beer and the driver didn't seem to be wearing any deoder... what, dear? OK. Phone me will you and tell me all about... Don't be nervous. I remember when Frank and I..., oh."

Emily's hearing aid buzzed as the dialling tone warbled in her ear. *His money must have run out*, she thought. She then sighed as she pictured little grandchildren running around their house. *What a shame*, she thought before heading to the shed to relay every syllable of her conversation to Frank.

"Nate?"

"Yes, darling."

"Have you wondered why someone keeps ringing your mobile and who owned it before you?"

"No, why?"

"Oh, I thought there might be a mistake, that's all."

"A mistake?"

"Yes, that you shouldn't have been sold the phone."

"What do you mean?"

"That maybe it was stolen or something."

"You think I stole it?"

"Of course not, it's just that... that call the other night. The man seemed quite desperate."

"To get his phone back, is that what you're thinking?"

"Oh no, it wasn't his phone but it belonged to someone called Alexis. She's missing."

"How do you know that?"

"That's who he asked for."

"Then she's the one that sold it to the guy on the market. Maybe he's an old boyfriend and she was pissed off that he kept calling her."

"Isn't that rather drastic? Couldn't she have changed her number or bought a new card for it?"

"Maybe she wanted an upgrade or a different model. You girls get tired of things easily."

"Maybe, but don't you think that it's…"

"I don't see how it's my problem."

"You're right. You bought it fair and square, only… The guy from the market might have records."

"What is this? Why are you playing Miss Marple? She's nothing to you."

"I was just wondering."

"You think too much."

"Where's the mobile now?"

"In my jacket pocket, where it's always been. No one has the number yet. I was going to swap my old sim card with the one in–"

"I thought you said you lost your old phone."

"Er, yes, I thought I had but I found it."

"So you needn't have bought this one. I needn't be worrying about this woman, if she's gone missing or not."

"I still can't understand why you're worrying anyway."

"Maternal instincts, I suppose."

"Already?"

"Someone's in distress and…"

"Oh come on, Beth, that's so melodramatic. The hormones have gone to your head. Why don't you have her phone and I keep my old one if you're so…"

"Oh could I?" Beth jumped off the sofa.

"If I'd known you were that keen, I'd have given you the bloody thing when I first got it."

"Thanks, love!" Beth called from the hall as she rifled through his pockets.

###

Chapter 40: Rick

Not known for his patience, Rick sat crossed legged on Jessica's lounge floor. He tapped his right index fingernail on the floorboards and chewed the inside of his right cheek. He frowned and stared at the ground. He'd not let Daniel down before and wasn't going to this time.

He looked around the room and took in his surroundings. The chances were that the bank would ask 'Mr Price' for some passwords or confidential information so Rick needed to do some digging and have everything at his fingertips. He'd got copies of the bank statements he'd accessed online but he'd not been able to get login paperwork and security details, so that meant looking for an office.

Opening the connecting doors from the lounge into the dining room yielded no such place and there was only the kitchen yet to be explored downstairs so that meant a room upstairs had to be his key. He bolted up the stairs, missing every other step, and headed for the smallest room; the room usually converted into a study, leaving the bigger rooms for bedrooms. The house was a typical 1930s layout so likely that the box room would be above the hall.

Rick frowned as he put his head round the door and saw nothing but a bed and two chests of drawers. The room didn't look as if it had been used in months. The bed was made but there was nothing on top of the units, as if the room was for show and nothing else.

Next door was the master bedroom and this was equally sparse although there was some evidence of a recent life. Three huge wardrobes dominated the main wall so Rick headed for these. With his mission for paperwork temporarily distracted, he opened the left door so slowly as if not to wake any moths that might be sleeping inside. A plethora of colour greeted him. There were evening dresses of every colour, bags neatly stacked into side shelving like soldiers on parade. A glut of shoes balanced on racks on the floor almost seemed to quake with excitement at seeing daylight. Yes, he was definitely in the right place; a tart's wardrobe if ever he saw one, and he'd seen a few in his time.

The second was similar so he moved on to the right wardrobe which was disappointingly monochrome by comparison; business suits and pencil skirts lined in order of shade from black to light grey like a minimalist's paint chart. *A tart with a day job*, Rick thought.

Shutting the doors, he went to the back bedroom. One wall was lined with bookcases, full of self-help and 'airy fairy' books in Rick's opinion. He picked one at random. "'*You've quit your job, what's next?*' Pah!" He shook his head. You wouldn't catch me dead reading this..." On the top shelf he spotted a row of labelled ring binders. Two marked 'bank statements' caught his eye.

He pulled them out and sat at the desk. The first one was the standard current account. *Boring*, Rick thought as he flicked through the statements looking for confirmation of pin codes or jottings by one of the girls in an attempt to remember their codes. With nothing of use in that file, he moved on to the other. At the back of the file was a copy of the account application form. It contained both signatures, dated differently, and by one, Alexis', was 'buttons51' and 'Underwood' in red fountain pen. "Good girl," Rick clenched his fists and thrust them in the air like a celebratory football player. All he had to do was to ring the bank, pretend to be this Mr Price and play it by ear. Rick supposed that finding out what 'Mr Price's' first name was would be useful so he did a reckie round the room. People were predictable. They either had photos which they'd write on or leave note around the room reminding them to do things, with names of friends and family mentioned. It wouldn't be too difficult to find. Before too long he'd found a letter addressed to Mr S Price c/o 51 Berry Avenue and a note to 'ring Shaun' so armed with the information he needed, he fished the piece of paper from his jeans pocket and dialled the number for the bank.

"Good afternoon. Eversley Bank, Carol speaking, can I help you?"

"Hi, Carol. It's Shaun Price, can I speak to Mr Frizzell please."

"I'm sorry. You are?"

"Shaun Price, Jessica Price's brother?"

Carol hesitated. "Err..."

The old bag probably can't remember her. You'd think with an account that healthy, she'd remember, Rick thought.

"Certainly, Mr Price. I'll just put you on hold."

'Christ, it's bloody Greensleeves,' Rick said as the music came on.

It had almost played twice when Carol came back on the phone. "Sorry, to keep you Mr Price. I'm connecting you."

"Thanks." The phone rang and was answered almost immediately.

"Good morning... sorry, afternoon already. Good afternoon, Mr Price."

Rick pictured the manager's plastic smile as he was asked, "And how are you today, Mr Price?"

"Fine, thanks, Mr Frizzell."

"Please, call me John."

"Then you call me Shaun." Rick smiled. He liked being someone else.

"Shaun."

"Yes."

"OK. Mr Price... Shaun. I just need to ask you some security questions before I'm able to relay any information."

"Of course, I quite understand," Shaun alias Simon alias Rick said.

"Can I have your mother's maiden name please?"

"Certainly. It's Underwood."

"Thank you."

"And the password on the account?"

"buttons51."

"Thank you."

"And Jessica's brother's name?"

"Sorry?"

"Miss Price's brother's name?"

"Errr..."

"Who is this?"

The line went dead.

Rick slammed his fist on the top of Jessica's desk. "Shit! Shit! Shit!" He'd been careless and Rick Taylor didn't do careless. "You prick, Rick." He tapped his right middle fingernail against his bottom middle tooth. He winced as the finger slipped and his nail dug into his bottom lip. "Shit!"

He turned the study upside down and looked through the rest of the house. Apart from the shared bank statement, which yielded little other than deposits of cash, there was nothing to give away who Alexis was or more importantly, where she was. The only personal documents; birth certificates etc. were of Jessica and he saw little point in taking those.

In fact the only place he didn't look was the lounge drawers, which was a pity as there was something in there that would have suited him nicely.

###

Chapter 41: Simon

"He won't fancy you if you've got no fingernails left?"

"Sorry?"

"Andy. He won't fancy you if you eat your fingers to the bone. You like him, don't you?"

Simon nodded.

Marion smiled. "How did you leave things with him?"

"I'm not sure. Sort of good. I think he's interested but we've not talked about it. There… there was an awkward moment."

"Awkward? In what way?"

"We were talking about our jobs and he had his hand on my arm and kind of rested it there for a… bit too long long. It was nice but he seemed rather embarrassed. Oh God, I hope I'm not picking up the wrong signals."

"What was the last thing you said to each other?"

"I'll call you."

"Who said that?"

"We both did. At the same time."

"That's good. Great minds thinking alike and all that."

"If you say so."

Marion smiled. "Yes, Simon, I do."

Simon looked down at his ringing mobile and stabbed the green button.

"Hello is that Mr Price?"

"Yes."

"Mr Simon Price?"

"Yes. Who's this?"

"Sorry, Mr Price. It's John Frizzell from Eversley Bank."

"Oh, hello."

"I've just had a strange call about your sister."

"Really? From Alexis?"

"No, sorry. Do you have a brother called Shaun?"

"No. No brother. Just Jess."

"I didn't think so. A man rang me calling himself Shaun Price. He knew Jessica's password and your mother's maiden name but said he was Shaun not Simon. And his voice was different to yours. An east-end London sort of accent."

"Do you think it was a scam?"

"I'm certain it was, yes. Do you know who it might have been and how they would have come by Jessica's details?"

"No. No idea. Jess had a friend, boyfriend, called Shaun but I've only met him once. I think he's still in Australia. He's English though; they met here a few weeks before he went out there and she went with him. They didn't keep in contact after she came back, about a year later. Not quite sure what happened. She didn't talk about him after that but I got the feeling he was rather controlling. Anyway, his accent is, was, more refined. And his surname isn't Price, obviously."

"He could be pretending to be another brother."

"Why go to all that trouble?"

"You know how much money was in the joint account. He may have found out."

"Doubt it. It was a while ago, before she got her legal job. Can't see it being him."

"Can you contact him anyway – to make sure – and let me know?"

"I guess. His number must be at Jess' house somewhere or on her mobile."

152

Chapter 42: Rick

Tapping a couple of buttons on his mobile, Rick put the phone to his ear.

"Good afternoon, Cheshire Hotel."

"Tania?"

"Speaking."

"Hey, it's Rick."

"Hi."

"Heard anything more about this Alexis woman?"

"No, sorry. I've spoken to everyone who might know her and it's like she's disappeared off the face of the earth."

"Thanks."

###

Chapter 43: Simon and the Bank Manager

"Is that Simon?"

"Speaking."

"Hi. It's John Frizzell again."

"Ah, yes. I was going to ring you."

"I wasn't actually chasing for that, but how did you get on?"

"It wasn't him."

"Are you sure?"

"Absolutely. He says he didn't know anything about it and I believe him."

"OK. Do you have any idea who it might have been?"

"No, sorry. I've got to go back to Jess's house later so I can do some more digging if you like."

"That would be great."

"You said you rang about something else?"

"Yes. I've found an alternative address for Alexis."

"You have? That's great."

"Do you have a pen and paper?"

"Just a sec. Can you pass me that pad. And a pen? Thanks. Go on."

"Twenty-seven Waverley Drive, Mil–"

"Are you sure?" Simon interrupted.

"Yes. Why, do you know it?"

"I'm there now. Were you going to say 'Milton Keynes Village'?"

"Yes. How do you know it?"

"It's my mum's house."

"Mum. That was Jessica's bank."

"Oh yes?"

"Do you remember me mentioning an Alexis to you?"

"The other day, yes."

"They've found some more paperwork relating to the account that Jessica set up with her."

"That's good."

"I'm not sure."

"Oh, why?"

"Because it's got your address as a secondary contact address."

"Really? Maybe that was Jessica's idea."

"Could have been but it seems odd. The Manager said that the address by Jessica's signature was her home address but the one by Alexis' signature was yours. Wouldn't she have put her own mother's?"

"Maybe she doesn't have one or she lives further away."

"Could be, but he also said that they'd had a call from someone claiming to be a Shaun Price and asking for Jessica's private details."

"Shaun? You don't think…"

"No. I've spoken to him already. I think it's a coincidence."

"Maybe they have another Jessica on their books?"

"But this guy used Jess' passwords including your maiden name."

"Oh, no. I don't like the sound of that. Do they have any idea who it was?"

"No. But he didn't get far. John said his voice was nothing like mine, like someone out of Eastenders. He'll let me know if they get another call."

Simon opened the door of number fifty-one and looked at the floor. There was no sign of the book. He smiled. That meant that Alexis had turned up at last.

"Hello?"

No reply.

He went into the lounge then dining room, both of which looked much as they'd left them, though not quite as tidy. He returned to the lounge and looked in the unit drawers. The money was still there so she'd obviously not needed that – clearly a flying visit.

Simon headed into the kitchen to make a cup of tea and took the kettle off its stand. Looking out the window at the white-covered garden, he robotically filled the kettle for a couple of cups of tea. He turned off the cold tap and was about to turn round when he looked down.

"Eh?" He stared at the book looking back at him from the bottom of the sink. He picked it up and shook it. Luckily the bowl had been dry and he'd only splashed it from filling the kettle. "So Alexis moved it from the hall floor and put it in here?" Simon shook his head. "Where's your head at, girl?" It then dawned on him that she must know about Jessica. He returned to the lounge and looked at the answerphone. No messages. Maybe there was one and she deleted it. But from who? The only person that sprung to mind was Veronica.

Pulling his mobile from his jeans pocket, Simon scrolled down to V and clicked on the green phone button.

"Ziebis?"

"Veronica?"

"Yes. Can I help you?"

"Veronica, it's Simon."

"Simon?"

"Simon Price. Jessica's brother."

"Oh, yes. Any news of Alexis?"

"No, but I think she's been home."

"You think? Is she there?"

"No, but things have been moved and whoever it was had a key. You were going to ring?"

"Yes. Sunday evening. Did she get the message?"

"I think so. It's been erased."

"Oh."

"Oh?"

"I let slip about your sister."

"Shit."

"Sorry."

"Don't worry. She had to find out."

"Any idea of where she might have gone?"

"I don't know. I haven't looked round everywhere yet. I'll see if any of her clothes have gone."

"OK. Will you ring me if you hear anything or find something out?"

"Of course. I want to find her as much as you do."

Upstairs also looked different, with the exception of the study which had radically altered. There were files scattered all over the room. So she'd been looking for something too. Simon returned them to their shelves and tidied up some random papers. He switched on the computer, waiting for the password prompt, typed in buttons51 then went into the main bedroom. The only thing that looked out of place in this room was the bedside unit. The top drawer was open slightly; a chest of drawers he'd not got around to searching. He looked around the room and sighed. Although the house was neat, there was still so much to sort out. He made a mental note to get some cardboard boxes from the supermarkets and pack things away. He'd ask his mum if she wanted anything, keep a few bits for himself but sell the rest. He supposed he'd better ring a couple of estate agents and get the ball rolling on that front. Hopefully they'd find someone who'd buy the house to let it out and maybe then he wouldn't need to sell the furniture. It was decent stuff after all.

He pulled the drawer open and looked inside. There was a square box of tissues with the top tissue pulled out an inch or two. In front of it was a box of coasters then to the left was a stack of books behind a small open-topped silver mesh tray of pens and pencils. Pulling the drawer out until it threatened to fall, he noticed the gilting on the top book.

His heart thumped in his chest as he opened the front cover of Jessica's diary. Her writing was impeccably neat. Knowing that there were only going to be a few pages of entries, Simon sat down on the side of the bed and read. The pages week-to-view and while the weekdays were methodical; work in the daytime, watching TV, playing with Buttons and report of latest book in the evenings, the weekends were a mixture of lie-ins, reading the newspapers, sorting receipts and bank statements (that made Simon smile), watching DVDs and going to the cinema. Simon thought it a solitary life as there was no mention of anyone else… until January second. '*Saw Shaun in bar near 'BP' this evening.' Chatted for hours. So happy. Invited him up. Feels right.*' Simon's heart sank. This was how he wanted to remember his sister, not the image he had when he last saw her.

Within a few minutes he'd read the whole thing. She'd seemed really happy and the potential between her and

Shaun so poignant. She'd had relationships in the past, she'd mentioned some to Simon but 'feels right'? Life could be so cruel.

Simon opened the top drawer of her bedside unit to put the diary away, out of respect, but then saw the previous year's book beside the tray of pens and pencils. He swapped the books over and shut the drawer. Lying lengthways on the bed, he pulled the two blue pillows from the left side to prop himself up.

Starting at the beginning of the year, much of it was again mundane until he got to Tuesday eighth February. "Tonight: Alexis was born." That was the only entry other than a large smile. "Eh?" Simon said, staring at the page. The rest of the two-week spread was the usual work and relaxation mix so he turned the page. A photo fell out, face down on the bed. Simon picked it up then dropped it as if it had burned him. Again, it landed face down.

Picking it up again slowly, he turned over the picture … carefully, as if the reality of what he'd witnessed would change his life forever.

There in front of him was his sister smiling back. His sister by face, but the rest was new to him, though he recognised the clothes from the wardrobe just a few feet away. He looked up and stared at it, his eyes burning imaginary holes into it, through the outfit in the picture.

Beneath the self-portrait, in Jessica's handwritten blue pen, was one word: 'Alexis'.

###

Chapter 44: Simon and Veronica

"Hello?"

"Veronica?"

"Yes?"

"Veronica, it's Simon again. Jessica's brother."

"Yes, Simon. You've found Alexis?"

"Er, yes."

"Great! Where is she?"

"Dead. I'm afraid."

"What? When?"

"That's the complicated bit. You see I found a picture of Alexis."

"Right."

"She has ginger hair, yes?"

"Yes."

"So does Jessica."

"Oh? That's a coincidence. Isn't it something like four percent–?"

"It's more than a coincidence." Simon interrupted. "You see, this picture I found was Jessica."

"I thought you said it was Alexis."

"Yes."

"You've lost me."

"They're the same person."

"What?"

"Jessica is Alexis. My sister is Alexis. Was Alexis."

Silence.

"Veronica?"

"I'm sorry. What? Your sister, Jessica, is my girl Alexis."

"Yes."

"And your sister died, so Alexis is dead."

"Yes. I'm so sorry."

"Thanks for telling me. I'm sorry too. She was your sister. I'd only known her…"

"About a year."

"Yes. How did you know that?"

"From her diary."

"You've read her diary?"

"Yes, I know. It felt weird but I needed to see if I could explain everything that had been going on."

"And it did?"

"Yes. Well, that part."

"And the unanswered parts?"

"A man phoned Jessica's bank the other day pretending to be me, only he got my name wrong so he didn't get far."

"I see."

"And I don't know how to find out who he was. He knew things he shouldn't have known."

"I think I know who it might have been. Don't worry. He won't be troubling you again. I'll speak to him."

"You know him? How?"

"A private investigator, of sorts, that I'm sure Daniel hired. Daniel's like that."

"Oh. So you'll tell him what happened?"

"Sure. Leave it with me. Thanks Simon and again, I'm sorry about your sister."

"Thanks. It's a shame in a way that there's no Alexis. It would have been nice to meet someone else who knew Jess."

"Yes, it's a real loss to us too, believe me."

As far as Simon knew, the only other people who'd known of Alexis were his mum and the woman with the mobile, Beth. Only it wasn't Alexis' phone, it was Jessica's. Still she didn't need it and nor did Simon.

"Hello, this is Alexis. Sorry I can't get to the phone. Please leave a message after the tone."

Simon laughed. If only he'd heard that when he'd rung before, it would have saved a lot of chasing around. It was Jessica's voice to a 'tee'.

"Hi, Beth. This is Simon Price, Jessica's brother. I have some news about Alexis. Can you give me a call back please? I think I left my number the last time we spoke but if not, it's…"

###

Chapter 45: Veronica and Rick

"Yeah?"

"Mr…" Veronica realised that Rick had never told her his surname. "Rick?"

"Yeah. Who's this?"

"Veronica Ziebis of Frau–"

"I know who you are. How did you get this number?"

"You phoned me the other day."

"And you're phoning me now because…"

"You were after Alexis."

"You've found her?"

"Not exactly."

"Explain."

"She died recently."

"Shit! Sure?"

"Yes, sorry."

"How?"

"Car crash."

"No way. Shit."

"It's very sad. She was a popular girl."

"Is it usual protocol to phone all your clients to tell them?"

"Of course not but…"

"But?"

"We both know that you weren't phoning to book Alexis. You're working for Daniel Goldstein, aren't you?"

Rick frowned. He needed to up his game. He was slipping and that could only lead to trouble… or no work. "So why are you telling me and not Daniel."

Veronica kept silent.

"Because it's easier, yes?" Rick said.

"You need to report into him anyway, don't you?"

"Of course. He'll not be pleased."

"None of us are."

###

Chapter 46: Rick and Daniel

"Yes?"

"Daniel, it's Rick."

"Found her?"

"Yes and no."

"What the fuck does that mean?"

"She's dead?"

"Shit."

"My sentiments exactly."

"How."

"RTA."

"Rick. Speak fucking English."

"Road Traffic Accident."

"When?"

"'bout a week ago."

"I saw her a week ago. So that's that, is it?"

"'fraid so boss."

"Not the outcome I'd expected but it draws a line."

"Yes, boss."

"Thanks, Rick. Your fee…"

"It's OK, boss. I didn't get the result you wanted."

"Not your fault. I'll see you right."

"Thanks, boss."

###

Chapter 47: Daniel and his Wife

Daniel slammed down the phone, picked it up again, then repeatedly bashed it against the holster.

"Daniel?" his wife asked.

"Sorry. Just some bad news."

"Oh?"

"Work. I'll sort it out."

"Anything I can do?"

"Thanks love, but it's OK." He paused. "You know something, Kate, you're one in a million."

"Yes, Daniel," she smiled, "to put up with you, I'd have to be."

###

Chapter 48: Beth and Nate

"You don't have to squeeze so hard."

"Sorry, Beth."

"It'll be fine."

"I know. But I can't help being nervous."

"That's sweet."

"Mr & Mrs Morrison? You can come in now."

"Thanks, Doc," Nate said.

"Please, Mrs Morrison, lie on the bed here and lift up your top a little so I can get to your stomach."

Beth did as she was asked.

"I'm going to put a little gel on so it might feel a little cold."

Beth giggled as the sonographer squirted a tube over her stomach. Nate giggled as the gel farted.

"There we are."

"Where?" Beth and Nate said together.

"Here. Can you see the heartbeat?"

Both parents squinted at the screen.

"Never mind. The good news is that your baby has a healthy, strong heartbeat."

"Did you hear that, Nate?"

"Can you tell what it is yet?"

"I'm sorry. I won't be able to for another six to eight weeks and even then sometimes the baby can be in the wrong position."

"A boy would be lovely. We could play football."

"You don't like football."

"I would if I had a boy."

Beth looked worried.

Nate continued, "But girls are always the apple of their Daddy's eyes. As long as the baby's happy and healthy when it comes out, with bits in the right places, I don't mind."

"Would you like a DVD?"

"You can do that?" Beth asked.

"Oh, yes. This machine does 4D movies and stills. You can have both if you like."

"That would be lovely, wouldn't it Beth? We can watch it whenever we like."

Beth smiled. Maybe, just maybe, this was the side of her husband that would stick. Being realistic, he'd probably need some steering from her, without him knowing of course, but she had high hopes.

###

Chapter 49: Simon and Marion

Simon hadn't quite worked out how to tell his mum about Jessica's double life, who Alexis was, about Veronica, Daniel, Beth and co. Although he knew Marion was a calm and level-headed woman, he figured that telling her everything now would be too soon. She didn't need to know everything just yet, if ever, so he decided to tell her about the diary, the photograph and see what she said.

"She had what?"
        "A double life."
        "Like a spy or something?"
        Simon laughed. "No, not a spy. Quite the opposite."
        Marion put down her cup of tea and tilted her head as if she were an animal not understanding a given instruction.
        "How do I put this?" Simon pulled out the photograph of Alexis and put it in front of his mum.
        "Ooh. She's… was such a pretty…" Marion sniffed and pulled a tissue from a small square box on the opposite side of the kitchen table. She blew her nose, screwed up the tissue and walked over to the bin, depositing the tissue, then returning to the table. "I don't understand."
        "She was an escort, Mum."
        "Escort? Like a prosti… No. Not Jessica. Jessica wouldn't…"
        Simon nodded.
        "But…"
        "I know. I couldn't believe it either."
        "Is that why she had so much money? Why she'd paid off the house?"
        "Couldn't have done it so quickly as a secretary."
        Marion winced and drank more tea. "But that's so sleazy. How do you know?"
        "Too many things adding up."
        Marion gripped the side of the cup. "Was she killed because of it?"
        Simon shook his head. "No, Mum. That was an accident."

Marion put the nail of her left index finger between her teeth and rocked her finger back and forth, the noise reminding Simon of waves against stones at a Devon beach they'd visited as children. "Why do you think she did it?"

Simon shrugged. "Excitement? Being a secretary can't have been all that challenging."

"Not my idea of excitement." She shuddered.

"Nor mine. Not quite skydiving or…"

"Going off to Australia for a year like she did when she met Shaun. It's a shame how that worked out. Lovely to have had her back, of course. This doesn't matter. It isn't, wasn't her, not the real her. That was…" Marion pointed to the photograph. "That was Alexis."

Simon nodded again and smiled. "Yes, Mum. And she's gone too."

###

Chapter 50: Simon and Marion

"You look great."

"Thanks. I'm rather nervous actually."

"Ah, that's sweet."

"It's been a while."

"Where are you meeting?"

"Hemel Hempstead, it's about half way."

"Do you know anywhere in Hemel?"

"He said there's the Holiday Inn near M1 junction eight so that sounded like a good a place as any."

"So I may not be seeing you back tonight then." Marion smirked.

"Mum!"

"It's a hotel…"

"I know, but it's our first date."

"Not exactly. You've already met."

"That was hardly a date though, was it?"

"No, but you chatted for ages, so you have a head start."

"Yeah, you're right. I'd better go. I don't want to be late."

"What time are you meeting?"

"Eight o'clock."

"But it's only half past six."

"I know but…"

"You don't want to be late." Marion repeated, smiling. "Have a wonderful time. He's just the thing you need to take your mind off… what's been happening lately."

"Thanks. Will you be all right?"

"Of course. Helen's coming over for a game of Scrabble and I've won the last three times so she's determined to fight back."

"You have a good evening."

Marion winked. "And you."

Simon shook his head, smiled, and grabbed his car keys.

###

Chapter 51: Simon and Andy

The M1 was busy for a Tuesday evening and Simon pulled
into the car park just after seven thirty. His heart raced as he
switched off the engine. Pulling round the rear view mirror, he
switched on the internal light. His face was flushed so he
zipped down the window to let in some fresh air. He sat for a
while breathing deeply and fanning his face with his right hand
until he'd calmed down.

"This is stupid," he said, staring at himself. "Getting
worked up over a date. He's a nice guy. He likes you, you like
him. It'll be fine."

If nothing else, Jessica's death had taught him that life
was too short to not grab every opportunity that came his way.

Walking into the hotel bar, Simon spotted Andy sitting on a bar
stool, grinning like an X-factor winner.

Andy stood up and held out his hand. Simon shook it and
blushed. They ordered their drinks and went over to one of the
tables.

"This is probably a stupid question, Simon, but how are
you?"

"OK. You know. Got quite a lot done over the past few
days, a lot more to do but it's the reading of the will on
Wednesday then I guess it'll be easier to... And you? Back at
work or...?"

"Wasn't supposed to be but they had a staff shortage. I'm
not the only one to have..."

"Better keeping busy."

Andy nodded, changing the subject to hobbies and they
sat chatting like old friends, laughing and taking turns to buy
refills.

As the bar emptied, Andy said, "I have a room here. Didn't
fancy driving back. Would you...?"

"Oh. I'd not thought. I didn't bring..."

"Of course not. It's fine."

"But I'd like to."

Andy winked, put down his empty glass, and looked at
the exit to the rooms.

Simon smiled, finished his drink, and followed Andy out of the bar.

###

Chapter 52: At the Solicitor's

Simon opened the door for Marion and followed her into the solicitor's reception.

"Good morning," the receptionist chirped.

"Hello," Simon replied. "We're Mr Thomas' ten o'clock."

The receptionist's smile faded and she pointed to a couple of chairs. "Certainly, Mr Price. Mrs Price. Please take a seat."

"Thank you," Marion said, and sat beside her son.

The receptionist made a call and Mr Thomas appeared from a frosted glass office door.

"Good morning. Sorry to have kept you waiting. Please come this way."

Simon and Marion stood up and Simon paused, letting Marion go first.

Mr Thomas directed them to a couple of chairs then sat behind his large mahogany desk. "Firstly let me extend my condolences, on behalf of Thomas, Duckett and Peterson."

"Thank you," Marion said.

Simon nodded.

Mr Thomas picked up a thin cream stapled document. "As you may be aware, Jessica wrote a will which we have for safe-keeping. It's quite simple. She had a reasonable estate and kept all her affairs in order so it won't take me long." He coughed then read…

"This is the last Will and Testament of me, Jessica Price, of Fifty-one Berry Avenue, Hinsley, which I make this, the fourteenth day of November 2015. I revoke all former Wills and Testamentary Dispositions made by me. Subject to the payment thereout of my funeral and testamentary expenses and debts, I give devised and bequeath all my estate, both real and personal whatsoever and wheresoever unto my daughter, Holly Marion…" Mr Thomas paused at the expression on Simon and Marion's faces.

Marion said nothing, her bottom lip dropping open.

Simon looked at her then looked back at Mr Thomas. "What?"

#######

Hitman Sam

a British lad-lit

crime novella

This book is dedicated to 'Scottish Andy',

for his unyielding support and belief in me,

which he is learning to have in himself.

Table of Contents

Chapter 1 – Sam Ponders his Future   185
Chapter 2 – The Advert Entices   189
Chapter 3 – The First Package   195
Chapter 4 – Sam's New Life Begins   197
Chapter 5 – Preparation is Key   205
Chapter 6 – A Partner in Crime   209
Chapter 7 – Emma and the Post-it   213
Chapter 8 – Not All is as it Seems   217
Chapter 9 – So to Business   219
Chapter 10 – Emma Grills Sam   223
Chapter 11 – Emma's History   225
Chapter 12 – Something's Not Right   229
Chapter 13 – Emma and Paul   231
Chapter 14 – Organised, Sam, Get Organised   233
Chapter 15 – Beginning to Warm   235
Chapter 16 – Tom and Sandra   239
Chapter 17 – Sam's Research   243
Chapter 18 – Emma's Dad   249
Chapter 19 – Emma and the Italian   251
Chapter 20 – More Preparation   257
Chapter 21 – The Gun   263
Chapter 22 – It Just Won't Go Away   265
Chapter 23 – The Perfect Spot   267
Chapter 24 – Emma's in Charge   269
Chapter 25 – Josh Bradley   273
Chapter 26 – The First Date   279
Chapter 27 – The Dales   281
Chapter 28 – Caught   283
Chapter 29 – Deaf Ears   287
Chapter 30 – The Fake Misunderstanding   289
Chapter 31 – All Part of the Service   293

Chapter 32 – Duncote Mark   297
Chapter 33 – Walkabout Farm   303
Chapter 34 – Another Ice Maiden   305
Chapter 35 – Making Amends   309
Chapter 36 – A Partner in Crime   311
Chapter 37 – The Trial Run   315
Chapter 38 – Meeting Heather   319
Chapter 39 – The Smallest Detail   325
Chapter 40 – A Popular Choice   329
Chapter 41 – Head or Heart   331
Chapter 42 – Getting the Gun   337
Chapter 43 – The Deed   343
Chapter 44 – A Heart Grows Fonder   347
Chapter 45 – Things Change   353
Chapter 46 – The Pieces Fit   357
Chapter 47 – The Love Triangle   361
Chapter 48 – THP   363

About the Author   365

Note from the Author   366

Chapter 1 – Sam Ponders his Future

Click, click, click. "Sod this." Sam threw the remote onto the empty sofa seat next to him. "Who in their right mind watches daytime TV? Roll on Pointless."

He looked at the clock. Four-thirty. Too early for supper. "Cuppa and toast should do it."

Being his first winter at number five Greath Close, he was now realising how much 1930s houses cost to heat with the exposed floorboards and their gaps.

He looked round the kitchen. Maybe he'd spend some of his newly acquired time redecorating. He reckoned it had been quite a few years since the place had seen a paintbrush, the kitchen especially. Fortunately the units were quite modern, a fairly pleasing lime colour, but the walls were a drab blue, made especially cold by the season. The colour scheme reminded him of a phrase his mother used to say, "Blue and green should never be seen" or something like that. Sam didn't mind anyway, he was relishing having the place to himself since Michelle had left and he could now do whatever he liked. He was grateful she'd not invested any money when he'd bought the house and wasn't tied to paying her back.

"Never go into business with family or friends," was another of his mother's favourite sayings, Sam's dad having been stung with the latter. She'd then set up a small interior design company which had gone from strength to strength, until an offer from a local entrepreneur had been one she couldn't refuse. She and Sam's father were now on a Mediterranean cruise from some of the proceeds.

Sam digressed. That was something he'd become an expert at. He wondered whether he could make a living out of it. He'd upload his CV and profile into totaljobs.com as a 'professional procrastinator', minimum £30K per annum, click here to contact.

Putting on the kettle, he went upstairs and grabbed a jumper, returning to the kitchen as the kettle clicked off and he fetched the milk from the fridge. He shook the bottle, not noticing a lump hitting the side. Pouring the water on the tea bag, he added a spoon of half-calorie sugar (his mates had ribbed him about his small potbelly so he'd decided he'd better watch his weight). Like many people, Sam didn't think of checking the date or sniffing the milk as he unscrewed the top. It wasn't until the blob of congealed milk plonked into the black and red striped mug, that he'd figured it was time to get a fresh bottle.

"I suppose I can kill two birds and get the job paper as well. Can't live on fresh air and there must be more to life than daytime TV."

Taking the keys from the kitchen table, he put on his jacket and slammed the front door behind him. The local shops were only a few minutes' walk from his house, barely enough time to decide whether he needed anything else.

As Sam wandered down the aisles of the Co-op, he noticed two members of staff filling shelves; one bars of chocolate, the other struggling with getting oranges to stay still. The owner of the shop, Mr Shah, was at the till, staring out the window, his small head swivelling as if watching a tennis match. Sam smiled at the diminutive man in a beige jumper that seemed at least one size too large.

"Evening, Mr Shah. This milk and an Echo please. A bar of… mmm, Bournville. And I'll have a Euro Millions for tomorrow night please. Oh and I 'd better have… no it's okay, just kidding."

"Evening, Sam. How's redundancy suiting you? Bored yet?"

Sam laughed. "Not quite there, but I'm heading in that direction. Even contemplating decorating the house. Maybe there'll be something in the paper that'll lure me back to joining the gainfully employed. Don't suppose I'll find anything as exciting as designing photocopier software," he said, faking a yawn, "but I'm sure there'll be something eventually."

The shopkeeper wished him luck and turned to serve the next customer, an elderly white-haired woman wrapped in a red tartan scarf, who was too intent on her purchases to notice or return Sam's smile.

Deciding he'd better check his bank balance, Sam headed to the cashpoint and printed out a mini-statement; two grand. It wasn't a fortune but it would be enough to pay the mortgage and keep him in bread and tea bags for two or three months. He hoped long enough to find the ideal vacancy and go through the laborious interview, second interview and company tour bit. He longed to be his own boss but apart from the risks of setting up his own business, he didn't know what he wanted to do, or to be. At twenty-seven, did you need to make a decision about the rest of your life? He had plenty of time to go through another job or two until he found something exciting, challenging and well paid. He'd done okay so far. Software design had given him a deposit on his house, a not-too-old VW Golf and nights out with the lads, so he wasn't complaining.

Sam stuffed the statement into his jeans pocket and went home. He decided if there was nothing that grabbed him in the paper, he'd upload his CV on the internet anyway and wait for the calls to flood in.

"Hello, Mr Simpson. Google here. We've seen your CV online and you're just the guy we've been looking for. When can you start?" Sam chuckled.

ooOoo

Chapter 2 – The Advert Entices

Reaching his front door, Sam emptied his green metal post-box. Nothing but bills. "Story of my life."

Fresh cuppa in hand, Sam scoured the paper but nothing leapt out at him from the job pages. He'd almost written the section off when he got to the last row of small ads when the final one shouted at him.

Bored with your life? the text read.

"Yeah! Jeremy Kyle, Judge Judy, Rinder… blah, blah."

Do you want some excitement?

"Who wouldn't?"

Ring 07007 007007.

As Sam dialled the number, he sang the theme tune to his favourite James Bond movie, Live & Let Die "when you were young and your heart was an open book… dah nah nah, nah nah nah, dah dah… dah dah dah…" until he was interrupted by a recorded message in a woman's voice.

'Welcome to THP Services. You will be asked a series of questions which you must answer truthfully. After the final question, please leave your name and contact details. There are no right or wrong answers but they must be honest. If you pass this stage, you will then be sent an information pack. Good luck!'

After a prolonged silence, Sam wondered whether he should hang up but the voice started again.

'Please state your height. You may answer in feet and inches or in metric.'

"Six feet four" Sam said, not seeing the point in lying.

'What size shoes do you wear?'

"Ten." Sam wondered what that had to do with anything, thinking the advert a vacancy for an undertakers.

'Are you right or left-handed?'

He paused. "Right."

'Red or black.'

Red or black what? he wondered, but answered "black" as he thought of the percentage of black vs red clothes in the half-empty-since-Michelle-left wardrobe. He'd almost missed the next question, only hearing 'pockets'. He wasn't sure what he was supposed to do now so kept quiet hoping she'd repeat it.

'Do you own a pair of black trousers with pockets?'

"Ah, yes." Sam had a pair he used to wear to work, with deep pockets for the USB flash drives he'd had to carry from department to department. Although this still tied in loosely with the funeral home scenario, he found the question strange as surely they'd provide a uniform.

'Do you play computer games?'

"I'm a bloke. Of course I do… sorry, yes." Okay, so that ruled out undertakers. He didn't imagine they'd let him blat aliens, find desert island treasure or Pokémon in the off-peak dying season.

'And your eye colour please?'

"Brown."

'And now your hair colour please?'

"Brown but going a little..."

'Favourite film now please.'

"Um, how to choose? I'd say overall 'Leon', but 'In Bruges' and 'Collateral' were cool. And of course, 'Skyfall' and 'Casino Royal' the Daniel Craig version rather than the David Niven but he's very good too. I especially liked him in–"

The voice didn't wait for Sam to finish. *'What is your favourite flavour ice cream please?'*

Sam wondered what that had to do with the price of fish but answered "Rocky Road." If nothing else, she was polite. The subject of food made Sam's stomach grumble. He'd have some supper when he'd finished with this farce of a phone call. The thought had also crossed his mind that it was a practical joke but then why would someone pay to have an advert, albeit a cheap one, in the local paper? It had to be some kind of psych evaluation. Medical research perhaps? Or more likely market research for some consumer company packaged up as a job vacancy to boost their ratings.

The voice continued. *'Do you drive?'*

"Yes." Sam figured he'd take it seriously although wished the questions would get to the point as he was calling a mobile at peak rate and wasn't made of money.

'Two more questions to go,' the voice said, as if psychic. *'Do you eat pizza?'*

Sam screwed his face up at that one but answered, "Yes". The questions seemed to be getting more bizarre and not particularly unique. Surely everyone played video games, ate ice cream and pizza and had a car. He finally settled on market research. One more to go. What would be the harm?

'And the last question, do you live alone?'

Sam hesitated. He wondered whether if he answered positively to this one they'd send someone over to check him out or beat him up. He'd always loved dramatics and pictured the scene. *A dark figure skulking up the path looking around him (it was always a 'him') making sure he wasn't being watched. He looked for lights in the house. There were none. Good. He reached inside his pocket for the gun and twisted on the silencer. He fired at the nearest light, a good twenty yards away, and it smashed into pieces. He'd never missed a shot in his life. The victim would be in bed. Where else would he be at three a.m.?*

On the other hand, would it benefit him to say "No" to appear to make him more stable? But then they'd not asked for his address yet. He decided to stick with the truth and said, "Yes".

'Thank you for your time. Now please leave your full name and details and should you be successful, we will contact you in due course.'

Sam left his name, mobile phone number and, deciding it safer than giving his postal address, his email, then the line went dead. He finished his tea, which by now was a shade cooler than tepid but he wasn't paying enough attention to it to notice. The 'interview' had puzzled him. Who were THP Services? He could phone the Echo asking for their details but they were likely to quote 'client confidentiality' and 'Data Protection Act' to him. So he strode upstairs and powered up his laptop. Putting in the password, he decided not to wait for the screen to boot up so made a couple of slices of toast and a hotter cup of tea. Not exactly a proper supper but he was on a mission now, and proper food took time.

Typing THP Services into yell.com but leaving the location field blank, the screen brought up over a hundred possible matches the closest being a financial company in Essex.

Having assumed that THP was a local company, Sam refined the search to Northamptonshire but there was nothing even remotely close. He clicked on the 'back' button at the top of the screen which returned him to the UK results. Still not satisfactory but Sam waded through the list, shaking his head as he scrolled down the screen. He tried Google and Yahoo searches and dismissing accountants, a management consultant was the closest he got. Peterborough was local enough but why go the secret route? It all seemed bizarre so he'd not waste any more time on it but wait and see if he got a phone call or email back. Maybe he'd be entered in a competition and win a weekend for two in Scarborough, though it would be of little use to him since his friends where all hooked up with partners. Maybe he'd get a case of wine instead which would do nicely, thanks very much.

Then, while he was online, he checked out some job sites and put his CV on a couple of them. Although the IT field had slowed down, he was hopeful of something. With that done, he logged on to his instant message service and chatted with his mates Mark and Danny. Both their girlfriendsmailto: had plans for them that evening so the conversations were shorter than Sam would have liked but it was nice to catch up with them, and they made promises to meet up "real soon". He was coming off 'Messenger' when his mobile rang. The screen showed 'withheld number' which Sam normally let go through to the answerphone but he pressed the green button. It wasn't that late and he had nothing better to do.

"Hello?"

The smooth female voice asked, "Good evening… Mr Simpson?"

"Yes. Who's this?"

"Good evening. This is THP Services. You rang earlier and answered a few questions for us. Is that correct?"

Sam still felt as if he were on trial. "Yes. That was me."

"Excellent. I'm delighted to tell you that you've passed the initial test."

"Initial test. What's the job exactly?"

Clearly not listening to what he'd asked, the woman replied, "Certainly. We need your postal address and we will gladly send you an information pack."

A long pause followed.

"Mr Simpson?"

Sam wasn't convinced so remained quiet.

"Not a problem. You're welcome to think about it. Would you like me to call back tomorrow?"

Curiosity got the better of him. "No, it's okay. Send me the details. Five Greath Close, Kemsley, Northants NN30 4DP. Could you not send it by email?"

"Thank you. You should receive the information pack in the post in the next couple of days. Any questions, do contact us."

"Okay," was all he could say before the line went dead. In Sam's experience, most companies preferred email contact as it was instant and free but they obviously weren't technology minded. The woman had sounded more than capable, but he guessed that wasn't how they worked.

Opening up iTunes, Sam synchronised his iPod. He planned to go for a cycle ride the next day, all part of his new fitness regime, and it would keep him company. Computers had a habit of eating time and his stomach growling indicated that a few hours had gone by – that and the fact it had got dark outside. He looked at the small clock in the bottom right-hand corner of his laptop screen. "Bugger," he cursed. He'd hired a couple of movies earlier in the week which were due back and the shop shut in less than an hour. *I must get Sky,* he thought for the umpteenth time since moving in. And he'd walked past the rental store on the way from the Co-op to the bank. Why hadn't he remembered to take the DVDs with him, especially as he'd left them in the hall as a reminder? He'd be fined if he left them any longer but the rain belting against his 'office', the back bedroom, window didn't inspire him to venture out. However, the prospect of another day of rubbish TV won him over and he'd swap them for two more. Any excuse to see the lovely blonde who worked there.

Sprinting downstairs, he grabbed his jacket off the end of the banister, tucked the DVDs from the hall table inside his coat, then put the keys in his jeans pocket and went out into the dark.

Pulling up his collar shielded some of the elements of the autumn night although the odd drop of rain slunk down into the back of his neck. "Yuck! Who's idea was this?" He soon arrived at the parade of shops and passing the Indian restaurant, post office and hairdressers, he approached 'Prime Time Rental'. Chickening out of going inside, he discreetly posted the DVDs through the large outside slot and went home.

ooOoo

Chapter 3 – The First Package

Sam had put THP's advert and grilling to the back of his mind and had just returned from a cycle ride when the doorbell rang. He thought it was odd as he had few visitors, his parents were still on their cruise and his friends were at work. He was prepared to growl at a double-glazing salesman when he recognised the part-florescent jacket through the frosted glass of his postman, George.

"Hello, Sam. I have a recorded delivery for you. Sign here please."

"Thanks, George. How are you today?"

"Not bad. Arthritis giving me jip but mustn't grumble. It's not raining and I retire in a few months. No more early mornings. Iris is looking forward to it as much as I am."

Sam smiled, assuming Iris to be George's wife. He looked at the envelope. "Thanks a lot." Sam signed in the box next to his name and George wished him a good day before heading back down the path. Sam watched him go and thought it a good job to have in the summer, to wear shorts, get a tan, but couldn't be envied on days like this.

In a corner of the close, a mini tornado of leaves buffeted against a garage door. Sam shivered and went inside.

Placing the package on the kitchen table, he put the kettle on and leant against the sink, staring at the envelope until the kettle clicked off. He made a cup of coffee, then sat down and ripped open the parcel. The accompanying letter read *'Congratulations you've passed the initiation and are now on the THP programme. Enclosed is part one of your training manual – you will receive further instructions throughout your training and payment with the final instalment.'* This was the part that especially caught Sam's interest. So he was being sent this stuff he'd not paid anything for and was also going to receive money for it? He'd not given his bank details and didn't intend to until THP Services could prove they were legit.

He rang the 07007 number again but got the same recorded message. He was going to say something but decided to read the booklet first. He had his redundancy money to keep him ticking over until something came along.

Providing this fiasco didn't cost him anything, what was the harm in going along with it until he had a reason not to?

ooOoo

Chapter 4 – Sam's New Life Begins

Despite having spent the afternoon engrossed in the book, and still thinking it was all a game or part of something bigger, Sam was excited yet... How did he feel? Terrified. Yep, that was it. He'd never done anything illegal in his life. Not strictly true; the odd mile or two over the speed limit and the occasional cycling on the pavement when traffic was busy, but everybody did that, so they didn't count. Now he found himself reading up on, and potentially embroiled in, the underworld and was loving every minute; every sentence he read, every picture showing him the moves to being a secret stealth machine. He had suspected from the cloak and dagger approach that this was something far from run-of-the-mill and finally, the last page confirmed what the THP stood for. 'Trainee Hitman Programme'.

He sighed, wanting to know everything; what his future had in store. The last page also explained why he couldn't jump ahead. If he was given too much information he'd try to perform later moves too early and his training wouldn't be complete. If this happened he wouldn't be taken on as a member of the 'team'. Sam wondered how many team members there were and whether anyone else in Kemsley was an 'agent'... or whatever THP Services staff were called.

Looking at the clock, he realised why his back was aching and stomach rumbling; it was swiftly approaching tomorrow. Too late for food but that wouldn't do him any harm. He'd been snacking all day which, on reflection, wasn't the wisest of things to do. He needed to return to the DVD store and get the movies on the manual's list and the shop would shut shortly. Better go last thing, he'd decided, when it was quiet, and he didn't want to waste another day.

All he had to do tomorrow was find, or buy, two notebooks; one large, one pocket-sized, a pad of post-it notes, a noticeboard, three reliable pens; black, blue and red. Highlighters weren't mentioned but would probably come in handy. And a map. He wasn't sure of where yet but he was new to the area so a copy of his wouldn't hurt. He could use his board to tape the map again and drawing pins to mark his route. His territory, wherever that might be.

Sam decided that any missions he had to go on would be best done in the dark. He couldn't trust his face to not give himself away until his new profession had soaked into his skin and he could be sure of acting normally. He would be Sam Simpson by day and THP agent by night. A double life. A life with no turning back. And he couldn't wait.

The DVD rental shop was unusually quiet for a Friday night. Emma looked at the clock for the third time in as many minutes. Nine-thirty-three. She sighed and leant against the counter, tapping her pink varnished fingernails on the black melamine surface. There were three people in the shop and two had been there ages. Why did people take so long making their minds up? Behind her, she heard the kettle click off.

"Cup of tea, Emma?" Tom, the shop manager, shouted from the back.

"Love one. Usual gnat's pee please... sugar this time. Treat myself. Thanks, Tom."

She watched one of the male customers sniff, wipe his nose on his scruffy jumper sleeve then scratch his bum, while looking at the adult DVD section. He turned towards the counter and Emma dropped her head as if engrossed with something. The man approached her nervously with a DVD in his hand and put it on the counter, together with his membership card which, like him, was rather grubby.

"Thank you." Emma picked up the card with her index finger and thumb and swiped it into the till system. She waited for the screen to divulge his information. "Mr Rogers... O... Oliver."

Mr Rogers nodded meekly.

"Can you please confirm your address, Mr Rogers?" Emma raised her eyebrows.

"Okay." He paused.

Emma waited, eyebrows still raised.

"One... one... seven... Lewis... Road." The man's speech was painfully slow and he whispered while looking at his feet, still sniffing.

"That's it. Thanks. Bear with me, I'll get your disc." Emma pulled out a drawer and swapping the original case for a plain blue 'Prime Time' one, she glanced at the title and smiled. "Tina and Jane Go Wild," she mumbled, then in a normal voice, "Enjoy your movie, Mr Rogers."

Emma's smile expanded into a synchronised-swimmer's grin as he walked away from her. Tom brought the teas through to the counter and as she mentioned the film title, he winked at her as the customer scuttled out of the shop. Anyone seeing him would have guessed from his mannerisms that he wasn't renting out a U-rated Disney movie.

Picturing the state of his membership card, she was hoping that she wouldn't be the one to open the post-box when his case came back, when Tom whispered, "All he needs now is a raincoat."

"He does look the type, doesn't he?" Emma sighed. "It's sad. He's obviously quite lonely."

"Probably too shy to meet real women."

"What do you think he does for a living?"

"Something dull but he thinks is vital. A civil servant or tax inspector."

"Let's have a look." Emma went to the computer keyboard and tapped a couple of keys. "He's a Credit Control Clerk... does that count?"

"Not really, unless the credit he controls is tax... and ours. Best of three?"

"Okay, what about her then?" Emma looked at the female customer browsing through the chick flick section.

"I reckon she's a secretary or typist. She's been here nearly an hour so she's the patient type."

They stood looking at the woman who was reading the backs of cases with the occasional machine gun laugh which seemed to be unnerving the remaining male customer. Finally, she chose a film and brought it to the counter.

"Good evening," Emma said, "Can I have your membership card please?"

The woman looked surprised, then fished around in her small beige handbag and put the card on the counter.

"Thank you… Mrs…" Emma swiped the card and brought up the relevant details. "Miss Abbott. 'Me Before You'… a lovely film… Have you seen it before?"

Taking back her card when offered, Miss Abbott shook her head.

"I'm sure you'll love it." Emma continued, "but do have some Kleenex handy!"

Miss Abbott nodded and left the store.

"So, what is she?" Emma asked.

"Apart from painfully shy and apparently unable to speak? We should get her and Mr Randy Rogers together, start a Prime Time dating club."

It was Tom's turn to raise his eyebrows.

"She's a… secretary. Wow, Tom, all your years as a copper haven't been wasted."

Tom smiled. "I have my uses."

With one remaining customer, a man dressed in black, Emma's attention was drawn to him. She recognised him from a few days earlier but couldn't remember his name.

Looking at the clock, Tom said before heading back towards the staff area. "It's nearly ten. I'll go and lock the back door."

"Thanks, Tom. I'll deal with this guy then get my things." She then approached the man in black who seems startled. "Excuse me… I'm sorry… but we shut in ten minutes. No hurry but so you know."

"Er, okay, sorry. Won't be long. Can't decide. How many can I have?"

Emma paused, thinking the question odd as he'd been in recently but pointed towards a card on the wall, situated below the clock.

"It depends on your membership card level. If you've got a bronze, see, you can have three at once, silver is four and gold is five. DVDs or Blu-ray – makes no difference."

"Okay, thanks. Not sure what mine is." He flushed. "Er, not used it for a while. I'll have a look."

The man shuffled in his inside jacket pocket and retrieved his card which he showed to Emma.

"Yours is a bronze, so three."

They looked down at a small mound of cases on the floor by his feet and laughed.

"I'm not supposed to, but I could let you have four. Can't stretch to anymore than that though or I'd get shot."

The man laughed nervously while Emma retreated to the counter, leaving him to put some of the films back. Emma hummed Oasis' Wonderwall while she waited.

A couple of minutes later, the man brought over his selection of DVDs. She looked through them and read the titles while she swiped his card.

"The Assassin... good choice, I love Bridget Fonda. The Assassins... another good one... Antonio Banderas is great. The Specialist... Sly Stallone again, not so good, I'd leave this one 'til last if I were you, in case you run out of time... and The Life Story of Al Capone... nothing like a bit of non-fiction after three shoot-'em-ups. Interesting selection – you could be a hitman or something."

Emma laughed but stopped when she saw the man smiling a little too much. She dropped her head to look at the computer keyboard, allocated the DVDs to his card and put them in a bag. "There we go. Mr Simpson. Have a good evening."

"Thanks..." Sam stooped to look at a name badge on her chest, a little longer than Emma would have liked, "...Emma."

She watched him leave the store then tapped a few keys on the computer keyboard. "Software design engineer. Yeah, nerd, could have guessed." She tapped a few more keys, closing down the system. An audible sound confirmed her request as she retreated into the back of the shop to collect her belongings.

A moment later, Emma and Tom returned to the front of the shop with their coats on and bags in their hands, Tom switching off the back room's lights as he followed her.

"That last man was strange." Emma hesitated. "Said on his records that he's in I.T. but he was borrowing most of the shoot 'em up films. All assassin type."

"What's strange about that? Maybe he wants a change in career and is interested in law or on a drama course, or he's writing a book."

"Yes, maybe. He was acting funny. Went weird when I joked with him."

"Probably shy, like the other two. How about a Prime Time Dating Club for Shy DVD hirers?"

"Yes, Tom. A new sideline for you." Emma thought more about Sam. "I suppose it's not unusual for a guy around my age to be quiet but he said he'd not used his card for a while and I'm sure he came in a few days ago. On Friday or around the weekend."

"Perhaps he's in love." Tom laughed as Emma blushed. "Come on, let's go home. Wanna catch Sandra before she goes to bed."

"Sure. Say 'hi' to her for me. While I remember, will you tell her my mum's still looking out for some wool for the blanket she's doing. I'm taking my mum charity shopping on Wednesday so we might find some then."

"Will do. That's kind of you and your mum to think of her."

Tom switched off the lights and locked the front door, top and bottom, and they went their separate ways.

As Sam arrived home, he thought the first part of his first 'mission' had gone well. He'd appeared nerdy enough not to arouse suspicion and had got all the films on the list. They were old so he knew he was lucky to have got them. He could have waited and got them in two instalments but he needed to be discreet. Despite looking no different to a week earlier, he felt different and wanted to go out in his new 'guise' as little as possible until he was more used to it. Behind his front door he could do whatever he wanted, be whoever he wanted but in the outside world he needed to be on his guard, appear normal.

He stacked the DVDs by the lounge TV, alongside one of two pads of post-its he'd unearthed in his 'office' and went upstairs, switching off the downstairs lights on the way. The THP book was still on the bedside table and he repeated the previous night's ritual of re-reading it until he had memorised the next stages. '1. Watch one movie of trainee's choice; 2. Choose one scene; 3. Make records of that scene on post-its; 4. Use board to make plan of area; 5. Make bullet point lists of where the character stands in relation to the 'mark' (the book was precise on not using the words 'criminal', 'felon' or 'villain'); 6. Study the scene and make notes in the large notebook (use the small one only for external missions); 7. Could you have improved the scene?' Sam stuck one of the post-its in the page, closed the book then switched off the bedside light.

In the morning he'd go through the book and follow the details, step by step. Size tens by size tens. With plans in place for the following day, he quickly went to sleep. There were no dreams of desperados aiming him or mountain car chases. No exotic women seducing him. It would be no wonder he wore a frown, but then he didn't know that; he was too busy sleeping.

ooOoo

Chapter 5 – Preparation is Key

Sam spent the weekend watching and re-watching the DVDs, picking a scene from each one, making notes from them which were destined for the boards. He was used to being thorough. Software design had to be accurate. One slight mistake and the whole programme would stall.

He laid the boards out on the kitchen table and wrote more comments into the book. He'd arranged to go out on Saturday night with Danny and Mark but they always piled back to Danny's house so he could leave everything where it was without fear of discovery.

The last meal of the weekend was a homemade Spaghetti Bolognese, one of a host of plastic boxes in his freezer, courtesy of his mother. Sam had moved out of his parents' home in Market Harborough some six months earlier but like all mothers, his was convinced he wouldn't eat properly while she was away. Sam wouldn't complain. It beat shop-bought TV dinners.

Again under cover of darkness, he took the films back to the store. All he had to do was drop them through the door so they registered on the Monday morning.

He only saw his neighbour, the white-haired Mrs Ellison walking her dog on the green. She was too busy cleaning up after it to notice Sam walk out of the close and round the corner to Singleton Parade.

The Co-op was closed which was a pain as Sam could have done with some more milk. Even the Indian restaurant and 'Pizza di Verona' were shut. The only traffic going past was, Sam reckoned, people on nightshift or returning from an evening out.

Unwrapping from the cold, he switched on the kettle and made a mug of hot chocolate. He'd had enough tea and coffee over the weekend to sink the Titanic and wanted to save what was left of the milk for the morning, plus he didn't want to stay awake any longer than he needed to.

He took one final look at the boards on the kitchen table and smiled. It was all coming together. He'd decided on sheets of thin metal and had the carpenter at Homebase drill holes in the corners so Sam could thread string through them.

He took them upstairs; his 'office' now his 'planning room'. Having earlier cleared the desk of CDs, snacks and other junk that always seemed to clutter the place, and deposited it, for the time being at least, in the bin, he set down the boards and measured pieces of blue string of equal lengths so they would hang in a row behind his monitor.

Standing back to admire his masterpieces, he noticed that one of the post-its was missing. He shrugged and assumed it to be downstairs so switched off the light above the desk then the main light. He brushed his teeth and went into his bedroom to change into his pyjamas. He looked in the mirror. *Need nattier clothes,* he thought, *James Bond wouldn't be seen dead in these.* But then James was way too cool to wear anything in bed, especially with a raven-haired Russian sharing it.

Sam put his hands together and stretched his arms out towards the long pine-framed mirror pretending to aim a Colt or Smith & Wesson at a villain lurking in the distance. He made a mental note to go on the internet in the morning and see what gun James used. It didn't matter, but if he was going to take this seriously he had to get into James' head.

Although he'd never thought of this as his new profession, it would certainly be more interesting than designing software for Panasonics, Xeroxes and Canons. His friends could never know.

Hitmen were solitary creatures and that suited Sam. Part of the thrill would be people thinking he was a mundane office worker or a boring something-or-other when all the time he'd know differently. He'd have the life they could only dream of. Hopping from country to country, being chased through the streets of Rome or Madrid with shots ringing out around him. Hopping from bed to bed, seducing various nationalities of beautiful women, all in the line of duty.

Sam sat under his blue striped duvet re-reading the second part of the THP book with his lamp's light showing up every line. The instructions were clear. It seemed he was going to be metaphorically taken gently by the hand, at least at first, into the world of the assassin.

Sam felt like a child on Christmas Eve; knowing Santa was going to leave goodies and being really excited but being so tired that he was battling to keep his eyes open.

With the orders instilled in his mind, he switched off the light and before unconsciousness took over, Sam thought how easy this was all going to be.

ooOoo

Chapter 6 – A Partner in Crime

Sam looked for the missing post-it the next morning but no joy. He assumed he'd thrown it out. It was no big deal. It wouldn't have meant anything to anyone anyway. He'd made notes in his A4 notebook so he'd write out another one and fill the 'Assassins' bit of the board. His 'planning room' was coming on a treat. He was sticking the replacement post-it up when he heard the post-box flap clatter.

He wasn't expecting any bills – they all seemed to come at once towards the end of the month and today was only the thirteenth. As he opened the box, he recognised the envelope. It was the second instalment from THP Services. He ripped it open and took out the booklet – similar looking to the previous one but not sent recorded delivery – then read the first page.

So you've watched the movies, made up the boards. Did you add many of your own notes?

Sam had made loads. The boards were now four squares in his back bedroom; to the point where he'd almost run out of post-its. He scribbled in his pocket notebook to buy some more, perhaps multi-coloured ones, if the Co-op stocked them, in case of the need for prioritisation.

Congratulations. The booklet continued. *Now the fun begins.*

"Promises, promises." Sam switched the kettle on. He flicked the switch back off again, mumbling, "I drink too much tea," and opened the fridge door, retrieving the last can of Coke. "Replacing one form of caffeine for the other isn't such a good idea but hey, can't sleep on the job." Sam passed the mirror in the hall and smiled. A James Bond smile; cool and sophisticated, something Miss Moneypenny would have approved of.

Sam dug out the small notebook again and made a note to buy some more Coke. Diet Coke was better for him, given his diet, but it tasted like tin to him. Taste over health any day. He was running short of milk again and might as well buy another paper. Job day was Thursday but there were oddments in the other days and although he wasn't desperate, especially in light of his current vocation and two uploaded CVs, he thought it was worth spending 50p to see if anyone needed his computer skills. 50p; the equivalent of a Snickers… he might get one of those too, which set him to wondering why no one did a bar like that in dark chocolate. They did hazelnut. Sam swiped at a blob of drool threatening to escape his mouth and wiped his finger on his sleeve. He shook his head then shrugged. There were worse things he could do. Would do. Had done.

He timed his visit to the shops badly. Despite being mid-morning the place was swarming with suit-cladded workers from the industrial estate. He didn't miss working at all, especially the 'dressing up'. He was more of a dress-down Friday kind of guy and wearing black, even if it was smart trousers on his mission didn't seem to count. Mrs Ellison had come out of the Post Office and was untying her Westie 'Hamish' as Sam walked by.

"Morning, Mrs Ellison. How are you today? And hello, Hamish. You're looking smart in your lovely red tartan jacket."

The dog wagged its white tail at the mention of his name.

"Hello, Sam," the old lady said, beaming at her dog. "We're well, thank you. Hamish recently had his yearly booster so he's fighting fit and we're off to the park. His jacket is Ellison tartan. Did you know that?"

"I didn't, that's fascinating." Sam hoped he sounded convincing. "Have a nice time, and you, Hamish." Sam looked down at the dog, who was now wagging its tail furiously. Sam had wondered at times whether or not to get a dog. In the absence of a girlfriend he figured it might be a way of meeting someone but that wasn't a good enough reason to get one. Besides, if he and the girl of his dreams had one **they** might not get on, and if he was going to be a 'man of mystery' and travel the world, it would be a wonderful life for him but not for a dog he'd never see.

Shaking his head to bring him back to reality, Sam watched the Ellisons walk away and headed for the Co-op.

A young boy was struggling to open the front door so Sam held it for him and shook his head again as the boy ignored him and ran off. "The youth of today," Sam grumbled then laughed, thinking it the sort of thing his parents would say.

Fishing the notebook from his pocket as he wandered in, Sam looked at the list. Passing the bread section he put a loaf of seeded batch, it made nicer toast, into his basket and made for the chiller cabinets. The half-litres of milk he'd been buying hadn't lasted any time at all so he picked up a litre container of semi-skimmed. Reaching for a packet of vintage cheddar (which made even nicer toast) when he came face-to-face with a girl he recognised; Emma from the DVD rental store, a couple of doors down.

"Hello… Emma."

"Mr Simpson isn't it? Hello."

"Yes. You remembered? But please call me Sam."

"Okay… Sam." Emma looked at her watch. "Sorry but I have to go. We open in a few minutes."

"Er, okay, bye!" Sam shouted after her.

"Good to see you again," was also meant for her but sadly only an old woman reading the ingredients list on a packet of chicken roll benefited from this statement. She smiled then carried on reading.

Sam picked up a newspaper, then went to the canned drinks fridge with a grin, head full of poppy fields, Emma in a flowing dress and Andrex puppy by her side.

ooOoo

Chapter 7 – Emma and the Post-it

Tom was often grumpy on a Monday morning and Emma had
learned to assess his mood before asking how his Sunday
had gone. Hers had been fairly uneventful.

The morning had been spent at a car boot sale. She had
been thinking of selling with her friend Libby, but Libby had hit
the town the previous night and hadn't checked in since one
a.m. Emma had gone to look round instead and picked up a
variety of bargains: two out of three DVD titles listed in the
'notes' section of her mobile were bought for the grand sum of
a pound each. Apart from loving films, she read a lot and
bought over a dozen chick-lit novels which she planned to
devour during the non car boot sale winter months.

Traipsing the shops of Northampton in the afternoon –
for an elusive pair of winter shoes that were big enough for
Emma's size eight feet or jeans that fitted perfectly – wasn't
her idea of fun. She could have done it before work any
weekday or on her day off but she'd picked this weekend for
some reason. As a line from her favourite film, 'Pretty Woman'
went: "Big mistake. Big. Huge. I have to go shopping now."
And she did. Along with everyone else from the county, it
seemed.

While Emma was holding down the switch for the front
window grate, Tom counted the float into the till. Emma kept
quiet until Tom spoke.

"Emma."

"Yes, Tom."

"While you're there, can you empty the post-box of
DVDs. I haven't got around to it yet."

"Sure. No problem." The grill clicked in place and Emma
let go of the button. She unlocked the back of the post-box
with one of the keys kept on a bunch on her waistband and
the cases piled out on to the floor. "The joys of a dull Sunday".

"That'll keep you busy. I'll stick the kettle on. Going to be
a quiet one, I reckon, today."

"Thanks. That would be lovely. I think you're right.
Mondays are usually deadly, aren't they? People overdosing
on movies at the weekend and the TV's good on a Monday
night." Emma soon realised, however, that she was talking to

herself as she heard the sound of boiling water from the back room.

"Overdosing on beer more like," Tom said, walking back to the till.

"You've got good hearing. Thought you were out the back."

"Sharp as a tack, as the saying goes. Always have been dear. I may be retired from the force but there's life in the old codger yet."

"Never doubted it, Tom. Good day yesterday?" Emma didn't think it would hurt to ask.

"Good thanks. Yes. Sandra was out at her *this, that and the other* club so I had the morning much to myself. How are you doing with the films? Need a hand?"

"No, I'm okay. Lots of scanning DVDs back in. How's the tea?"

"What was I saying about life in the old dog?" Tom laughed.

"Codger, but I know what you mean." Emma smiled. She liked working with Tom. He made the dull bits of the job more painless. She hoped he didn't retire properly for a few years although she knew Sandra had had her share of health problems. Someone new would no doubt insist on having the shop open on a Sunday and there would go her weekend day off.

Emma was getting to the last couple of DVDs when she noticed a yellow square post-it note stuck to the underside of one of them. She removed it and read the black biro scrawl. "Tom?"

"Yes, dear."

"Can you come and have a look at this? I don't suppose it's anything but thought you'd like to take a look before I chuck it."

"Sure. What is it?"

Emma handed the note over to a puzzled looking Tom who read it out.

"'Antonio aims at mark behind bar. Takes him out with one bullet. Five paces behind screen. Clear shot.' Then there's a diagram of some kind."

"Yes, Tom, look at it."

"Some kind of floor plan. Which case was it attached to?"

"The Assassins. I remember who took this out. The young guy in black. Mr…" Emma swept the DVD case under the scanner. Sam Simpson. Five Greath Close. What do you think it means?"

"The Assassins. Isn't that the film with Sylvester Stallone and Antonio Banderas. That's the Antonio then."

"But what about the other stuff?"

"I don't know, my dear. Oh yes, he's the man I said might be writing a book or be a drama student. I wouldn't worry. Either throw it away or keep it for him for next time. I'm sure he'll be back."

"Probably. I'll keep it under the counter and see what happens. See what excuse he has."

"What makes you think he needs an excuse?"

"Don't know really, something about him. Bit shifty. You watch him next time. See what your experience tells you."

"Sure, my dear. Glad to help."

ooOoo

Chapter 8 – Not All is as it Seems

Sam opened his front door then gasped as heat hit him.

He closed the front door silently. Why was the house so hot? He couldn't remember changing the dial on the combi-boiler. In James Bond mode, he snuck up on each room, edging his way around each door checking for signs of life.

Finally, he opened the corner cupboard in the back bedroom and checked the boiler's controls. The timer switch had moved from intermittent to constant and the heating dial had gone from half to full. He might have knocked **one** of them when getting a towel for his morning shower but to have moved them both? No. He can't have. But there was no other reason. Double-checking the external doors were all still locked and no windows broken, it was clear no one could have got in and nothing had been disturbed. He hadn't accumulated enough stuff in six months to get the place cluttered, especially minus Michelle's possessions. Not long enough to unpack either, his mind wandering to the remaining boxes in the loft.

Still, something wasn't right. He was sure of it. With no explanation other than his clumsiness, he reset the controls then logged onto his computer to type up the notes; the notes that watched him from the boards above his desk.

Flicking through the two THP booklets, Sam spent the afternoon jotting down more notes which he'd then combine with the typed up yellow post-its and create it into a plan.

The plan, he decided, would be best as a Word document so he clicked on the blank sheet icon. He typed out a header in bold but then decided the default Times New Roman font was too wimpish. He needed it to make a statement. Scrolling down the list of fonts, Bauhaus 93 appealed as it reminded him of one of his favourite eighties rock groups but it wasn't a clear one. It didn't matter for a header but 'attention to detail' was one of his mottos and if he didn't get it right from the beginning then it wouldn't flow.

"I should be a writer," he said to the yellow post-it notes. They seemed to wave their lower halves in agreement but Sam couldn't be sure. The thin blue cotton curtains weren't moving so it couldn't be windy outside – he made a mental

217

note to get double-glazing when he'd save some money – and there was no radiator near his desk. Besides, the heating wasn't on. Or was it? He was getting paranoid now.

He swivelled his chair round to face the boiler cupboard and leant over to check the dials. They sat exactly as he'd left them. The heating didn't come on until seven.

"I need an early night. I'm getting clumsy and seeing things. Get a grip, Sam."

He continued looking through the font list. Although tempted by 'Goudy Stout' and anything with 'Gothic' in the name, he finally settled on 'Bodoni MT Black'. THP Plan – Agent Simpson looked 'cool', he decided, and he liked that the font sounded Italian. The Mafia were Italian and they were 'cool'. At this pace though it would take him the rest of the night to type up his plan so he'd start with the basics.

He decided to write out the topics from the booklets and made an indented list (he laughed when he hovered the mouse over the icon and it showed 'bullets') to capture the highlights of his notes. He then scanned the dozen or so 'pose' photographs and cropped them with Paint Shop so they were small in physical and file size.

The basics turned into detail. He couldn't help himself. Once he got going he didn't want to stop and before he knew it, Monday became Tuesday.

"So much for having an early night. There's always tomorrow night. Er… tonight."

He wondered whether he was wasting his time with all this, and even thought that maybe someone was having a joke at his expense. He lived twenty miles from where he was brought up, so in theory no one had known him in Kemsley when he'd arrived. Could his past now been catching up with him? He racked his brain trying to think of what could have done in his previous 'life' that had warranted this? His brain came up empty.

Click. File. Save. Yes. Start. Shut down. Shut down again. Okay. The computer played its melodic 'goodbye' tune and went to sleep.

Sam got ready for bed before doing the same.

ooOoo

Chapter 9 – So to Business

Sam was woken by the noise of the metal letterbox. He wondered why the postman had delivered so early until he rolled over, looked at his clock and groaned. Nearly eleven. How had he slept so late? Why hadn't his mobile woken him? He'd set it to beep at a respectable nine a.m. but this time it had let him down. He stretched his arm out to the bedside unit to grab the phone but his hand landed flat onto wood. No mobile.

Semi-consciously, he felt around the top of the small chest of drawers, assuming the king-size duvet overlapping his double-size bed had knocked against it, moving it from its usual location, but the space was just that: space.

Dragging himself out of bed, he put on his dressing gown and pushed his feet into his size ten slippers. Having shaken them first. Ever since he was little, about ten, he had to check shoes and slippers. One of Roald Dahl's Tales of The Unexpected had changed Sam's life forever. Okay, so only in a small way but enough. He couldn't remember which episode it was but it had ended with a chap putting his slippers, or it might have been shoes… no, must have been slippers as the man had got out of bed as the programme ended. What the viewer had seen just before the slipper-putting-on moment was a scorpion skulking into the right one. So, slippers had to be checked. And shoes. One could never be too careful.

At the bathroom mirror, he groaned again at the sight that greeted him. Instead of a fresh-faced, dark haired, brown-eyed twenty-seven-year-old bursting with life, the man looking back at him resembled his father. He opened the cabinet door half-expecting to find his father in there. Sam shut the door again.

"Don't be so ridiculous, Sam." He laughed at his reflection. "Dad's on a cruise." Sam laughed again.

With no plans to venture outside, he didn't see the point in getting dressed. He was cosy in his dressing gown and slippers, he could stay in them all day. George the postman had been and gone. The only people who were going to get his attention today were Sarah-Jane Mee – Sam liked keeping abreast of news – or Silent Witness actress… erm, Foxy… yes, Emilia Fox.

Clearly, even the mention of the postman hadn't jogged Sam's memory that there was something for him in the box: THP part 3.

As he went back to his bedroom to search for his errant mobile, an image of Emma, Prime Time's prime totty, came into view. Sam sighed. They'd had some banter in the Co-op the day before but nothing of any worth, nothing that would make Emma jump at a date with him. She probably thought he was an idiot. An idiot who thought she was stupid. There was no way someone as sparky as her would fall for that 'Agatha Christie play' story. At the time he considered he'd been clever to think of something so plausible so quickly, but picturing her reaction, she'd seen right through it.

So, Sam Simpson, what's the plan of action now?

"Shit!" He remembered what had woken him so returned downstairs. It was probably a postcard from his mum but it could just be…

The now-familiar envelope sat invitingly in the box, the words inside almost yelling at him to be read. Sam ripped open the top of the envelope, scowling as he caught his right hand as he did so; a thin red line appeared on the soft pad of his index finger.

He sat on the bottom step and read. He'd been a little disappointed by the first two booklets and had higher hopes of this one. It was thicker and had more photographs. He took the package upstairs, switched on the 'planning room' light and fired up the computer. He typed in his new password ('holiday' deemed dull having been replaced by 'mission') and while he waited for the desktop icons to load, he nipped downstairs and made a cup of tea.

Settling into his office chair, his slippered feet playfully tilted the footrest backwards and forwards. Since he'd been made redundant he had sorely lacked exercise and even this small amount would be something. Okay, so it was only calf-orientated cardio but better than nothing. Maybe he could do some buttock clenches. He'd read it somewhere in a women's magazine in the doctor's surgery when he'd been there to register some weeks earlier.

Retrieving a clear plastic book holder from a shelf to his right, he propped 'part 3' open at the index and typed it into the 'plan'.

1. Preparation
2. Equipment
3. Methods
4. Routes
5. Targets
6. Words of advice
7. Shooting practice
8. How not to get caught
9. How to stay legal
10. Relationships

Now someone really was taking the piss. Number nine. Staying legal? How could any aspect of being a hitman, trainee or not, be legal? This was a section he would take great interest in reading.

So, to business.

ooOoo

Chapter 10 – Emma Grills Sam

The next time she met Sam, Emma jumped straight in. "Sam, I've got a question for you. One of the DVDs you borrowed the other day, and put through our post-box, had a post-it note on it. A rather odd one?"

"It did?" Sam tried to look surprised which wasn't totally unconvincing as he'd pictured it in a recycling centre somewhere. "Was it definitely mine?"

"Yes. It was stuck to the 'The Assassins'. We only have one copy of the older films."

"Ah, yes." Sam was quickly trying to think of an excuse. "A friend's doing amateur dramatics up in Northampton, an Agatha Christie I think, and I said I'd do some research for him".

Ah, the old 'friend' excuse. Emma thought. "I said there'd be an explanation."

"You… said? To whom?"

"Just my manager, Tom. We were chatting about it."

Emma let herself into the shop and repeated her usual chores. The grill came up with the usual squeak (followed by Emma calling to Tom to buy some WD40) but the mountain of posted cases was now a molehill. Tom slammed the till drawer shut as he filled the last segment with change. "WD40. Right. Noted."

"And how are you today, Tom?"

"Fine thanks, Emma. Sandra's a little lame. She stubbed her bad toe on the edge of our dining room table last night."

"Poor thing. I bet that hurt. Ouch. By the way, I ran into Sam Simpson."

Eyebrows raised, Tom was clearly none the wiser.

"The man in black? Who left the post-it. Said it was research for a friend's play. But said it like he was making it up on the spot."

"Do you still have the note?"

"Yes, under the counter. Why?"

"Best to hang on to it for now. Just in case."

Emma wasn't sure what the 'just in case' might be but she was happy to go with whatever he said. He was the expert, after all.

ooOoo

Chapter 11 – Emma's History

Emma loved her job, but she treasured her days off. She'd promised to take her mum shopping and drop her brother off at school but apart from that, the day was hers to do with as she pleased.

She was a morning person. Always had been. Couldn't understand people who stayed up late then slept in half the day. What was the point in being awake in the dark when you couldn't see anything, and staying under the duvet when there was so much going on in the outside world? Mrs Dale, Emma's mum, was the same. Emma remembered, as a child, waking up and hearing her mother whistling in the kitchen doing the cleaning, washing up, cooking; raising Emma while her importer / exporter father, Alan, was away on business. As he so often was.

Then Paul came along. Emma had celebrated her tenth birthday a couple of months earlier and it was naturally to be expected she would be jealous. And she was for a while but soon adored her little brother and helped her mum with every aspect of his care. Three years later, everything changed.

One phone call shattered the three lives that had been ticking along quite nicely.

"Hello. Kemsley 4 2 9 1 2 9, Teresa Dale speaking."

"Mrs Dale?"

Teresa couldn't picture the man's accent, and she was usually good at accents.

"Yes. That's me. Who's calling please?"

"Mrs Dale. I'm phoning from Toronto. I'm afraid I have some bad news."

"Canada?"

"Yes, Mrs Dale. I'm Sergeant Iverson calling from Toronto Police Service."

Silence.

"Are you there, ma'am?"

"Yes." Teresa sat down. "Go on."

"It's about your husband. Mr Alan Dale."

"Alan? What? Has something happened?"

"I'm sorry, Mrs Dale."

"Is he OK? Please tell me–"

"He's missing."

"What? What do you mean missing? Where?"

"Here in Toronto, ma'am."

"No. He's in New York on business. It can't be him."

"I'm sorry, Mrs–"

"Stop saying you're sorry! You're wrong. It can't be him."

"I'm…" the Sergeant paused. "Mrs Dale, a man fitting your husband's description–"

"Then it's definitely not him." Teresa interrupted, "My husband looks like many people. He's normal looking; five-feet-ten." Teresa's left hand touched her hair then said, "Brown hair, average weight. It could have been anyone."

The man, continued. "Your husband checked into the Four Seasons Hotel in downtown Toronto two days ago."

"No." Teresa shook her head. "You're mistaken. You are. He wouldn't stay at the Four Seasons, we don't have that kind of money."

"The hotel has his passport, Mrs Dale. Your husband is Alan Ian Dale, born Leemington Spa 1947. Is he not?"

"Leamington Spa." Teresa corrected, a tear descending her now-red right cheek. She wiped it away, still refusing to believe that it was her husband that this man was talking about. Someone had stolen his passport and was the one that was missing. It couldn't be Alan. Alan wouldn't leave her. Them. He just wouldn't.

"We understand your husband went for a walk and didn't return. We've not found a body…"

Teresa yelped at the thought of Alan lying somewhere strange. Miles from his family. His family miles from him. She couldn't bear it.

"Are you alright, Mrs Dale?"

"Of course I'm not alright!" Teresa barked then burst into tears. She was only glad that Emma was at school. What would she tell her when she came home? She was old enough to understand but **how** would Teresa tell Paul that he might never see his father again?

"I'm sorry, Mrs Dale."

"No, I'm sorry. You're only doing your job. Do you… do you have any idea where he might be?"

"We understand he went down Yonge Street, in the direction of Lake Ontario."

"Lake Ontario. It's huge, isn't it? Maybe he got lost."

"Yes, maybe, Mrs Dale." The man paused, not sounding convincing. "Is there anyone you can call? Have someone stay with you until we have more news?"

But the news never came. The Dale family got on with their life. Teresa, with a glimmer of hope like embers in her heart, never remarried but instead concentrated on her family, her part-time supermarket job and to helping others. She convinced herself that keeping busy would take her mind off Alan and while this worked in the daytime, it was at night that the memories came flooding back. She would lie awake for hours then finally fall asleep. She'd dream of him leaving the hotel. Of walking down Yonge Street with a beautiful winter view of Lake Ontario. He'd buy a coffee then looked at the water, partially frozen, with people around him walking their dogs, and children laughing, not a care in the world.

But that's what children should do, Teresa thought. *It's up to the parents to worry.* So Emma and Paul never saw her cry; Teresa took great pains to appear normal. Emma also spent the first few nights crying to sleep. Paul asked questions but eventually their father was no longer a topic of conversation and Teresa liked it that way. Reminders in her sleep were exhausting enough. He still came to her every night, and every morning there would be tearstains on the pillow. His pillow. The mismatching pillow that still contained his DNA because she couldn't bear to wash it. His jackets still hanging in the cupboards because she still believed that he would someday walk through the door and want to wear them. To pick up where he left off.

Some women in Teresa's position would be angry but she wasn't. What was the point? It wasn't his fault that he'd lost his bearings and ended up a John Doe in hospital somewhere. You hear of cases where someone loses their memory, starts a new life and surfaces eventually. Don't you? So why couldn't it happen to him?

She'd tried to find him. She'd spent their savings on trying to find him. Neighbours had told her of their relative Pamela who lived in Buffalo and had offered to let her stay. The flight ticket had been bought thanks to a whip-round at Teresa's work. She'd only been there a couple of years and it was a relatively small shop but somehow they'd found the money. She'd left the children with the mother of a babysitter and spent a week knocking on doors, walking round the Toronto side of the lake shouting Alan's name. No one had seen him. No one knew anything. The police told her that they'd done everything they could – with the exception, Teresa presumed, of calling out for him – and suggested she go home.

With three days left before her flight, she was determined to use the time wisely, planning to visit every hospital in Toronto. There were twenty-four listed in Pam's directory but as three were children only, that still left twenty-one. Pam worked also part-time and had willingly driven Teresa to the distant hospitals but each one had been a brick wall. She realised Alan might not have had any identification on him. He hadn't taken his driving licence as he was supposed to be flying to New York and doing some business in London on his way back. If his hotel had the passport then he'd only have his credit and cashpoint cards. The chances were that they were being used elsewhere, although the police had said they had no record of any action on his account. So where had he gone?

On the last evening, Teresa sat at the desk in the hotel room and stared in the mirror. Her brown hair was showing signs of grey in only a matter of weeks. She'd heard that stress could do that to a person and one of the most stressful things in life was… death.

Except she knew in her heart that Alan was alive. They were soulmates. She'd know if he was dead. And she wasn't going to give him up without a fight.

ooOoo

Chapter 12 – Something's Not Right

Sam jolted awake. He'd fallen asleep at his keyboard and now it was light. The thin curtains, though closed, betrayed the day. Sam looked at his watch: nearly ten-thirty.

"Shit!"

Though he had no deadlines, he'd lost valuable planning time. He looked at the screen…

1. Preparation
2. Equipment
3. Methods
4. Routes
5. Targets
6. Words of advice
7. Shooting practice
8. How not to get caught
9. How to stay legal
10. Relationships

"Eh?"

He looked at the word count figure at the bottom left of the screen. '30 / 30'.

"Eh?"

The page numbers at the bottom left of the screen showed '1 of 1'.

"What? Shit!" he said again.

He couldn't understand what had happened to the hours, probably three or four hours, of notes he'd made. Even if he'd fallen asleep on the keyboard, which he didn't think so considering he'd woken up drooling with his head hung back over the rear of the chair, there would be rows or pages of complete nonsense.

Sam pressed the 'Page Up' button. Nothing. He pressed the 'Page Down' button. Nothing but blank space which he knew already from the statistics.

"Shit! Shit! Shit!"

He pressed the 'Start' button then selected 'Recent Documents' in case he'd saved the work as something else before he'd nodded off, but the other Word documents on the list were ancient. He opened them all but they were exactly as he'd left them.

"What's going **on,** man?" First the heating, now this. Was twenty-seven too young to start losing your marbles?

Sam also couldn't believe it was Wednesday again already. He'd answered the advert almost a week earlier and in that respect, the days had flown. On the other hand, he'd received three booklets (the third only being a proper instruction manual in Sam's opinion) and his life had changed in a short amount of time. But it can, can't it? People meet their soulmates and their lives alter in a second. Okay, so it takes longer for them to realise they are soulmates but it only takes the second to meet them. Eyes locking and all that. A little like him and Emma at the Co-op yesterday morning. He giggled. Maybe it was time he hired some more movies. He'd go tomorrow, get the job paper. Kill two birds and all that.

ooOoo

Chapter 13 – Emma and Paul

"Mum!"

No reply from inside the house.

"Mum!"

Silence.

Emma followed her brother into the house, carrying the shopping. She kicked the front door closed.

"Paul, Mum's at work. We were out at the charity shops up in Northampton when she got a call to go in. Staff shortage or something."

"But I'm hungry."

"We've only just got in."

"But I'm–"

"I know, you're hungry. I stopped off at the Co-op when I dropped Mum off before collecting you from school so I've got plenty here. Go upstairs and get changed and I'll do you something quick like cheese or beans on toast."

"O… K…"

"Don't sound so enthusiastic, you normally **love** beans on toast."

Another "O… K…" was almost lost as Paul trudged up the stairs.

"Boys!" Emma whispered as she walked to the kitchen. "Who'd be one? Yuk."

As plate hit table, Paul rushed into the kitchen and yanked the chair out almost tipping it over.

"Watch it!" Emma growled. He never seemed to look after things and although he was only thirteen, he was the man of the house. She'd tried to instil in him to be more responsible but this, she reckoned, seemed to have gone in one ear and straight out the other. But then with little in-between for the advice to get lost in, it wasn't surprising that it didn't rattle around in there long enough to stick.

"Boys," Emma said again, shaking her head.

With food eaten and plate licked (another disgusting habit in Emma's opinion), Paul jumped down from the table and ran into the lounge. Seconds later, the TV blared out what sounded like a western and the gunfire made Emma jump. There was something about guns that gave her the creeps. Whenever a car backfired, she'd feel her heart try to escape her chest. Gun crime was something that often appeared on the news but had thankfully mostly escaped Northamptonshire although Emma felt it only a matter of time. She switched her mind to her purchases and the crime was forgotten… for now.

ooOoo

Chapter 14 – Organised, Sam, Get Organised

After the head-back-drooling-in-the-chair episode the morning before, Sam had made sure he'd gone to bed at a reasonable time, taking 'part 3' with him to make renewed notes but going to sleep before getting too carried away. He was still kicking himself for being so careless for losing the original lot of notes from 'part 3'. His computer was a pain in the arse at the best of times so he guessed it was getting its own back for him swearing at it so much.

He was going to set his alarm clock for the morning but noticed the hands had stopped in an 'air traffic controller' position and the usual supply of spare batteries (AA) fitted everything except the alarm clock (AAA). Something else to get from the Co-op. Bread, yoghurts, local and national papers, batteries for alarm clock. Anything else? Brain cells? "Ah, yes, let's buy a few of those."

Sam shook his head. He reckoned he'd lost some brain cells when head-banging to heavy metal in his teens. *Organised, Sam. Get organised.*

***

List in hand, Sam set off the next morning for the Co-op then DVD store (for anything, he didn't care) then home to get cracking with the notes.

En-route he saw Mrs Ellison again, this time with Hamish minus the tartan. The old lady waved at Sam like he was a long-lost son before scuttling off in the direction of the park.

Sam laughed and shook his head. This head shaking seemed to be becoming a regular thing. At least it was exercise. He laughed again.

He stuck with his plan to go to the Co-op first, a little early he thought for the local paper but the van pulled up as he arrived. He watched a little brown-haired lady scuttle out to take the bundle from the van driver, chat with him for a moment, laugh then scuttle back inside the shop. The driver watched her until she disappeared, sighed, then drove off down the road. Sam sighed too. He could tell the driver had the same feelings for the woman as Sam had for Emma. But would either man act on those feelings?

ooOoo

Chapter 15 – Beginning to Warm

Emma was surprised when she arrived at work on the Thursday morning that there was no sign of life. She had keys but Tom had always been there before her. She unlocked the outside padlock and pushed the button to lift up the outer grill. It was as tired as Emma felt and groaned almost as much as Kevin would have, had he been there. Emma laughed and wondered where Tom was. His day off was Tuesday and he was always reliable on the other days.

Once the grill had risen far enough to unlock the front door, she did so, locked it behind her, then went to the back room to stock up the till.

As she approached the safe, she saw the light flashing on the office phone. Just once. Emma hit play, then unlocked the safe and pulled out the float money.

"Hello, Emma. It's Tom…"

Silence.

Quieter, Tom's voice continued, *"Yes, dear. I'm calling her now. It'll be all right. She won't mind. Yes, I'll ask her about the wool when I get there."*

"Emma, sorry. Sandra's had a fall in the night and she's twisted her ankle. She won't let me take her to hospital… *No, dear. He's on his way."*

"Sorry, Emma. The doctor's coming here so I've got to wait for him. I probably won't be with you until lunchtime. Sorry. I know you can cope. You're a real trouper. Will be in as quickly as I can, love."

Emma smiled. Despite the age gap, the two of them got on really well. She let the message play until it finished. This ended up being longer than expected as Tom hadn't put the receiver back down properly so she heard his and Sandra's 'discussion' going on in the background.

"Poor things," Emma said as she filled the till.

She had the post-box to empty, shouldn't be too bad on a Thursday. Wednesday night TV's quite good. No actually, priorities right. Kettle on first. Her mum had got home late the night before so she'd had to get Paul ready for school. No easy task at the best of times. So no time for a morning cuppa. "Boys."

After stacking up the returned DVDs on the floor, she then shut the post-box door and transferred the cases to the counter for scanning back onto the system. She heard the kettle click off, so made her 'gnat's pee with one sugar' and, at a minute before opening time, eleven a.m., she unlocked the door. There was never a queue of jostling customers to get into the shop in the mornings and today was no different. She'd thought it had been particularly quiet on the way in so hadn't got high hopes for it being a busy morning.

She'd just scanned the last DVD in when the shop door opened. Emma looked up and saw Mr Nerd-Dressed-In-Black-Because-It's-So-Cool Simpson. Her heart sank.

"Morning," Sam said cheerfully.

"Morning," Emma replied, somewhat less so.

While Emma was busy scanning, Sam pretended he needed something from the rack nearest the counter so he could start a conversation with Miss Emma Flowing-Dress-In-A-Poppy-Field-With-A-Puppy Surname Unknown.

"Are you on your own today?" Sam scratched around for something witty to say but could tell by her lack-of-interest expression that he'd failed miserably.

"Only 'til lunchtime. The manager's wife needed him this morning."

"Nothing wrong, I hope." He didn't want her to think him a complete loon but to come across as caring and sharing. He'd be happy to care for, and share anything with, her. But he wasn't doing a very good job of it. He scolded himself for not having prepared a speech before he came in. Worked out what he was going to say and be natural about it instead of being a dork like now.

For a reason unknown to her, Emma wanted him out of the shop a.s.a.p. With no other customers or Tom, she felt vulnerable. She supposed Mr Nerd was harmless enough but he had a shifty look about him. The kind that 'tea leafs' (as her nan used to say) get and Emma had caught her share of those in the past. They were the thickest of the thick. What good were empty cases to anyone? Unless you also took an original DVD from under the counter or out the back, the original cover from the shop floor was no good to anyone. Tom said once that trade had decreased since DVD-writers on home computers and car boot sales as outlets to sell pirate copies but Emma didn't imagine Mr Nerd to be that smart.

"I'm sure she's fine. A fall at home, I think. Shock I suppose. Accident prone. I think his wife is older than he is. Not sure, something he said once… Anyway, have you made your choices, Mr Simpson?"

"Sam. Please. Your badge only says Emma so I don't know what else to call you so please, call me Sam." *Call me anytime you like,* he thought but daren't say. For someone who was training to be a hardened criminal, he wondered whether he was cut out for it.

"Okay, Sam."

Emma began to warm to him. Only lukewarm, mind; as cool as her tea probably was. "What sort of movie are you looking for today?" She was hoping to at least point him in the right direction and get him on his way. With Tom out, she'd have to deal with the snacks delivery which would keep her busy, customers or no customers.

Sam wanted another selection of hopefully-soon-to-be-work type films but he was trying the 'sensitive' tack so found himself saying, "Something kind of chick flick but not to the Titanic scale." At least he sounded vaguely intelligent. He laughed, trying to guess what was going through her mind. Her lovely, beautiful, clever mind.

Oh boy, Emma thought, *I think he's trying to impress me. Help!*

I think she's suitably impressed, Sam thought. *Oh boy!*

ooOoo

Chapter 16 – Tom and Sandra

Doctor Philips rang the doorbell of twenty-three Beacon Close, Kemsley. It was an old-fashioned chime with a slow, melodic rhythm. He didn't see any movement behind the frosted glass so rang the bell again. A moment later, he saw a tall sturdy figure walking down the hallway.

The door opened and the two men stared at each other. Neither spoke. Finally the doctor broke the silence.

"Good morning. I'm Doctor Philips. I understand your wife has had a stumble?"

"Yes. Sure. She's through here."

"Thank you." The doctor felt a little disappointed by the cool welcome. People these days seemed to be getting that way which he felt quite sad, especially in someone of probably pensionable age. He put it down to the man worrying about his wife although it seemed to be a bind to the husband. Doctor Philips followed him into the lounge and saw the man's wife sitting in a chair with her right foot in a washing-up bowl of soapy water. The doctor presumed it was warm although from the temperature of the atmosphere in the room he wouldn't have been surprised if the man had filled it with ice.

"Hello, doctor," the lady boomed. For someone so small she certainly had a voice to make up for it.

"Hello. I'm Doctor Philips. Can you tell me what happened and where it hurts?"

"It was my own stupid fault. I got up in the middle of the night to go to the bathroom and I'd left my sewing box my side of the bed. I didn't see it as I didn't switch the light on, Tom's a light sleeper you see, and I didn't want to wake him up, and–"

"Sandra, he doesn't want to hear every last detail. Just tell him what happened."

"Tom, I'm explaining."

"Don't worry." Dr Philips looked at Tom who'd turned his attention out the window. "Please go on."

"I'd already hurt my foot the other day and it was getting better when I went and did this. It's not too bad. It's all a fuss over nothing. Some rest and I'll be fine. I don't want to be a burden to anyone."

Tom turned to his wife and sighed. He'd had decades of endless chatter and wondered how he'd not learnt to switch off years earlier.

"Don't worry. You're not a burden to anyone." The doctor looked at Tom who'd returned his gaze to an old woman walking her dog on the other side of the road. She stopped briefly, looked in the direction of the house then walked out of view.

Sandra smiled and continued talking. "Tom's busy. With the shop and all the paperwork and…"

Tom shot his wife another glaring look and she dropped her head. He then faced the medic. "It's fine, doctor." Tom paused and returned to look at his wife. "Sandra, I think he just wants to know nothing's broken so he can get back to work."

"It doesn't hurt as much as it did the other day," she explained. "The box of sewing is only cardboard, although it seemed quite heavy at the time."

Tom shook his head. He'd never known a woman talk so much. Forty-seven years earlier, he had the chance to date Cassandra Mildani or her twin Carmela. Sometimes he wondered why he hadn't picked the other sister.

Dr Philips knelt before the woman and lifted her injured leg. She winced as he did so and Tom felt a pang of guilt as sharp as his wife's pain. Then he remembered why he'd married her. Though she talked too much, she never complained. He didn't even see her cry when she'd scalded her foot. She'd topped up their twin tub with boiling water and had knocked the washing up bowl against the machine, the water spilling onto her, burning the skin as it contacted. Tom recollected the phone call to come home. Sandra's trembling but calm voice. The vision of her when he went to the kitchen. She was sitting on one of the chairs, wearing just one chiffon-coloured stocking. He asked her why only one and felt sick as she told him it wasn't a stocking.

Tom shuddered, went over to his wife and held her hand. Even after all these years her foot had to still be more sensitive than the robust other. He'd been so wrapped up in his life that he'd only seen her as a wife… and a mother, until they'd been told they couldn't have children. That was another occasion when her strength had outshone his. Maybe it was about time he valued her for the strong woman she was. He'd always acted tough and maybe that's what it had always been; an act. He listened as the doctor told her it was probably just a sprain, said she would need plenty of rest. She could walk on the foot but would need it bandaging and not to put unnecessary pressure on it until it had healed properly. The couple thanked the man and Tom escorted him to the front door, giving him a warm handshake as he left.

Doctor Philips walked down the footpath of number twenty-three with renewed hope. Maybe he'd misjudged the old man.

Behind him, Tom had shut the door, returned to the lounge, knelt in front of his wife and kissed her hand. "Sandra, I love you so much and I'm sorry. I take you for granted. Lean on me from now on and I won't let you down."

Sandra looked at her husband, just before he hugged her, and burst into tears.

ooOoo

Chapter 17 – Sam's Research

Armed with new movies, Sam settled down to re-typing the notes. He thought maybe having something going on in the background would give him some inspiration. He'd typed them once so he could do it again but the screen still only had those ten numbered bullet points. Although he knew it was childish, he couldn't help laughing again.

The cursor flickered encouragingly. Sam sighed discouragingly.

An hour later, the cursor was still flashing and Sam still sighing. He decided he was getting nowhere and switched off the screen. What good was 'Elizabethtown' to him anyway? A great film it maybe, but there were no shoot 'em up scenes, no assassins. Okay, there was a dead body but it had been snubbed out due to a heart attack, and that hadn't even happened on screen, so that didn't count.

Sam's fingers hovered over the keyboard. He looked at it, then at the screen. Finally the words appeared in his brain and were transferred through his body to his fingers. The screen soon filled up with text, some from the booklets, some from the films, and some from Sam's imagination. With the bottom of the screen now saying 'Words: 1,583', he felt better.

Heading to the kitchen, he returned with a glass of milk. Seeing as he'd been to the Co-op countless times, often as an excuse to go to the DVD rental store, he thought he'd better use it up.

He looked at the word count: 1,583. He pressed Ctrl S to save then F9 to refresh the screen. 1,583. "Good. Still there then."

Sam wasn't sure why the text he'd typed would have vanished again but he couldn't explain the first time so there was nothing stopping it doing it again. Ah, but this time he had his work backed up. If the computer's C drive decided to wipe it then he could copy it off his external hard drive. Good old (young) faithful D drive. The drive with his iPod's music on it, with the 'Top Gear' and 'Gadget show' podcasts he liked to listen to on his walks to the shops. The podcasts that he actually only half listened to as he was usually thinking about Emma.

He sighed again. The girl of his dreams. The girl who probably thought he was a sensitive wimp. Better than a nerd, Sam supposed, but not far off. His selection this time had supported this theory. 'Elizabethtown', '50 First Dates' and '27 dresses'. Chick flicks of the highest order. And a waste of time. Apart from the aforementioned heart-attacked stiff in Elizabethtown, there were no real fatalities in the others, just good old fashioned sugary schmaltz.

The cursor reminded him that he should be putting a plan into action. Enough time wasting. He'd finished work three weeks earlier and had nothing to show for it. Okay so he was currently in training but he had no clue as to who exactly he was working for, how much he was going to get paid, when he was going to get paid or even, if. Still, he was having fun. Apart from the weird goings on, but he wasn't exactly doing a run-of-the-mill profession. And that's what he was, a professional. Maybe he was being tested. Could he keep his cool while strange things were happening around him? But that was exactly the point. It was going on around him; in his house. No one else had a key. He scratched his ear. Didn't that mean something? That someone was talking about him? Probably his parents. They were due back from their cruise in a few days maybe they were in the middle of buying him a present. More likely wondering whether he was out looking for a job. He'd show them. He'd be a success. Get the Aston Martin and jet-set lifestyle that James had. Of course he couldn't tell them but it sure beat photocopiers.

After a great start, Sam slowed down to a crawl. He double-clicked on the blue 'e' icon and got the Google home page. He loved seeing the ingenious ways they'd change the letters to suit current events, and was especially in awe of the characters when the Olympics were on but they were plain and simple today. *Obviously nothing going on in the world* Sam thought before typing 'assassin' into the 'pages from the UK' advanced search options.

One of the links showed Wikipedia's page on 'Assassinations'. Wiki was one of Sam's favourite websites and he often referred to them for a variety of topics. Not letting him down, this particular page was packed with information.

Just the first paragraph contained nearly a dozen blue underlined words which implied links to other pages and were too irresistible for Sam not to click on. There was also two small superscript numbers, '1' and '2' which Sam promised he'd come back to later, if he remembered.

The first was 'murder'. Sam read the page out loud. "*Murder is the unlawful killing of another human person with* <u>*malice aforethought,*</u> *as defined in* <u>*Common Law*</u> *countries. Murder is generally distinguished from other forms of* <u>*homicide*</u> *by the elements of malice aforethought and the lack of lawful justification. All jurisdictions, ancient and modern, consider it a most serious crime and therefore impose severe penalty on its commission.* Oh God, more blue links."

In turn, Sam clicked on them all and was led further and further away from the first page. Then even further away as he clicked on the blue underlining links under the headings of 'reference', 'bibliography' and 'external links' at the bottom. The screen was rapidly filling with more and more website pages to the point where it resembled an underground station poster wall, each competing for air.

Shutting down the non-vital ones, he saved the rest into Favourites and clicked on the blue backwards arrow at the top left-hand side of the screen until he returned to the Assassination page. He felt this was the most relevant page and continued working his way through the blue links. Finally he spotted 'contract killing'. "Now you're talking!"

Again, he read this page out loud. It seemed to sink in better.

"Contract killing occurs when a private contractor or a government hires someone to kill a specific person or persons for a sum of money. <u>Assassins</u> have been hired for many different jobs, but casual society rarely sees contract killings being carried out. Usually such a contract involves a <u>crime syndicate</u> hiring a professional killer, termed a *hit man*. However, governments and individuals also issue contracts to kill, though it is a part of some major organizations that is kept quiet. It also should be noted that an <u>executioner</u> has nothing to do with the concept of contract killing, even though an executioner is indeed paid to kill people. The difference is that a contract killer can be hired to kill for any particular reason, while an executioner kills as <u>punishment for a crime</u>."

He paused.

"No... yet more blue links."

He persevered.

After stopping to make a cup of tea, he returned to the Assassination page and clicked the little blue raised '1', to the top of the References section. He was greeted with a list of thirty-five links. At this rate he'd never get any work done. Looking through the list though, he quickly decided that most of them had no relation to his plans, not that he knew what they were at this stage, but he'd made a note of the links so he could always go back to them for future assignments.

Just below the list, at the bottom of the page were three 'external links' and the first grabbed his attention by its throat and shook him hard. Assassinology.org a website dedicated to study of assassination.

He clicked on it and was directed to a picture of former US president Ronald Reagan waving and smiling. Sam guessed that RR was walking towards whichever hotel it was that he got shot outside. Below the picture was the heading 'Assassination Prevention'.

"We don't want that," Sam muttered to the screen, "I'd be out of a job twice."

The final link to 'Assassination Research' was another part he liked as it contained facts and figures and he was a facts and figures guy, he read on...

"Many exclusive assassination facts put together from the detailed analysis of thousands of assassinations can be found here. For example, guns are by far the assassin's weapon of choice. They were used in 64.9% of high-profile assassinations (9% of these were snipers) carried out between 1950 and 2000 with a 68.3% success rate. The next most favoured method was bombing at 11.2% followed by poisoning at 7.9% (source: How to Kill)."

"Ah, this Kris Hollington seems to know his stuff. Only 9% snipers? 68.3% success rate. That's not good. Bombing, nah too noisy. Poison, too intimate."

There was a cool picture of a shot-through window at the bottom which Sam clicked his mouse's right button on and selected 'Copy'. He then pasted it on to the plan, selecting 'tight' text wrapping so he could move it around the page easier, and returned to Wikipedia.

The link to 'Assassins in fiction' appealed to Sam's literary side as he had always fancied writing the novel that was "inside everyone". Maybe his first could be semi-autobiographical. *Okay, maybe not,* he thought. He saved http://en.wikipedia.org/wiki/Assassinations_in_fiction into his Favourites and continued back on the main page.

History wasn't one of the best subjects for Sam at school but he knew Caesar had been assassinated. What Wikipedia taught him though was that Assassination is one of the oldest tools of power politics, dating back at least as far as recorded history. Perhaps the earliest recorded instance was the murder around 586 BC of... blah, blah, blah. Even just five and a half lines of old names lost Sam's interest. He made a note of the date, that Julius Caesar was in the list, and ignored the rest.

The 'military doctrines' and 'tools of insurgents' didn't do much for him either so his mouse scroll wheel spun into action.

"For money or gain, now we're talking!" Sam shuffled upright in his chair. His back was aching again and his backside going numb. He would have thought that his body would be used to the sitting position after his years of software design.

Ignoring the 'for racist reasons', he skipped to the 'targeted killing'. Again this concentrated on political and military so was skimmed but the psychology and techniques proved interesting.

"Ancient methods... stabbing, strangling or bludgeoning. Ooh. Substantial planning... oh, maybe not. Infiltration... poisons... yeah. As I said, too intimate."

Sam read on, concentrating on the words highlighted in blue.

247

"Modern methods. Okay. Ranged weaponry, check. Firearms, check. Gunpowder, car bomb, grenades… Land mines? Where does Average Joe get landmines? Middle East. Ah. Rocket propelled grenade… RPG… pocket change." Sam smiled.

"Sniper… sniper rifle… expensive, hard to acquire. No wonder only, what was it?" Sam held down the Alt and Tab buttons and switched over to his Word document.

"Ah yes. Nine percent. Easy to acquire and difficult to trace handguns. That's more like it. Radioactive polonium-210… no, too dodgy. Counter measures? Suppose I'd better read this so I know what I shouldn't be doing. Not that I know what I'm doing, but hey."

Then he was back to the links and references.

With all the to-ing and fro-ing with pages, he hadn't noticed it get dark. He looked at the clock: nine p.m.

"This is frigging ridiculous! Where does the time go? Man!"

He'd forgotten to look up the little blue '2' and wasn't going to bother but it wasn't that late, and it was the last thing to research.

"Go on then."

He clicked on the number and was immediately zipped down to the second 'References' entry, a Washington Post article.

Sam looked at the clock.

"Two a.m. You've got to be kidding."

ooOoo

Chapter 18 – Emma's Dad

The water was flatter than Alan had imagined. He wasn't sure why he'd thought it to be anything but flat but it still surprised him. The weather was similar to the UK. Again this surprised him but then he thought of the latitudes and it made sense.

He spotted a bench and sat down. A little boy in a navy and white striped t-shirt and blue jeans was chasing his dog along the edge of the lake and laughing. It had been a long time since Alan had laughed. He thought of his family at home and sighed. He didn't want to be doing this but he stood up.

"Sorry, Teresa," he whispered as he walked along the edge of the lake. "I have no choice."

ooOoo

Chapter 19 – Emma and the Italian

Emma woke up with a horrible feeling. She wasn't sure what it was but she felt sick. She didn't feel like breakfast before going to work so had a cup of tea and would get something from the Co-op later if she got peckish. Her mum had often said breakfast was the most important meal of the day and normally it wasn't a problem. Not starting work until eleven meant she'd be having breakfast while office workers were having brunch.

She looked at the clock and didn't have to leave for at least half an hour; had plenty of time for food. She opened the cupboard above the cooker and stared at the boxes. Even the Cocoa Pops monkey couldn't tempt her. She sighed and shut the door.

She thought maybe some fresh air would do her good, so grabbed her coat and bag and headed out the door. Her mother had taken Paul to school so Emma had no commitments that morning. The park was kind of on the way so she decided to detour and watch the dogs chasing sticks, pre-school kids on the roundabout and industrial park 'suits' on their mobiles.

The whole area was quiet. Just a woman, who she vaguely recognised as a customer from the Co-op, walking her little Scottie dog. It looked so cute in its jacket. No, hang on, it wasn't a Scottie, it was a Westie. Emma knew it was a Scottish breed of some kind. Weren't Scotties black and Westies white? Yeah, that was it.

Sitting on the park bench, Emma watched the old lady and her dog approaching.

"Morning." Emma smiled at the woman and patted the dog on the head as it probably wouldn't have felt any contact via the coat. She remembered the dog she'd had as a child. It was a little feeble thing, a Chihuahua with a curly tail. It did make her laugh. Her mother had tried to put a coat on it but it wriggled so much as it walked, that she'd taken it off. For some reason it was happy to wear a red felt with white trim Santa-style jacket on Christmas Day but refused to wear one of any kind at any time of the year. Perhaps it had something to do with the house being full. As full as it ever got; the four of

251

them. Emma wished sometimes that she'd had aunts and uncles, grandfathers and grandmothers to show her presents to, cousins to play with, but both her parents had been an only child, and their parents had died before Emma was born. Despite early reservations about her new brother, she was delighted to have a playmate and doted on him, despite his foibles although she'd never admit it.

"Morning, dear. Emma isn't it?"

"Yes. Sorry, you do look familiar."

"Bridget Ellison. Your mother works in the Co-op, doesn't she?"

"Yes, on the tills and shelf-stocking. Everything actually. She's been there long enough."

"Of course. She's lovely. Not married is she?"

Emma thought this was a strange question and didn't answer.

"I'm sorry I didn't mean to pry. She seems a little sad."

Again Emma was silent but smiled weakly.

"I'd best be off. Come on, Hamish."

"I'm sorry, Mrs…"

"Ellison."

"I didn't mean to be rude."

"That's alright, dear. None of my business. Come on Hamish."

No, Emma thought as she watched the pair leave, *it's not.*

Tom was already at the shop when Emma arrived. He was in the middle of his pre-opening ritual of making the tea when she let herself in.

"Hi, Emma," he shouted as she walked through the shop, "we're almost out of milk. Would you be a love and pop next door. I'll get some petty cash…"

"It's okay, I've got some money." With that, she re-locked the front door and popped to the Co-op.

"Hi, Mum."

Teresa Dale, tidying up the newspapers near the front of the shop, turned.

"Hello, darling. Off to work?"

"Just been but we're out of milk. Catch you on the way back."

"Sure. See you in a minute."

Emma went to the chillers and grabbed a pint of milk. As she came face-to-face, literally, with Louis di Marco who owned 'Pizza di Verona' the other side of the DVD rental shop.

"Buongiorno, Emma."

"Buongiorno, Louis."

"Come siete?"

"Er... buon, grazie."

"Il vostro italiano è molto buono."

"No, è diffettoso, realmente."

The little Italian chuckled and went towards the drinks aisle, Emma noticing a slight waver in his walk.

With milk in hand, she returned to the newspapers for a quick chat with her mother.

"Emma, you look ever so pale. Are you alright?"

"Yes, Mum, a tad hungry now actually. I couldn't face breakfast earlier."

"Doesn't Tom let you eat at work? You need to have something."

"He does. He's always munching something, forever popping in and out of Pizza di Verona. I'll grab a pastie or something," she said heading back to the chiller, buying two buy-one-get-one free Cornish pasties, paid separately to the milk, and went back to work.

Louis di Marco was in the shop when she arrived back. Tom was chatting to him and was laughing at something the Italian was saying. They stopped when Emma walked past and Louis slapped Tom on his lower back before walking in the direction of Louis' pizzeria.

Emma guessed he was going off to prepare for the lunchtime rush; assuming they had one as they also sold kebabs, burgers and fish and chips. She couldn't imagine people eating pizza for lunch although it was Friday so why not have something special. Either that or they went to The Nutcracker pub at the other end of the parade of shops. She was a little envious actually as her job was rather solitary. Okay, so she had Tom for company but the atmosphere was like a library. People chose their films in silence. Tom was always busy doing something; the accounts, ordering or making cups of tea. The back room was his domain and Emma was usually ushered out of it at every opportunity. That didn't bother her. She was good with figures but accounts bored her rigid. PAYE, gross and net, no thanks. She'd leave that to the expert until she needed to get involved. Until then, she was paid to serve, smile and scan and he was paid to manage. So she kept to the front of the shop and he the back, and they worked well like that. Keeping out of each other's way and friendly when together.

Tom went to return to his office.

"Tom?"

He stopped by the counter. "Yes, Emma."

"Do you speak Italian?"

"Some. Why?"

"You seem to get on well with Mr di Marco. I wondered if you knew him."

"He runs the pizza parlour next door. You know that."

"Yes, but I didn't think he spoke much English. I thought he did the cooking and left the dealing of customers to his wife."

"He does but he knows a few bits and pieces. We muddle through."

"How do you know the language?"

"I've visited a few times, Rome, Naples, Verona. A few friends and family there, picked bits up along the way."

"Could you teach me what you know?"

"Sure. I'll jot down a few things and we'll go through them."

"Thanks. It's always been something I've wanted to learn. I only know the basics but I practice the accent. I love accents."

Tom looked at the milk. "Shall I put the kettle on?"

"Yes. Thanks, Tom. That would be lovely. You know the way I like my tea."

Tom laughed. "Yes, I do. One sugar, like gnat's pee."

As he walked through to the back, Emma wondered what the two men had been chatting about. They seemed to be more than muddling through.

Her mind had wandered to the back streets of Milan or Firenze, she wasn't sure which as she'd never travelled past Lyon and that had been on an exchange trip, when the shop door bell went.

"Oh no," she said as she spotted the first customer of the day.

"Morning, Emma, and how are you today?" the man in black asked.

Adopting the synchronised swimmer's smile, she replied, "I'm good, thanks. Not had enough of our movies yet?"

"Never enough of you, Emma." Sam smiled weakly.

Emma's stomach lurched and the feeling of that morning returned. Suddenly microwaved Cornish pastie didn't seem so appealing.

ooOoo

Chapter 20 – More Preparation

Sam slammed his front door and dropped back against it, slumping to the floor. Wanting a hole to swallow him up, his flushed face matched the hall rug and he wished he could fly away on it.

"Why the fuck did I say that stupid, lame, clichéd... 'Never enough of you, Emma.' My God. She'll think I'm a complete loser and want nothing to do with me. Ever. Shit."

Sam sat in silence, his mind whirring faster than the second hand on his watch.

"Ah! I know. Get my act together and do my first hit."

He revived his laptop from its sleep mode and looked at the notes he'd made. Sighing with relief as the list, and contents, were still there. He printed out the text on the screen and got his highlighter ready.

"Right, here goes... plan into action."

"*1. Preparation. A professional operative lives alone.* Check. *A professional operative tells no one of his profession.* Check. Who would believe me anyway?"

A picture of Emma came into his head. She was throwing hers back, laughing. She'd be stunned into silence though when he walked into the rental shop wearing his flash black suit. The black suit he hadn't got yet. He knew he'd have to invest to look the part, but that could wait until they paid him.

He carried on reading, highlighting the key words.

"*A professional operative is suave.* I'm tall, not butt ugly but will have to practice on the suave. Not doing a very good job so far, am I Emma? Guess if I get into the role it'll all come flooding to me. That's fine. Next. *Number 2. Equipment. Your hardware will be supplied to you in the next instalment. Once we are sure that you are ready.* Ready? What does that mean? How will they know when I'm ready? *Your hardware...* yeah, done that bit. *It is essential that you blend in with your environment. You will therefore need black trousers.* Check. *Black jumper or t-shirt and outer clothing.* Check. *You will not require headwear although a hooded top will be acceptable. Do nothing to become obvious to the people in the vicinity of the project.*"

"It's a project now is it? Not a hit? Anyway," he said, looking at the clock which now said two p.m. '*Number 3. Methods.* Great! The training finally begins. *While hitmen usually use guns to 'wipe' out their target, there are other methods of eliminating undesirables. From the films you have been prescribed, make a note of the possible other methods.* What? The films I saw were just gunmen. Man, this is hard work. Right, perseverance, Sam. You've gotta win your girl with this stuff."

With a sigh, he read on. "*4. Routes. You will be provided with maps of your surveillance areas. These will be forwarded to you in your next package, along with the first instalment of the equipment.* Man, they don't mind paying postage, do they? Man, I must stop saying 'man'."

He chuckled then continued. "*5. Targets.* People. Real live people that won't be live when you're done with them. Can you do this, Sam? Can you?" He read on. "*Your targets will be selected according to your abilities. Initially a practice target will be allocated to you. If this project is successful, you will then be allocated your first real target. This will be someone unknown to you and will be someone who has earned the project.* What? 'Earned the project'?"

"Next. *6. Words of advice.* Yes, that might be useful. *Keep calm in all situations. If a project fails, simply walk away. Do not get recognised. If you see someone you know, appear normal and do not show any emotion. Talk as little as possible and laugh.* Eh? *Laughter causes confusion.* Ah. Oh. Maybe that's where I'm going wrong with the lay…dees!" Sam said imitating a scene from Little Britain. He moved on to the next section.

"*7. Shooting practice.* Yee hah! *A five-session course has been paid for at Northampton Target Sports Club under the name of Josh Bradley. Telephone the number given on the website to arrange your sessions.*"

Sam typed the website address listed in brackets: www.ntsc-online.org.uk and clicked on the tabs at the top; home, how to find us, facilities, ignoring membership which he wouldn't need that if it had all been paid for.

"Actually how much does it cost?" He thought that perhaps if it was expensive it would give him an indication as to how serious they were about the whole thing and more importantly, how much he would get paid. He scrolled down the membership page and was sorely disappointed.

"*One-off fee £25. Membership £80 per year.* Shit, that's cheap. It would be worth joining just for fun. *Members per visit £3… increased on last year due to diesel prices.* Yeah, okay whatever."

There was no mention of costs of ammunition, pellets or whatever. And guns. Would he have to take his own? That would be okay. He'd get sent one anyway.

The caption at the bottom of the page made him roar with laughter "*Enjoy shooting in Northamptonshire*".

"Yeah, I will!"

He read on.

"*8. How not to get caught.* Now this is important." He was itching to get his highlighter to work on this section. "*Taking note of the advice mentioned above, ensure no one sees you enter the target property, no one sees you affiliating with the aforementioned undesirable, that the project is accomplished in complete silence, save for words that you will be sent with the details of the project, and that you leave under the cover of darkness with no witnesses.*"

Sam re-read the passage '*save for words that you will be sent with the details of the project.*' "What the hell? Someone's having a laugh."

He read on.

"*Please note that there are reasons for these words to be uttered and it is imperative that you tell no one of these words. All will become clear as the projects and your training evolves.*" Okay. Right."

"*9. How to stay legal.* Now this is the interesting bit. *Follow the advice above and call us if you have any questions.* Great. On what number? I've only got the 07007 one."

Sam decided to give it a ring just in case it was different to the answerphone message he'd been getting before. He was greeted by the same woman's voice asking him to leave his password and a message and an operator… or was it operative? …would call him back.

"Oh yeah, there's one more section. Number... *10. Relationships. It is advisable for our operatives not to have serious relationships to ensure that secrecy is maintained at all times. You will have been selected on this basis.* How...?"

So Sam decided to call NTSC to book in his sessions. It was unlikely he'd get any hands-on done in the next day or two but at least he could get the ball rolling. He clicked the 'back' button to bring up the 'Contact Us / Links' page and dialled the number. While he was waiting for someone to answer, he scrolled down to the links section. "*Airguns online...* not sure. Aren't airguns rather tame? This is more like it... *practical pistols uk...*"

"Good afternoon, sorry, good morning, Northampton Target Sports Club, Elizabeth speaking. How may I help you?"

Sam liked the sound of her voice. Definitely a receptionist's voice. Calm and soothing. Sounded quite young too. Maybe if things didn't go well with Emma...

"Hello?"

"Ah, hello. Sorry. I have a five-session course booked under the name of Josh Bradley. It says on your website to speak to your Membership Secretary, Mr Binns, but if it's already paid for, do I need to speak to him about it?"

"Hello, Mr Bradley. No, that's fine. I can deal with your enquiry. Can I ask a few questions first?"

"Sure. Fire away." Sam chuckled but soon stopped as the woman clearly hadn't got the joke. Either that or she'd heard it a million times before. He was seriously losing his touch.

"Are you over eighteen?"

"Yes. Twenty-nine." Sam hoped she'd say something if hers was similar but she continued her questioning.

"Have you ever been shooting before?"

"Not really. I used to watch my dad shoot clay pigeons but I never had a go. This is... a present from him... my father." Sam smiled at being so quick with the lies.

"That's nice. Do you own a' gun or have a licence for one?"

"No. Neither. Presumably I can hire one though right?"

"Yes. That's not a problem. You pay for your hire and ammunition. Are you interested in the pistol or rifle range?"

"Pistol." Sam thought he perhaps sounded too keen but Elizabeth didn't pick up on it. Besides he was a bloke and it was a bloke thing to do, so she was probably used to it.

"Okay. Mr Bradley. When would you like to begin your first session?"

"In the week sometime? Presumably the weekdays are quieter."

"They are. We are busy in the winter months though as our ranges are indoors so not dependent upon the weather."

Sam was warming to her voice. He hoped she'd be there when he checked in for his lessons. He wondered how he could find out when she worked.

"Which days would you suggest… Elizabeth."

"If you are free any day of the week then I would pick a Tuesday or Wednesday. Obviously days either side of the weekend are busier as some people have a longer break."

"And the time of day?"

"We do get some in their lunch breaks… helps them unwind from a bad morning at work, I think."

"I guess it beats those rows of stainless steel balls or squeezy ones."

Elizabeth laughed.

Sam thought she was sincere. At last, he'd cracked the icing.

"Our instructor Adam Warner will be free at ten-thirty on Tuesday. How does that sound, Mr Bradley?"

"That's perfect, and Josh, please. Call me Josh."

"Okay… Josh. We look forward to seeing you on Tuesday morning. Enjoy your weekend."

"Thanks, Elizabeth. And you."

With Tuesday to look forward to for more than target practice, Sam wiled away the rest of the day flicking between his notes, Wikipedia's assassination and hitman pages, and making cups of tea.

He presumed THP Services knew what they were doing sending him to Northampton under a pseudonym. He knew he was relatively new to the area and didn't know anyone in the town but how would they? What if a neighbour from

Kemsley went there and recognised him? Or even from Market Harborough. He guessed it would be a long-shot (this produced another giggle) and he'd have to be quick-thinking if his cover wasn't to be blown. He'd say the lessons were bought for a friend who couldn't go or had lost interest. He'd cross that bridge if it came to it. The notes were by this time getting lengthy but he wanted to be ready when the first instructions came through.

And, as it turns out, he didn't have long to wait.

ooOoo

Chapter 21 – The Gun

Sam was still asleep when the doorbell went. It rang three times before Sam reached the front door. It was George, the postie.

"Sorry to disturb you, Sam. It's another recorded delivery."

Sam yawned. "That's okay." He looked at the package and recognised the label immediately. "It's worth it."

"Sign here then please and I'll let you get back to bed." George smiled.

Running up the stairs and missing every other step in his hurry to get to his desk, Sam ripped open the package. This one was bigger than the others and considerably heavier. A booklet of similar size to the previous ones was accompanied by a DVD, a balaclava and a gun (http://en.wikipedia.org/wiki/Pistol). The pistol landed with a heavy thud on the solid pine desk as Sam dropped it in horror. The office chair flew back as he jerked away, expecting the gun to fire as it made contact with the wood.

Sam stared at the shiny black metal object. The enormity of what he had got himself into had finally sunk in. He was in for the long haul now and there was no going back.

Slowly approaching the desk, he pulled in the chair and sat down. He ignored the gun and read the book while shielding his eyes, obscuring his view of the gun. *Out of sight, out of mind*, he thought.

The front page greeted him with fewer headings:
1. Shooting practice;
2. Equipment and research;
3. Target.

Curious of less content, he flicked through the booklet and found most of the pages were filled with diagrams. A man dressed in black, reassuringly not dissimilar to Sam in stature, posed in various positions of combat.

The middle pages showed pictures of a Browning 9mmx19 Hi-Power pistol matching the gun sitting on Sam's left. Below the picture of the Browning was a disassembled Taurus Millennium series PT145 pistol. The research section led him to Wikipedia's http://en.wikipedia.org/wiki/Pistol page on which he recognised the pictures. "The cheapskates. They don't even use their own photographs."

Finally curiosity got the better of him and he picked up the gun with the tips of his left thumb and index finger. With the booklet propped up between his keyboard and raised monitor, the notes showed him how to open the gun magazine for loading and cleaning. The magazine on this one however wouldn't open. He looked around for signs of a catch but nothing. He bounced the gun up and down in his left palm. It was lighter than he'd imagined. He read the first part of the equipment section in detail. "Bugger. It's not real." He read on.

You may have expected to receive a real gun but do you seriously think we would have sent one in the post? You shall receive your equipment after your professional training. You can however practice on the equipment enclosed with this booklet. You may wear the balaclava with your black attire if this assists with the role-play but it must be carried out either in the comfort of your own home or in an area of your choice with complete confidentiality. Practice makes perfect and as you can appreciate, there is no room for error in this profession. Errors lead to capture or extermination by operatives on either side.

"Extermination by operatives on **either** side? You mean my guys can kill me too? Holy shit, this is serious stuff, ma..."

Sam's stomach rumbled so loudly that the chair went flying again. "What am I doing? I can't do this life or death stuff. It's ridiculous."

Throwing the kitchen cupboard doors open and wanting something quick, Sam settled on a bag of Bombay mix he'd bought on his last shopping trip. Picturing Emma again, Sam sighed. He had it all so wrong. Surely James Bond didn't have this trouble. He wasn't James Bond but he was Josh Bradley and he was going to toughen up. Eat the Bombay Mix, hot bits and all, and do some gun and stance practicing before his first lesson on Tuesday.

ooOoo

Chapter 22 – It Just Won't Go Away

Emma, in the meantime, sat staring at the TV screen in the movie rental store. If anyone asked her what the film was about though she'd not be able to say.

Although her customer, Sam Simpson, was nerdy, she couldn't get him out of her head. The way he smiled when he came in seemed eerie but there was something in the sincerity of his eyes that had an appealing quality.

"Come on, Emma, you're not that desperate."

But the feeling wouldn't go away and Emma spent the weekend wondering, while picking out the dried peas in the Bombay mix that the Co-op had had on special offer.

ooOoo

Chapter 23 – The Perfect Spot

Sam was in the middle of a lovely dream about his next visit to the movie shop when a ringing interrupted. When it was clear that it wasn't going to give up, he stumbled downstairs to the hall phone, the only one in the house. "Yes?"

"Hello, Sam darling. How are you?"

"Mmm…"

"Sorry. Did I wake you?"

"Mum?"

"Were you asleep? Would you like me to ring back?"

"No, it's fine."

"I thought you'd like to know that we got in safely from our holiday. Len, three doors down, got up at four o'clock this morning to collect us from East Midlands. We've had a wonderful time, your dad and I. He sends his regards."

Silence.

"Sam?"

"Sorry, Mum. Yes, I'm listening. Len, the neighbour, four o'clock, East Midlands airport, lovely time. Len sends his regards."

Sam's mum sighed. "I thought I'd let you know we're okay. Did you get our postcards?"

"No. How many did you send?"

"Three. One from Florida, one from the Bahamas, and one from Jamaica."

"No, she went of her own free will." Sam giggled.

"What?"

"Nothing, Mum. No, I didn't get any of them but the post has been rather irregular." Sam lied. *Regular as clockwork if you're training to be a hitman.*

"I'm sure they'll get there eventually. And how are things with you? Do you have a new job yet? Dad said he'd help you find something if you don't mind a bit of a commute."

"Thanks, Mum, but I think I've found something. I'll let you know how I get on."

"Is it well paid?"

Why did mothers always think of the money first? Sam had given up trying to guess how his mum's brain worked but supposed that she just wanted the best for him.

"Not bad," was the only answer Sam could give as he didn't have a clue. He reckoned he'd be on a danger money rate which should be good but he guessed he'd have to prove himself before being put on the real-deal dosh. Prove his worth before the fast cars and brunettes in slinky dresses. He pictured Emma with a brunette wig in a satin or sequin dress. His mother then brought him back to reality.

"Let us know. Keep in touch, won't you."

"Yes, Mum. Sure. As soon as I know, you'll know."

Seeing as he was awake at just after seven, he decided there wasn't much point in going back to sleep. He had to be at the rifle range, or rather, pistol range, in three hours. He'd need more practice in the mirror before then. And have a shower and look presentable. He thought he'd better not go for the all-in-black look but be casual with jeans and a smart sweatshirt or fleece. Something with some 'give' in it although he imagined the only position he'd stand is straight with both hands outstretched.

He leapt in front of the hall mirror and struck the pose in more of a Madonna / Clint Eastwood fashion than James Bond but thought himself cool all the same, albeit in a white and blue striped towelling robe.

"Hello, Mish Moneypenny. Have you mished me?" Sam whispered in his best Sean Connery accent. He pictured Miss Moneypenny swooning and him racing over to catch her in his arms while throwing his trilby on the hat stand.

Heading into the kitchen, he spotted the calendar with its big, black, bold circle around the thirty-one. Ten days before the latest Bond movie. Sam had already booked the tickets; middle row in the middle two seats. The perfect spot. He'd bought two tickets thinking he'd take one of his friends but they'd likely be busy with their girlfriends on a Friday night, but if Emma played her cards right... Or if she didn't, maybe Elizabeth might like to go.

"Decisions, decisions. So many women, so little time. How I feel for you, James." Sam smiled as he walked up the beige-carpeted stairs and into the shower.

ooOoo

268

Chapter 24 – Emma's in Charge

Tuesday was Tom's day off so Emma was in charge. They had a part-time relief who worked their two days off plus Saturdays but he was as useful as a paper dishcloth.

Jacopo di Marco was the neighbouring pizza shop owner's grandson. Despite a history of the di Marco family working in the food industry, Kevin had obviously decided he'd rather watch movies than cook, and however much grandpa Louis had complained, which Emma suspected had been little, Kevin had ended up being an employee of Prime Time rather than Pizza di Verona. Emma also suspected Signor di Marco's decision had been somewhat monetary, preferring Prime Time to pay Kevin to sit on his backside, rather than the money come out of the di Marco earnings.

"Kevin."

No reply.

"Kevin?"

The teenager was hooked on the umpteenth showing of Casino Royale.

"Kevin!"

"Huh?" Kevin, his jaw open a couple of inches, continued to stare at the screen.

"Will you unpack these tubs of popcorn and put them in the dispenser by the ice-cream fridge?"

"Huh?"

Emma repeated her request, adding a please at the end, and the boy finally turned in her direction.

"Uh, yeah. Sure."

"Thank you." Emma shook her head as he turned back to face the screen.

She stood and waited. "Kevin?"

"Yeah?"

"Can you do that job for me?"

"Eh?"

"Popcorn?"

"Yeah, love some. Thanks."

Emma stormed over and tipped his chair, just enough for him to slide off.

"Hey! What did you do that for?"

"The popcorn?"

"Yeah, okay. I said I'd do it. It's not like they're going anywhere."

"Exactly," Emma muttered as she walked back to the counter. She turned back to the lad, pointed at him, then the box of popcorn tubs and said one word. "Now!"

Kevin sighed, turned up the volume on the TV in protest, grabbed the box and stomped over to the dispenser. Throwing the contents into the rack so the round tubs battered against each other, then saw Emma's scowl. He dropped the empty cardboard box on the floor and arranged the tubs so they stacked neatly, adjusting the last one precisely as if making a point.

"Thank you," Emma said, sarcastically.

"Welcome," Kevin said, equally so.

"I'm not happy about your attitude, Kevin. I'll have to have a word with Tom."

"Sure. Feel free," he said aloud followed by a mumbled, "Little Hitler."

"I will," Emma said aloud followed by "Little sod" under her breath.

Less than a mile away, Sam was running back down his stairs dressed in his planned sweatshirt and jeans. He'd gone for the sweatshirt rather than fleece as he reckoned that the adrenaline running around his body would be heat-overload if he wore anything heavier. Besides, he was prone to getting a red face quite easily, and if Miss Elizabeth was on duty, it wouldn't take anything more than a smile from her to turn the corpuscles in his face to the colour of one of his fluorescent highlighters. If there was anything more than a smile he'd need to wear a bikini, shudder the thought. That was assuming that her face matched the voice. But then what was to say that someone as lovely as her wouldn't already have someone… or Emma for that matter? How did he know **she** was single? She did look rather sad but then it could be a man making her that way. Then she should ditch him. Fair and simple. Another bridge to cross if need be.

Grabbing his car keys, he slammed the front door behind him. The door which he'd de-latched earlier to put the recycling out and forgotten to click the lock back down. The door which then bounced open which, in his hurry, Sam hadn't noticed.

ooOoo

Chapter 25 – Josh Bradley

As was the story of his life, Sam was running late. Not only had he wanted to spend a few minutes chatting to the lovely receptionist, there would be the matter of the instructor waiting for him. Most of the roads between Kemsley and Northampton were national speed but sod's law, the shooting club was the Kettering side of Northampton. This meant going round the A45 / A43 ring road which was fine, average speed cameras on a fifty limit, but the A43 was a single carriageway hell-hole. If you got stuck behind a lorry, tractor or even worse, a JCB, it could add at least another ten minutes. In his new guise, Josh would want to make a good impression and being late for your first lesson does not a good impression make.

By some miracle, if not cutting a few corners and exceeding a non-camera'd road or three, Sam made it with two minutes to spare. Just enough time to throw the Golf into a parking space and walk coolly into the building. Pulling open the front door, he was welcomed by a brightly lit reception behind which sat a brightly-lit receptionist.

"Hello," she beamed.

"Hello. I'm Sa... sorry, I'm late. I'm Josh Bradley for my ten-thirty lesson with Adam. Sorry I can't remember his surname." He knew it was Warner but just wanted the vision behind the counter to speak."

"That's quite alright. Mr Bradley. You're booked in. It's my turn to apologise actually as our nine-thirty was also late, stuck in traffic, and will be another few minutes. Would you fill this form in while I get you something to drink."

"That would be lovely. Are you the lady I spoke to on the phone? Elizabeth."

"Yes, you rang on... Friday, wasn't it?"

"Yes. I... I thought you might not be here."

"I have a mid-week weekend, Wednesday and Thursday. I'm off when everyone else is at work, which comes in handy when you want to go shopping or book appointments or get things done around the house when you know you won't get any phone calls. And I work when it's busy so the days go so quickly. I hate being bored. The time goes slowly when there's nothing to do. I'm sorry, I could talk for England."

273

"That's okay. You have a lovely voice."

Sam smiled as he watched her blush. Perhaps she was the one who needed the bikini. The thought of this then made him blush so he coughed as a disguise.

"I'm sorry. I was offering you something to drink. We have a water dispenser in the corner here, and they're also in the corner of each of the firing ranges. Or we have tea and coffee in the members' lounge."

"Water will be fine, thank you, Elizabeth." Sam's brown eyes smouldered into her hazel eyes.

"Please, call me Liz." She smiled, looked down at her feet then resumed eye contact. "Perhaps you'd like a guided tour of the facilities before Adam joins us?"

Hey, hey! Sam thought, his flush returning. He coughed again and drank his water. "Thank you… Liz, that would be lovely. And I'm Josh." As Liz started the tour, Sam followed her like a love-sick puppy.

Despite reading about the club on their website, it wasn't how Sam had envisaged it. The solitary photograph on the simple design website, and Sam knew a thing or two about website design, did not do the place justice. He'd obviously missed the bit about the multi-lane outdoor range, the relaxation lounge and training room. Before the THP paperwork had arrived, he'd never even known the range had existed. When he'd lived in Market Harborough, worked in Kettering, and sometimes had to run errands in Northampton, he'd driven past the main gate and assumed it was a farm. He might have joined before if he'd realised. But then he could say that about a lot of things. He liked swimming but never went. There were plenty of things he'd do if he had the time, and now he had the time, didn't do them. Except for this.

They'd just returned to the reception when Sam, still mesmerised by Liz as he followed her down narrow corridors, failed to notice Adam appear.

"Thanks very much, Mrs Hall. See you next time. Right. Hello Mr Bradley. Sorry to keep you waiting. I hope Elizabeth here has been looking after you." The instructor winked at Liz and her blush returned.

"Yes, very well, thanks, Adam." It made a change for Sam to have a conversation with someone as tall. He even felt intimidated as Adam was built like a rugby player compared with Sam's footballer physique. Maybe this was what the women preferred; a little meat on the bones. Still, once Sam got into THP training he'd be able to take Adam on any day. He'd still be lacking the piercing blue eyes and Mediterranean tan but nothing that contact lenses and a sun bed wouldn't cure.

"Okay. Are you ready? Just through here to the training room then, please." Adam put his right arm out pointing the way for Sam to go. Turning to the reception area, Adam whispered, "See you later, Lizzy," and winked.

Liz laughed but her smile soon disappeared after the training room door had closed. Adam might be handsome and athletic but she didn't care for his manner and doubted he had many brain cells between those leather-tanned ears either. What she wanted was a man who knew how to treat a lady and be respectful, like their newest member Josh Bradley. Being just under five feet ten, she liked tall men. He had to be another five or six inches taller than her; the perfect height, and the few men she'd dated had all said how lovely it was to date a tall woman. No need to get neck ache talking down to their women. And she hated men who talked down to her. Like that loser she met the previous weekend. She should have known. And she'd blown a trip out with her best mate for him. Tosser.

While Liz engrossed herself in Sam's paperwork, he was having a blast in the training room. He'd been given some ear defenders, which didn't look dissimilar to the Sony headphones attached to his lounge stereo except these had William Evans written on the sides and Sam guessed they were considerably more expensive.

Adam spent the first forty minutes of the hour's lesson explaining the basics of guns to Sam, with examples of a 'Browning' (similar to the gun sitting on his office desk), a 'Colt', 'Smith and Wesson' (which Sam had always thought was called 'Smith and Weston') and a Remington. Adam did mention model numbers but said Josh didn't need to remember them as he wouldn't be using them. Adam then produced a black standard model pistol, far more ordinary than the ones Sam had already seen.

"These are all single-shot pistols," Adam explained. "You may have seen semi-automatic pistols used on TV or in the movies but we only use single-shot here."

Sam opened his mouth to ask "why?"

Adam pre-empted him. "Good question, Josh. This is for accuracy. We feel there is no point in aiming at the target and getting one in the inner area and five in the outer." He seemed pleased to see that Josh was following him. "We would rather you concentrate on each shot and get five near the inner area and one outside. Think of it like the bull's eye on a dartboard. If you have three darts but throw one at a time slowly, you are more likely to get all three in the centre than if you throw them together or separately in quick succession." Adam paused, waiting for Sam to answer.

"I agree. Can't play darts for toffee… to save my life, but I see what you mean."

Adam laughed. The pun wasn't lost on him and that won brownie points in Sam's book.

For the final twenty minutes of the lesson, Adam loaded up the 'Smith and Wesson' and after showing Josh the best stance, let him take a few shots. To their surprise, four out of six bullets landed in the inner target area.

Adam slapped Sam on the back. "Well done, Josh. You're a real natural!"

Sam was warming to this man. Rather than the jerk he imagined him to be, Adam was a great teacher and all-round nice guy.

Once the hour was up, Sam followed Adam into the reception and shook his hand firmly, thanking him for such an enjoyable session.

"You've got four more although I think the last ones will be a waste of money but hey, better too much training and we make you safe, than not enough and you do something stupid."

Wham! There it was again. Adam seemed to be two people: genuine and patient as an instructor in the training room but as soon as he got outside he was the arrogant schmuck – yes, Sam admitted he watched too much American TV – he'd appeared to be on first meeting. Sam guessed this was for Liz's benefit although she clearly didn't appreciate it. She was busy with a new member, form-filling but stood behind the counter shaking her head. The customer looked puzzled as if there was something wrong with her form but Liz's smile soon reassured her. It also made Sam melt. He was surprised how women there were at the club, but thought perhaps this was for self-defence.

Adam took the new lady through into the training room and seemed just as smarmy as he had before. Sam chuckled and Liz nodded.

"I know. He's actually a nice guy. He just seems to have something to prove. God knows why because he's a dish. Shame there's…"

Sam waited for the rest of the sentence but when it wasn't forthcoming said, There's…?"

"Let's just say, I don't think he'd get very far in 'Pointless'."

Sam laughed which set Liz off. She had such a lovely laugh. If Sam could melt any further he'd be a puddle on the floor. He thought of Emma and knew she had a soft side, but it seemed to come easier to Liz.

"Speaking of Adam, did you want to book another lesson?"

"Yes, I would please. Any gaps on Thursday?"

"I'll have a look. We don't have the same time but how about the one after, eleven-thirty?"

"Eleven-thirty is perfect."

"Not working this week?"

"No, no work. Made redundant recently but making the most of it."

"Sorry to hear that. I'm sure you'll get another job soon."

"Thanks. There is something I'm interested in." He paused, gathering the nerve, "Liz?"

She frowned at Sam's serious expression. "Yes?"

"Do you mind me asking you whether you're free tonight?"

Liz laughed. "No."

"No? You don't mind or you're not free? Or both?"

"Sorry. No and yes. I mean, I don't mind and yes, I am free tonight. Oh, no, I'm not. Sorry. I promised to babysit for a neighbour. How about tomorrow night?"

"Sure. Anywhere in particular?"

"Do you know The Nutcracker at Kemsley? It's a few miles south of here but quite easy to find."

Was that a trick question? The Nutcracker was about three doors down from the Co-op and therefore Emma's shop. His mind raced. He'd not booked the course so he hoped whoever had done had given a false address so Liz didn't know Sam lived in Kemsley. "Er, sure."

"It's just that I've promised to spend the afternoon with friends who live near there and they've always told me how nice it is. What do you think?"

"Sure. No, that sounds great. What time?"

"Should be done by around six. So about half six. Is that too early?"

"Perfect. Shall we eat or…"

"Love to. But we go Dutch, okay?"

"My kind of woman." Sam laughed. "It's a date then."

"Yes, a date. Lovely. Look forward to it."

"Me too. Bye."

"Bye. Oh."

"Yes."

"Forgot to ask you how your training went. Did it go well?"

"It did, thanks. A perfect start to the day all round."

Liz smiled and Sam headed to his car.

His day was only going to get better. Complicated, but better.

ooOoo

Chapter 26 – The First Date

Sam was on a high driving back to Kemsley. He thought he'd pop into the Co-op and pick up a bottle of good wine to celebrate. He didn't know much about wine so usually went by the price or sometimes the design of the label. A very girlie thing to do he admitted, but girls were often right.

He was scouring the bottles and had just picked up a Jacktone Viognier when a familiar voice said "Hello". He turned and there, in the flesh, was Emma.

"Hi, Emma. How are you?"

"Apart from a pipsqueak of an assistant, I'm good, thank you. I'm glad I've seen you actually because I wanted to apologise."

"Really. Why?"

"I think I was rather rude to you the other day."

"I don't think so. If you were, it passed me by. No apology necessary. In fact, I…"

Emma looked at the bottle of wine. "Not drinking alone?"

"I'd planned to but you're welcome to join me."

"Thanks, that would be lovely. I'm working today though."

"No problem. How about later?"

"Don't finish 'til ten and… How about tomorrow? It's my day off."

"Er…" Sam thought of the plans he'd made with Liz.

"Or not. It's not a problem."

"No. Great plan. Erm…"

"I'm busy during the day so how about after supper. About eight o'clock at The Nutcracker?"

What was it about The Nutcracker? He'd been in there a couple of times and it hadn't struck him as anything special. And what about the wine? Wasn't the plan to share the bottle he was now holding? He looked down at it.

As if she'd read his mind, Emma continued. "Yes. Sorry. I just fancy getting out. Do you mind?"

He'd been dreaming of this moment for weeks so how could he mind? He'd just have to make sure he'd made his excuses to Liz and get her out the way in plenty of time. If she'd been visiting friends she'd be tired and want to go early. Maybe he could get one of his mates to call him on his mobile with an emergency. Clichéd but it had worked for him in the past.

"Could we say half eight. I have something to do beforehand and I might run a little late."

"Sure. No problem. It'll give me time to do the Dale household chores."

"Okay." Then putting two and two together, Sam said "The Dale household. You're Emma…"

"Dale. Yes, I know. I guess my parents didn't watch much TV."

Sam smiled. "I think it's lovely. I shall say goodbye and look forward to seeing you tomorrow evening."

ooOoo

Chapter 27 – The Dales

As Wednesday was Emma's day off, she'd left a note for Tom about her issues with Kevin. She didn't like telling tales but didn't see the point in employing him if he didn't do any work. Favour or no favour.

She decided she needed to do something relaxing to take her mind off Kevin so, as it was half-term, she took Paul swimming in Northampton.

Afterwards she treated him to a burger and fries in Happy Harry's in York Road on the edge of the pedestrianised shopping area, then headed through 'Abington Street Arcade' where Paul bought a couple of Warhammer figures, and Emma a floral skirt from Monsoon. Having spent so many months wearing the regulation Prime Time sweatshirt and black or navy trousers, which at times bored her rigid although it saved her a few minutes every morning deciding what to wear, she relished in the fact that she might now have a social life. Besides, the skirt was reduced from £85 to £25 in their (early) winter sale, so how could she not buy it?

Driving home, they passed the row of shops at Kemsley, so Emma slowed down outside Prime Time, where Tom was joking around with Kevin.

"No hope of him getting a telling off then," Emma said.

"What?" Paul wondered whether that should have made sense to him but then little his sister said ever made sense.

"Nothing. Just work stuff."

"Okay," Paul said, turning back to the window out of which he'd been staring for the past twenty minutes.

Teresa Dale was refilling the baskets outside the shop when she saw her children go by. She'd recognised the splutter of Emma's car exhaust and turned. For some reason they were going at a crawling speed so she had plenty of time to catch their eye.

Emma was oblivious, looking in the direction of her shop rather than her mother's but when the car was level with the Co-op and she saw her mum, Emma waved furiously like a five-year-old, while keeping half an eye on the road.

Emma shouted, "Paul, look there's Mum!" by which time they'd driven past and he'd missed his chance to acknowledge her.

"Do you want me to stop so you can get out and speak to her?"

"Nah, it's okay. I'll see her later. Is she cooking dinner?"

"Is your stomach all you think about?"

"Eh?"

What is it with boys? Emma thought recalling her similarly-stimulating conversation with Kevin less than twenty-four hours earlier. Kevin was a few years older than Paul but somehow they'd been cut from the same mould, or was it cloth? Emma couldn't remember.

Still retaining the five-year-old mentality, Emma abandoned Paul and the car in the driveway, unlocked the front door, then dashed upstairs to try on her new skirt. Although she'd hung around Game Warehouse for what seemed like an eternity, Paul had seemed distinctly reluctant to wait for her in Monsoon. It could have had something to do with the bustle of women around the shop, especially at the underwear rack, that Emma felt ever so slightly sorry for him. So she'd bought it, hoping it fitted. It was her size, a twelve, and although she had a long body, her legs were quite short so at least the skirt would be a reasonable length. Not that it mattered these days. She wasn't keen on at-the-knee so providing it was just below (or just above, at a push) that would be okay.

Thankfully it fitted perfectly and she jumped around her room like a mad thing. Or quite possibly like a five-year-old… until Paul shouted up the stairs, "What's for tea?"

ooOoo

Chapter 28 – Caught

Sam looked at his watch. Quarter past six. "Shit." Late as always. He'd wanted to be early so they could hurry with their meals and the shifts could change, with some time to spare but at this rate he'd be pushing it to make it on time. He'd planned to walk but going by car would save him a few minutes. Wearing a smart but casual shirt and clean jeans, he checked himself in the mirror and was pleased with what he saw.

He drove into The Nutcracker car park with less than a minute to spare. Liz was nowhere in sight so he was hoping she'd not arrived yet rather than be waiting for him inside. The front entrance led to the main bar and he planned to have a quick look around inside before waiting in the foyer. He'd scanned the room and was going to head back outside when he spotted Liz at the bar with a part-glass of Coke.

"Hi, Liz. I'm so sorry. Am I late?"

"Not at all, Josh, right on time. I was early. I wasn't as long at my friends as I'd thought. She had to get ready for a date. I couldn't complain could I, given the circumstances."

Her winning smile returned and Sam felt a warm glow in the pit of his stomach as he sat on the bar stool next to her.

"Shall we order?" he said wanting to speed up proceedings and asked the barman for two menus.

"Shall we find a table first though? It's a bit cramped at the bar."

"Sure. How about in the corner away from the door? Nice and cosy."

"And warmer no doubt. I sat here so I could see you come in, I thought it was warmer than standing outside but it wasn't by much."

Sam laughed and carried her Coke and the menus to the table they'd spotted.

"So you know this place then? Have you eaten here before, Josh?"

"No. I've actually never been in here. I'm fairly new to the area but…"

"You live around here?"

"Not here no," he backtracked, trying to recall what he'd put on his form. "Market Harborough, but I've driven through a few times." Lying on a first date wasn't the smartest of moves but this was his home territory and it wouldn't do to have Liz becoming too familiar with Emma's neighbourhood. He couldn't run the risk of Emma seeing him with another girl and vice versa. Then he'd lose them both.

Looking at his watch, he grumbled, "Where's the waiter?"

Obviously speaking louder than he thought, Liz said, "There isn't one. You pick what you want then tell them at the bar your table number, as on this wooden spoon… and order the food and pay for it there and then. Are you in a hurry?"

"I'm sorry that must have sounded so rude. No hurry although I do have to get up early."

"I know, for an eleven-thirty training session. It'll still be dark. How will you be able to see what you are shooting at?"

So Liz had a sarcastic side too. More brownie points in her favour. Emma had some catching up to do. Which reminded him…

"I have an… errand to run before I go actually. Something I'd promised to do."

"I see." Liz didn't look convinced.

"I'm so sorry. I'd forgotten about it yesterday. It's quite a way away so, I… er, need to do it tonight." His plan for Danny to call him on his mobile in an hour was unravelling. "I could call and cancel, but it's been…"

"No, don't worry. could do with an early night. I didn't get as much done at my flat today as I wanted to and being out all afternoon…"

"Okay. Let's order and have a nice, early evening."

"That sounds like a good plan, Josh. We'd better skip starters then. I'll stay here to keep the table but if you could order me the Lasagne with side salad, that would be great. Here's a tenner which is just over."

"Are you sure about this? I don't mind paying."

"Thanks but I did say Dutch. I've always thought that if I'm working I can pay my way. Besides you're not working at the moment so I should pay for yours."

Sam laughed, reluctantly took the ten-pound note and brought back two fresh glasses of Coke. "At least let me buy you a drink."

"You're a gent. Thank you."

The food, much to Sam's relief, was served quickly, possibly helped by the fact that they'd both ordered the same thing. They tucked in and were scraping the remnants around their plates when a voice from behind Sam said, "Libby…?"

"Hi, Emms!" Liz jumped to her feet. "I'd like you to meet someone. Emma this is Josh. Josh this is Emma."

Sam felt his neck flush. "Er… hello, Emma."

"Hello…er, Josh." Emma's head tilted slightly as she said the name. "It's funny I have a date tonight with a chap who looks just like you. Except his name is Sam."

Sam looked at the two women and the colour drained from his face.

ooOoo

Chapter 29 – Deaf Ears

Emma unlocked the 'Prime Time' front door, yanked it open then slammed it shut behind her as she walked into the shop. To say she was pissed off was an understatement.

Tom was counting the float as she walked past the counter, towards the back of the shop. Silently putting her jacket and bag into one of the lockers, she turned towards Tom and was about to wish him a good morning when he interrupted her.

"I know what you're going to say. Sorry, Emma. I'll have a word with him about his attitude and I'll ask him to pull his weight. I can't do any more than that. Kevin's here as a favour for Louis."

"But why? You don't owe him anything."

Tom hesitated. "No, but…"

Emma put her hands up and decided to let it slide. Providing Tom was aware there was a problem it was up to him to sort it out. The money wasn't coming out of her pocket. Besides she just wasn't in the mood.

Tom shrugged and returned to counting the money. He'd already lost count twice while thinking about Sandra but would get it right this time if it killed him.

Right on cue. The doorbell went.

Emma headed for the door, expecting to either sign for a parcel or tell the early customer that they didn't open for another twenty minutes, but turned away when she saw it was no ordinary customer but Sam, aka Josh, standing outside.

"I'm sorry!" was barely audible through the glass.

Emma ignored him and carried on walking.

"Emma. I'm sorry!" fell on selectively deaf ears.

"Emma. Please!" was unheard as she was now out of earshot.

Tom approached the counter as Emma walked past. Tom pointed to Sam. "Didn't you tell him we're not open yet?"

"He's not the sort to listen, Tom. Thinks he knows everything. Let him stew."

Sam was by now just mouthing the words he wanted Emma to hear but knew she couldn't. The previous night couldn't have gone worse if he'd invited the two women on a date at the same venue and the **same** time. How was he to know the friend that Liz had visited was Emma? Of all the women living in the area, he had to pick two who knew each other. Not only that, but were best friends. What were the odds?

Banging his head against the proverbial brick wall, or in this case, a glass door, he decided he couldn't wait until they opened as he had to get to the shooting range before eleven-thirty and if he was late he would definitely blow his chances with Liz... Libby. The chance might be a slim one but if he lost Emma, he couldn't face losing Libby as well.

ooOoo

Chapter 30 – The Fake Misunderstanding

There was no sign of Libby in the reception when he arrived at
the Target Club. He'd forgotten she didn't work on Thursdays.
He could ask the young lad on the reception desk for her
home address or phone number (which he'd forgotten to get
before things went pear-shaped in The Nutcracker) until he
was blue in the face, but he knew there was no chance of
getting it. These days the Data Protection Act meant even
your inside leg measurement was Governmentally classified.
Unless it happened to be on a laptop or data stick in which
case it was probably travelling solo on a train somewhere.

He could try Adam but couldn't think of a reason he could
give for needing it and that was surely to be a dead end as
well. The only thing to do, he realised, was to book another
session for the next day and go early and speak to her
beforehand. That would give her another twenty-four hours to
calm down and him to have worked out what he was going to
say to her. Plus it would be more time for him to tackle Emma,
even if it meant hiring out Titanic to show he was a real softie
and that it was all a huge misunderstanding.

Adam appeared right on cue and went through the
basics from the previous day but in a digested format, leaving
much more time for some hands-on. Again 'Josh' was the
model student, despite his mind being elsewhere – not a good
habit to get into.

As Sam left the club after booking a session for the following
morning, he realised what the fake misunderstanding could
be. Josh had booked the course so what if Josh hadn't been
able to do attend but sent Sam in his place. So why did Sam
say he was Josh? This is something he had to work on. The
most logical excuse would be of using Josh's name because
he didn't think the course was transferable.

"What the hell. Let's just try charm."

Heading back to Kemsley, he decided to have another go at
trying to sweet-talk Emma. No easy task judging by her
attitude that morning. Not just cold shoulder treatment but
freezing. "Ice cold from Alex... Emma."

When Sam arrived at the parade of shops, he popped into the DVD store but there was a distinct lack of Emma. The man, who Sam assumed to be the manager, was behind the counter.

Sam hovered around the pre-owned sale display near the front door and picked up a couple of cases pretending to read the blurbs, keeping his eyes on the door. It wasn't long before he spotted her carrying a ½ pint carton of milk. Sam stepped forward and opened the front door.

"Hi, Emma," he said, hoping to start in a light mood.

"What do **you** want?"

"Just to talk. Can we?" Sam looked around the shop which was deserted except for the old man now hovering around the ice cream fridge, clearly eavesdropping.

But Emma didn't seem bothered, ranting "What is there to say, Sam... or is it Josh? You obviously don't think one woman is enough. But you could have at least had the decency to have a gap in the middle. And with my best friend? She'd told me she had a date at The Nutcracker so I thought I'd surprise her by turning up early and thought if we all got on, we could double-date. Little did I know that you already were. How greedy can you get? Was there another one before Libby or another after me?"

Sam let her blow off steam.

Emma waited for him to speak. "Well?"

"I'm sorry. It was a misunderstanding," was all he could manage, his brilliant plan having eradicated itself from his brain.

"Go on. Explain this one away."

"Erm." *Plan B, Sam, Plan B.*

"You can't, can you? You've been caught out pure and simple. And why **did** Libby think your name was Josh?

"Ah, yes, that's the misunderstanding. You see a friend's father had booked a course for him, Josh, my friend, and he couldn't go so he asked if I wanted to. He'd, er, broken his leg and wasn't all that interested anyway but didn't want to hurt his dad's feelings so I went along instead. I didn't tell them my real name in case he got into trouble with his dad or the course wasn't transferable." *Even better than plan B!*

"Right," Emma said suspiciously, "and the double date was just an accident was it or had you forgotten about me?"

"Not at all. Libby had asked first and–" Sam blurted out without thinking.

"Great. So you thought you'd get her out the way before moving on to me?" Emma's face now matched the colour of the emblem on the milk carton.

"It wasn't like that."

"Go on, then what was it like?"

"I got chatting to Liz… Libby, at the rifle range and she mentioned The Nutcracker. She seemed to be getting stick from one of the instructors and…"

"Adam, presumably. Yes, I've heard all about him. So it was a sympathy date. And me?"

"I saw you in the Co-op and have wanted to ask you out since my first visit here then when you asked me, I just couldn't say 'no'. When you suggested The Nutcracker I couldn't say I was already going. I didn't think for a second you two would know each other. Kemsley's a small place but I've only just realised how small."

"So it would appear."

"So, Emma, I'm sorry. I'll explain the situation to Libby tomorrow and…"

"And what, carry on seeing both of us? Libby was furious, needless to say. What makes you think she'd still be interested? Or me for that matter?"

"Because you like me?"

"Don't flatter yourself," Emma said, before storming off to the back of the shop.

By this time, Tom had disappeared and Sam heard the kettle click so left Emma to her tea and sympathy. She was a tough nut to crack but he'd not give up on her, or Libby. Besides, why was she getting so worked up if she didn't feel something for him? Let the two girls battle it between them and they make his decision for him. *Now there's an image,* Sam drooled.

ooOoo

Chapter 31 – All Part of the Service

One of Royal Mail's finest, George, was walking up Sam's path as the Golf pulled up. Sam honked the horn and George turned and nodded, walking back down the path to meet him.

"Morning, Sam. Another recorded delivery for you. You are popular."

Sam, practicing his lies, replied, "Thanks, George. Yeah it's early Christmas presents for my parents. They collect old stamps and stuff."

"Mine did too. I think I've got my dad's old albums up in my loft. Maybe your folks would like to look through them?"

"I'll mention it, thanks." *God, what ball have I set rolling this time? Why do I open my big mouth?*

"Anyway, here we go. One recorded, one normal. Looks like a bill, the other one."

"Gee, thanks, George. I'll look forward to that."

"You're welcome. All part of the service."

Sam signed for the parcel and watched George head off down the road, his bare legs oblivious to the late autumn day. *How could he wear shorts in this weather?* Sam wondered, preferring to keep his legs covered. Apart from the fact they were too thin, he felt the cold so they rarely got an airing. Although wearing shorts all day in the summer, he supposed, would give him a decent tan, it would probably be the early mornings that would kill him. Speaking of which, he ripped open the recorded delivery and pulled a card out of the envelope.

'Congratulations. Mr Bradley is now ready for operations,' the typed card read. "Is that it?"

He turned it over. "Ah ha." 'NN12 3ZY. V Fellini. 25/10/08. 11pm sharp.' And underneath, 'collect equipment from gent's toilet of The Nutcracker pub two hours before first operation begins. Ceiling tile four in from door, third from the right-hand wall. Don't look before then, it will not be available. Equipment to be returned within twenty-four hours of the successful operation.'

So there it was. Successful operation. No option but to succeed, clearly.

Sam's heart raced. He had forty-eight hours before he had to kill someone. And with the sketchiest of details to do it with. A time, a place, a plan. And that's why they'd not sent him a proper gun. He'd only have the responsibility of it for a day. They knew what they were doing then. But why pick a Saturday? It would be the busiest day in the pub and the busiest time on the streets. Eleven p.m. is turf out time so NN12 3ZY, wherever that was, was bound to be busy.

He went upstairs and switched on his PC. He put in his password then returned downstairs to make a sandwich and cup of tea while the computer warmed up. It was his first cuppa of the day and he was gasping. As usual, he'd been late to the rifle range despite wanting to get there early to speak to Libby. He looked at the instructions on the card again. '11pm sharp'. They must have known he was always late. For once in his life he wouldn't be this time. He'd get the gun just after nine p.m. and head straight over to NN12 3ZY and lie in wait for V Fellini. Valentino? Vito? Whoever he was. Assuming he was a 'he'. Veronica? "God."

With card tucked under the plate in his left hand and mug in right, he headed, somewhat more carefully, upstairs and back to the computer which was now showing a picture of him, Danny and Mark on a Malaga beach. They'd been going to Spain for the last few years but had such a good time each year it didn't seem to matter. Despite knowing them since college, Sam didn't feel they'd understand his new choice of career. He didn't know what he'd tell them when they asked, so maybe he ought to get a part-time job as a cover. If his 'work' was only going to take place at night he'd have time for something. He'd always like animals so maybe he'd get something at a nearby farm or vets in Northampton or Towcester. Ah, Towcester. That's where he knew NN12 from. It was somewhere near Towcester.

He placed his belated lunch on the desk and double-clicked on the blue 'E' symbol which brought up Google's home page. He then clicked on 'maps' and was greeted with a picture of the UK with major cities the size of the sweeteners he used in his tea. In the search bar he typed in NN12 3ZY and a pinned 'A' appeared in what looked like the middle of the countryside slightly north of Towcester.

"Bingo! Right, better check it out to see what I'm up against."

Tapping the left-hand mouse button on the '+' symbol a few times enlarged the scale and revealed a farm between Duncote and Caldecott, just to the left of the A5.

Mark lived in Duncote so Sam decided he could pop over and see if he knew anything about the farm, discreetly of course. Say he'd not noticed it before or had decided to go the scenic route or something.

He then printed off the map and went to put it with the card in the envelope which was leaning against the monitor stand when he noticed another card in the envelope. A plain white one. That is, until he turned it round: a photo. A black and white photograph of a slightly dark skinned man in his fifties, talking to someone out of shot. He was exactly how Sam had pictured a target to be; the photo not looking out of place on Crimewatch. He imagined he'd be doing the world a favour by 'rubbing' him out and was sure that once the first one was over, it would get easier. The fact he wasn't feeling sick or in the least bit horrified by what he was planning on doing, scared him.

Sam looked at the photo again. Being black and white it was difficult to tell what nationality the man was but with the surname, Sam guessed him to be Italian. Again comparisons with the Mafia came to mind and a shiver ran down his back. Sam thought he **was** getting into something heavier than he bargained for but there was no going back now. He'd not signed a contract but they knew where he lived and although there was no evidence against him as such, they could no doubt make him the target for other operatives. The cold feeling returned and he tried to shrug it off.

The clock clicked to five-thirty around the time Mark would be finishing work so Sam sent him a text message to see if he could pop over that evening. He remembered that Kelly, Mark's girlfriend, had a night class on a Thursday so she'd not be there to get in the way.

Sam's phone beeped and vibrated seconds later. He clicked on the centre button twice which said '1 message received' then 'view'. It read simply, 'Sure, mate any time.'

In true espionage fashion, Sam wanted to go when it was dark which wasn't difficult as it already was, but the roads would be busy, so he did some investigating on the internet on V Fellini. There was nothing on a V Fellini, a few on other Fellinis including the Italian film director Frederico Fellini but he'd died in 1993 so it couldn't have been him and Sam couldn't imagine any of his relatives living near not-so-sunny Towcester somehow. Just in case Fellini was a common Italian surname, Sam did a search on www.italiannames.com but it wasn't there so obviously not a Smith equivalent then. He used other search engines but got similar results and felt that if Google didn't know the name then no one would.

ooOoo

Chapter 32 – Duncote Mark

Sam left for Duncote just after six-thirty, figuring the rush hour would be over by then. He'd decided to drive slowly past the farm on the way over then see what Mark knew and go armed with, hopefully, more information for a detailed reconnaissance on the way back.

"Hey buddy, how's the diet going?"

"Hi, Mark. Not bad. Storing some fat for the winter but you know, up and down."

"Yeah," Mark giggled. "I know." And winked.

"Too much information. How is the lovely Kelly?"

"Yeah, she's… lovely. You've only just missed her actually. She's gone off to her class."

"What's she studying this time? More computing?"

"No, she's moved onto languages. She's doing Italian first as we plan to go there next year then said she'll probably brush up on her German or Spanish. I think it's an excuse to get out of the house."

"The perpetual student. Bright little thing, isn't she?"

"Very. Puts me to shame sometimes."

"Ah, you're smitten." Then recalling a scene from Miss Congeniality that his last girlfriend had made him sit through, Sam said in his best Sandra Bullock voice, "You really love her. You want to marry her".

"That's the plan."

"Really? I was only kidding. But you are? You're going to propose?"

"Shit. I shouldn't have said anything. You're hopeless at keeping secrets."

Little do you know, Sam thought. "That's not fair! So when are you going to do it? Where?"

Mark hesitated.

"Go on. I promise I won't tell."

"You'd better not or I'll kill you then she'll shoot me!"

Sam laughed, "I'll take that risk."

"Italy next year. The hotel and flights were booked weeks ago but I did some research on the net for the perfect place."

"Which is?"

"Come on. You want to know all my secrets?"

"You know all mine."

Mark laughed. "There's a remote vineyard outside Verona which apparently has the most amazing views. They do lunches there and trips around their vines…"

"Yeah. Sounds really romantic. Coach trip for you lovebirds and fifty-two others."

"As I was saying…"

"Sorry, do go on."

"Their website is in Italian and English so I emailed them, from work so Miss Nosey Knickers doesn't get wind of my plans. Anyway, I emailed them asking if they could arrange something unique over Lake Garda, and they sent back some fantastic photos. So on June thirtieth next year, Kelly's birthday, we'll get collected from the hotel in a limo – so no fifty-two other lovebirds, thank you very much…" Sam winked. "…driven through Verona, then off to the vineyard where there'll be a picnic waiting for us in a secluded spot.

Sam thought of the pizza shop on the parade at Kemsley. Pizza di Verona. A popular place. "Verona as in Romeo and Juliette?"

Mark nodded.

"You old romantic slush bucket, you."

"You're only jealous."

"You could be right. Hey, speaking of farms…"

"Which we weren't."

"No, but I noticed on the way… an old farm on the back road from the A5."

"You saw it in the dark?"

"The driveway leading up to it. I'd not noticed it before. Any idea who it belongs to?"

"Why, interested in buying it?"

"No, nothing like that. I'm…er just thinking of new career options."

"So now you want to be a farmer. We'll have to start calling you Old Fat McDonald."

"Hey, not so much of the fat, thank you very much."

"You know I'm only kidding. Chicks like men with meat on their bones. Or is that a bone…" Mark sniggered.

"Too much information! The farm?"

"Oh yeah. Not sure. Looks run down to me. Never much sign of life. I'll ask Kelly as she's lived here longer than me."

"Thanks. Just curious. Keeping my options open. I fancy a change. Get my hands dirty for once."

"Do you want a cuppa or something stronger?"

"I'm driving. I've been drinking so much tea recently but only had one today so yes please. The usual: little bit of tea, little bit of milk, little bit of sugar. Thanks, mate."

"All part of the service."

Sam and Mark were deep in a battle of 'Mortal Combat' on Mark's Wii when Sam realised how much shooting practice he'd actually had on all the games he and the lads had had over the years; the various Playstations, X-boxes and Nintendo Cubes. The pizzas they'd consumed, the beers they'd swigged. Happy times.

"Mate. You're losing."

"Sorry. Miles away."

"Or wishing you were. Keep up!"

Just after nine, they heard the front door open followed by a "Honey, I'm home".

"Hi, Kell. Sam's here. We're in the lounge blatting a few baddies. I got most of them but Sam's useless…. ouch!"

Kelly laughed. "Be right there. Just dump my college stuff upstairs and be with you. Either of you want something to drink?"

"Coffee would be lovely, and Sam wants tea if it's not too much trouble. Weak, one sugar. He's such a pain… ouch!"

"Sure thing. No problem. Was going to have tea myself so you're the pain, Mark."

Kelly heard Mark and Sam laughing and felt the happiest she'd been in a long time. Sometimes she had to pinch herself. After so many losers, she finally thought, at the ripe old age of thirty-five, she'd found 'the one'.

A few minutes later, she headed into the lounge with two mugs for the boys and hers left in the kitchen to cool while she did the washing up from a hurried pre-college dinner. One of the many things they ensured they did together was to eat their evening meal regardless of their commitments. Mark was always keen on leaving work on time. Kelly knew he wasn't happy there but being a Financial Adviser was well paid and he was looking to reduce the mortgage so that seemed to take priority. Kelly had reminded him numerous times there was more to life than money and he said he'd look for a new job but he didn't seem to get round to it. "I'll do it in the New Year," he'd say or "Sure, when we get back from holiday". It can't have been that bad for him to not even look. Still, Kelly figured he'd start looking when he wanted to and the topic was forgotten.

Getting stuck into the washing up, she listened to the boys battling out against their enemies and each other. She smiled at the occasional "Get in there" and "No!"

With the chores done and the crockery left to drain, she grabbed her mug of tea, popped her head round the lounge door. "I'm off to bed, taking my study books, so no hurry to wind things up."

Sam looked up. "I should be going actually. Thanks you two for a lovely evening… as always."

Mark switched off the TV. "You're welcome. It's getting late and **some of us** have work in the morning." He laughed.

"I don't lie in bed all day you know. I'm busy."

"Yeah, sure. Busy watching TV, busy playing on your X-box, busy drinking cups of chicken soup-coloured tea."

"Don't forget busy reading the job papers," Kelly piped in.

"Yes, the girl's got it!" Sam clapped. "Anyway, I'm off. Look forward to more abuse next time."

"I thought there was a funny smell in here."

"That joke is almost as old as you, Mark!"

"Night, mate."

"Night, you two lovebirds."

Kelly shot a questioning look at Mark as if Sam had meant something by it.

She laughed as Mark blew her a kiss. "Can't we talk about you while you're out?"

"Only if it's good." She smiled.

"Always my darling, always."

"That's officially bucket-worthy," Sam said, heading for the front door. "See you both anon."

Mark wrapped an arm around Kelly. "Night mate. Drive safely."

"Always," Sam grinned as he waved goodbye, then walked back to his car, his mind on the farm and what... who, lay behind its rusty iron gates.

ooOoo

Chapter 33 – Walkabout Farm

Sam slowed down the Golf as it approached the farm's left-hand side. The road was eerily quiet for just after ten-thirty so it didn't matter that the car was half on the driveway and half on the road. Sam leant over the passenger seat to peer behind the gates. In the dark, he could just about make out a name, 'Walkabout Farm'. That sounded more Australian than Italian. He remembered a scene from Crocodile Dundee where Paul Hogan says something about going for a walkabout or was he talking about someone else on a walkabout. Sam couldn't remember but it didn't matter.

He saw a light go on in an upstairs room and a figure walk by. He couldn't see the face but it definitely looked male, thick-set. Sam wondered whether it might be Mr Fellini or perhaps another member of the criminal fraternity that was living and thriving in the Northamptonshire countryside. In such a remote location they could have been up to anything and who would know? Sam had read many sting operations reported in The Echo where innocent enough looking houses, often terraced ones, were dens of iniquity producing various illegal substances. He'd tried a little dope at college, and didn't know many people who hadn't, but didn't do anything like that now; he was a respectable member of the Kemsley community. That was a fool's game, he knew, and he'd rather play the only kind of games that came with a remote control, mouse or joystick.

The upstairs light went off again and the figure disappeared. In the dark Sam couldn't see much. He'd have to come back in the daylight and look for any other entrances. He couldn't park here to do the hit so it would need to be better planned if his first project was going to be a success. He headed home, thinking of ways of happening to walk past the farm in the dark. He'd need a dog. Who did he know with a dog? His parent's neighbour had a boxer called Rocky but what excuse could he come up with borrow the dog? He couldn't think of anything feasible enough to drive the twenty-five miles to Market Harborough, get Rocky, have him for at least an hour or two then drive him back. So, he needed someone nearer home. The only dog owner he'd ever chatted to was old Mrs Ellison and he didn't imagine she'd part with him for a second, let alone a couple of hours. This would need some thinking about.

The hallway was cool when he got home. The heating would have been off for at least an hour and being a 1930s house with wooden floors, the warmth escaped quite quickly. Sam kept his jacket on while he filled a hot water bottle. Without the body heat of another person sharing his bed or a dog lying on top of the duvet, he'd have to make do with a red rubberised substitute. He envied Mark. Despite all the ribbing Sam gave him, he was lucky to have Kelly. They made a good pair. Although Sam liked his independence, it was at times like this that he missed his old girlfriend. Michelle was a fiery Taurean and bullish at times but she had been great company at night. Not a reason to stay with someone though, and although he'd tried to ignore the cracks in their relationship, she'd been the one brave enough to leave. His thoughts then turned to Emma and Libby. He'd not handled the situation well ("an understatement, Sam") and didn't know whether he'd end up with either of them but would have his chance to speak to Libby in the morning. Whether she'd be any more reasonable than Emma remained to be seen but he'd try at least.

With little more that could be done about the farm, Sam slept like a baby. A baby with a dog for company.

ooOoo

Chapter 34 – Another Ice Maiden

Sam got up early determined to get to the rifle range before his slot and chat to Libby. He imagined she'd have snatches of time between customers so he wanted to make the most of it. NTSC was the opposite direction to the farm so he wouldn't have a chance to swing by there, and he'd not managed to get a dog yet so wouldn't have a reason to 'walk' past. He had less than thirty-six hours; he couldn't wing it. Not feeling confident enough to go unprepared, Mrs Ellison was the only option.

With an hour left before he had to set off to Northampton, he made some toast and a cup of tea and logged into his computer. He revisited Google's map page for the farm's postcode and clicked on the '+' symbol until they had the farm in better detail. Then a 'light bulb' moment...

"Ding! Google Earth. Why didn't I think of that before? It'll show me the farm in full 3D colour."

Clicking on the Google Earth option the screen immediately changed to an aerial view in colour, and in 3D. Exactly as Sam had expected. Wanted. He printed off the page but decided he'd still need to check the place out for real, to borrow a dog if he could. He could pretend he was a vaccine salesman or something but that would mean meeting them face-to-face and he wouldn't have the bottle for that. Not yet anyway.

Sam left the house early allowing for any traffic he might encounter on the notorious A43. Thankfully there were no lorries, JCBs or tractors so arrived in plenty of time. He liked how that felt and made a mental note to do it more often. He was therefore on a 'high' when he opened the front door into the club. His heart sank as he saw Adam behind the counter. He was talking to a young female customer and was his usual smarmy self which made Sam cringe, although she seemed to be lapping it up. He waited his turn, dying to ask where Libby was when she walked out from a door behind reception which Sam guessed led to an office.

"Hi Libby. Have you got a minute?"

"Not really."

Another ice maiden. Sam thought.

"It's okay, Libby," Adam butted in, "take all the time you need."

Libby shot Adam a 'gee, thanks' look and pointed to a small table with two chairs in the corner of reception by a water cooler, which Sam imagined freezing when she approached it.

"Go on then," Libby said when they'd sat down.

"I'm sorry about the other night."

"So you should be, playing Emma and I off against each other."

"Who won?" Sam said, immediately regretting it.

"You certainly didn't...Josh, Sam, whatever your name is."

"I explained that whole mix up to Emma."

"I know, she told me. Some crap about your friend breaking his leg."

"He has... in five places... hurts like hell apparently... plaster up to his shin... feels sorry for himself." *I should win an Oscar for this*, Sam thought.

"If you say so."

"He's accident prone, used the wrong type of ladder putting up a security light. He didn't want the course to go to waste so said I should go."

"And here you are. So, what are your plans for Emma and I then? Do we fight for you?"

"If you'd like to." Sam laughed but soon stopped when he saw the look on Libby's face hadn't changed.

Adam came over to the table and hovered for a moment. "Sorry to interrupt, Josh, but your lesson is due to start in a minute."

"He's not—"

"Thanks very much, Adam. I'll be right with you," Sam blurted.

Adam left them to it and returned behind the desk and to a phone that was ringing.

"Libby. I'm sorry for all this but I really like you and would like to at least be friends. I tried to talk to Emma yesterday but she wasn't keen on speaking to me. I'll pop and see her after the lesson. I'd like to be friends with her too. Is that possible?"

"I can't speak for her but it's okay, I suppose, with me. I liked you too, Josh… Sam, and I'm disappointed but I can't tread on Emma's toes and she agreed to do the same. Of course she's going to see more of you than me."

"Because…?"

"Because you live nearer and once the course is over here you'd probably not come back."

"I don't know. I like it here. You have regular members, don't you? Who come over for practice. Aren't there events listed on your website that everyone can go to?"

"There are. It's just that I thought movies would usually be more popular. I suppose you're right."

"It has been known."

Libby laughed and Sam felt they'd gone some way to patching things up. So the outcome wasn't what he'd wanted but get involved with two women, especially friends, and there are bound to be consequences.

Sam's third lesson went even better than the previous two. Adam seemed suitably impressed with the speed at which he'd picked everything up. Sam asked for more details of the types of guns he could hire. Adam seemed to be in his element, stripping down the ten pistols and rifles that were available before rebuilding them, then watching while his protégée did the same… to perfection.

"You're a quick learner, Sam. You could be a professional."

Sam flushed and stuttered, "Err…"

"I mean a trainer or perhaps take it more seriously, enter competitions."

"You had me going for a minute there," Sam said half-jokingly.

"You're not too old for the Olympics, you know."

"You can do shooting in the Olympics? I thought it was only archery?"

"Oh, no. There's rifle and pistol shooting. Not such a popular sport with viewers so it doesn't get much airtime. Bit like Octopush."

"Octo… What's that?"

"Underwater hockey. My friend Martin plays it. Does it all over the world. Been to Tasmania and South Africa this year. He lives in Switzerland and it's taken seriously there. Quite a dangerous sport by all accounts, busted ribs and he often gets kicked in the…"

"I think I'll stick to this, thanks. Not a great swimmer so prefer dry land."

ooOoo

Chapter 35 – Making Amends

Having used the last two pieces of bread for his toast that morning, Sam headed for the Co-op on Singleton Parade on the way home to buy another loaf and some milk. He was sure he was drinking too much tea but as he didn't like coffee or tap water, tea wasn't exactly an indulgence. Parking in the only free space, outside Pizza di Verona, he saw Mr and Mrs de Marco behind the counter trying to fulfil all the lunch orders before the customers went back to work.

"Maybe," Sam said to himself, "if I can't work with live animals, I could work with dead ones." He shuddered and imagined what his mum, a staunch vegetarian, would say to that.

As he walked past Prime Time, he looked straight ahead but strained his eyes to one side to see if Emma was in the shop. He spotted a couple of customers browsing the shelves but no staff. The old man was probably out the back counting their money. If Sam was lucky, Emma would be next door buying the milk they always seem to run out of. He knew that scenario well.

He did a quick reckie of the Co-op as soon as he walked in the door but couldn't see her. He grabbed a basket, added a Guardian (he was hooked on their G2 crossword) and loaf of bread before heading for the chilled cabinets at the back of the shop. He was just approaching the milk and cheese section when Emma appeared from the 'Employees Only' door.

"We must stop meeting like this." He grinned. "Do you work here now?"

Emma rolled her eyes and tutted, "No, my mum does."

Still the ice maiden treatment then. "I've just seen Libby at the rifle range."

"That's nice for you. How was she?"

"Yeah, good. She seemed happy with just being friends."

"Is that what you want?" Emma said, her sad look returning.

"Is there an alternative? For you, I mean."

"I don't know. I guess we'll have to wait and see."

A light at the end of the tunnel.

"I have to get back to work. Just popped in to give my mum a message."

"And how is she?" Sam was now getting desperate to keep the conversation going.

"Fine, thanks."

"Great!" Sam tried to be cheerful. "I'll let you get back to work. I'll be there in a minute actually, I fancy some Arnie action."

"Great." Emma seemed less than enthusiastic but then, as if cutting him some slack, said, "See you in a minute then."

He smiled. "Sure. See you in a minute."

With his bag of shopping stowed in the boot of his car, Sam pushed open the movie rental shop door. He nodded at Emma standing behind the counter, who nodded back. It made a refreshing change to be on good terms and he recalled the chink of light she'd offered a few minutes earlier. Heading for the action section, he looked for films with Arnold Schwarzenegger in them. Anything would have done but he settled for Eraser and True Lies rather than Kindergarten Cop and Last Action Hero. He wasn't a fan of kids movies and although he preferred KC he wanted to stick to shoot 'em up.

Emma was pleasant to him while she checked out the movies and said she hoped he enjoyed them. He'd actually seen them so many times before that he knew the plots inside and out, and could recite some of the lines by heart. They might just help to keep him in the right frame of mind; a mind that would probably now view them differently.

ooOoo

Chapter 36 – A Partner in Crime

As he turned the corner from Northampton Road into Greath Close, he spotted an ambulance outside Mrs Ellison's house and went over to investigate. He walked up to one of the paramedics who was standing by the driver's door.

"Hello. I live a few doors down. Is Mrs Ellison alright?"

"No sir, she's had a fall, I'm afraid. She'll be out of action for a few days. She's worried about her dog. There's no one to look after the little fellow."

Sam's face lit up.

"I don't mind. He knows me and we get on well. I'm not working at the moment so I could give him plenty of walks. Will you ask her if it's alright?"

"You can speak to her. She's conscious, just a little bruised and shaken."

"Sure".

Sam headed over into the back of the ambulance where Mrs Ellison was lying on a stretcher.

"Hello, Mrs Ellison. Do you remember me? Sam from a few doors down."

"Hello, dear. I'm afraid I've been a bit careless. I wasn't looking where I was going and took a bit of a tumble."

"I just wondered if you'd like me to look after Hamish. The paramedic said you didn't have anyone else and were getting quite agitated."

The old lady beamed despite her obvious pain. "Would you? That would be lovely. One of the men said I could ring a pet sitting service or dog walker but they don't know Hamish and he would worry about me. But he knows you. Would you do that for me?"

"It's not a problem, Mrs Ellison."

"Thank you, Sam. That's ever so kind of you. The front door is open. There's some dog food in the pantry, just help yourself. Bags and lead in the hallway. There should be plenty of everything… and there's a spare key in the jar above the kettle."

"Jar above the kettle. Don't worry, Mrs Ellison. Hamish will be fine with me. You just get better and I'll drop him over to you when you get back."

"Thank you so much, Sam. Where is he?"

Sam went into the house, calling out Hamish's name. Sam heard a bark and headed for the lounge where Hamish was still sitting in his basket, not at the least concerned that his 'mother' had disappeared.

"Hi, Hamish. Let's go see your mum."

Hamish barked again and followed Sam out of the house. Hamish wasn't allowed in the ambulance but could see Mrs Ellison who reassured him that she wouldn't be long.

"You take care, Mrs Ellison, and we'll see you soon. I'm at number five so just pop by when you come home." Sam turned to the paramedics. "Will she come back in an ambulance or…"

"Oh yes, sir. Don't worry about that. Someone will bring her home."

Sam thanked them for taking care of her. Although she was only a neighbour she'd always been pleasant to him and unknowingly, now helped him with a problem he hadn't known how to overcome.

Hamish and his new carer watched the ambulance leave. Sam gathered up everything he thought he'd need, got the key from the jar and returned to his house, having ensured that the old lady's was secure.

Hamish trotted along by Sam's side and settled quickly into his basket in the lounge of number five. Mrs Ellison didn't have a car so Sam hoped Hamish travelled well in his as he had plans for him over the next couple of days but then he'd probably have more walks, so shouldn't complain.

With Hamish fed and watered, Sam stared at the Google earth map, working out area of the land adjoining the farm. He decided there was no time like the present to head back there. He found a lane a few hundred yards away where he could discreetly park his car and could walk the dog while checking out the area on foot.

"Shall we go in the car, Hamish?"

He'd only said the word 'shall' and Hamish's ears pricked up. With 'we go' he jumped up Sam's calves then with 'car' he went loopy, running around in circles as if trying to catch his tail. He went over to his basket, picked up his lead and brought it over to Sam who took it from the dog's mouth.

"Good boy!" Sam clapped. "That'll be a 'yes' then."

With Hamish restrained, in the absence of a proper harness, by the lead wrapped through one of the rear seatbelts, Sam set off for the A5 towards Towcester. The dog was in his element looking out the window and making a line of drool from his wet nose a few inches from the bottom of the glass as he wobbled with the motion of the car.

I hope he's not going to be sick, Sam thought as the Golf had cream interior fabric, not conducive to vomit or muddy paws. Still, he'd have to put up with the latter if they were going for a walk in the countryside. He made a mental note to check to see if there was anything in the boot that he might be able to use to cover the back seat then concentrated on the journey. He'd have a last good look at the printed map before leaving the car, to memorise the entrances to the farm's land and any outbuildings there might be. The note he'd received didn't say where V Fellini was going to be at eleven sharp so he'd have to work out where the best place might be to hide. If Signor Fellini was worth his salt he'd have bodyguards so Sam only had one chance to get it right. Stuff this up and Josh Bradley would be history. Stuff it up really badly and so could Sam Simpson!

ooOoo

Chapter 37 – The Trial Run

Twenty minutes later, Sam drove past the farm, took the next right into Orchard Lane, an unmade up lane, and pulled into a wider part of the road, some way down. It was daylight for at least another couple of hours so there shouldn't have been a problem with him leaving the car there, and there was still enough room for two cars to get by. He unbuckled Hamish who leapt out and followed him up the lane. It was a relief to have such an obedient dog. He'd not had terriers before and had grown up with Border Collies who had amazed him with their intelligence and loyalty and of what he'd seen from Hamish so far, they would have had some stiff competition.

Only one vehicle, a generic white van, passed them on the ten-minute walk up to the main road and Sam thought such a secluded area could only be a good thing for his 'operation'. He'd spotted a small gate leading to what he presumed was the back of the farm estate. He made a note in a small notebook in his pocket to check this out as an entry point on the way back to the car. The front entrance too obvious, the side would probably be the best vantage point as it was too small for a vehicle, but he'd reserve judgement until he checked out all the options.

Their progress was slow as Hamish liked to stop, sniff and wee every few yards but Sam was happy to plod along as it gave him the perfect cover to scrutinise the surroundings. Even though it wouldn't get dark for a while Sam was grateful that Hamish was a Westie as he would be seen from a longer distance than Sam in his dark navy zipped fleece and blue stonewashed jeans. His black clothes were slumped over the chair in his bedroom ready to be worn, together with a pair of trainers which were dark grey rather than black, but were the most comfortable pair he had and would serve him well in a quick getaway.

In the quiet of the deserted road, Sam heard his stomach rumble. In the excitement of his plans, he'd forgotten to eat anything since breakfast but would get something when he got home… if he felt like it. He was also getting back the excited but nervous feeling but couldn't have the rumblings give away his presence the next evening. If he had a late lunch that should do. He was rambling again.

"Rumbling, rambling… That will never do, will it, Hamish?"

The dog looked at Sam, wagged its tail, then continued sniffing.

When they reached the farm, Hamish went mad, barking at something behind the gate. Sam couldn't see anything but decided to walk on just in case someone came out to investigate them. He was dying to know who the figure at the window the previous night had been, but couldn't run the risk of being seen.

As they continued, Hamish quietened down and the walk brought back old memories. Sam wanted a dog of his own. Whatever had been behind the gate at the farm had spooked Hamish and it was going to be interesting to see if the same thing happened on the return journey.

Finally the pair returned to the farm. Sure enough, as they approached the gate, Hamish's head went down and his tail stopped wagging. He started growling but then stopped and was back to his normal self when they got to the gate.

"You're a funny dog," Sam whispered. "What do you make of all this then?" Hamish wagged his tail again, although not as enthusiastically as before. *You're one smart cookie,* Sam thought, *a definite contender for Border Collie status.*

Sam stopped at the gate for as long as he could and was grateful that Hamish was now more interested in the grass verge than anything on the property. Having covered the left-hand side and front of the land from his walk up to the house, he'd hoped to find another lane or pathway adjacent to the right-hand side of the house but there had been nothing but road. He hadn't remembered ever seeing one on his drive from the A5 to Duncote but then he'd never noticed the farm before. So, his interest now turned to the house. It had certainly seen better days. He guessed it as late nineteenth century but wasn't very good at guestimating. A light flickered on in a very small window to the right of the front door and this freaked Sam out more than the upstairs one the night before.

Retrieving the map from his pocket, and using a trick from the previous day, he stood looking at the road with the house on his left but strained his eyes towards the house so he could see the land to the right-hand side of it. There didn't seem to be much there; a gravelled parking area, no cars, some unkempt grass and a greenhouse with several panes broken. Like a normal residence really.

Suddenly the lead jerked as Hamish pulled towards the gate and growled again. Sam heard raised voices from within the house and a door slam. At least he thought it was a door slam. He could have been paranoid and thought it was a gunshot but that would have made him redundant, for the second time in as many months. He couldn't make out any of the words but there were two male voices and needless to say, they didn't seem happy.

"Right, Hamish, I think we'd better go. It's getting dark and I'm hungry." Sam wondered why people always spoke in a higher voice to animals as if they were children.

The little dog, happy to oblige, trotted by Sam's side, investigating the verge with renewed excitement. The walk back to the car seemed quicker, and once Hamish was secure, Sam decided to keep driving down the lane to see if he could get behind the farmhouse and glean any more information from the surroundings. He would be as prepared as he could, if it killed him. *Maybe I should rephrase that*, he thought.

As he drove, the white van that had passed them earlier, came hurtling towards them. The road had narrowed by this stage but it didn't seem to bother the driver with the wing mirrors missing by millimetres. Sam swore and looked at the van as it hurtled up the lane. There were no distinguishing features with a random '05' plate giving away its age, so nothing that Sam could remember it by should he ever see it again. The lane ended shortly after the parking place with two driveways into two houses. They both looked very well kept, in stark contrast to the farm. With no other pathways visible, Sam headed home.

ooOoo

Chapter 38 – Meeting Heather

The big day dawned and Sam woke up early. He'd hardly slept. How could he when he knew what was going to happen in… He looked at the clock… just over seventeen hours. He rolled over and almost screamed. There on the pillow next to him was a face. A certain white Westie's face.

"Hamish!"

Although a fan of dogs, Sam didn't fancy going anywhere near the pillow the little dog had been sleeping, and most probably drooling, on.

"I've got things to do. I'll deal with you later."

Hamish looked so sorry that Sam felt guilty but what the dog could get away with in his own house, he certainly wouldn't here. There would be rules.

"You hear that, Hamish? Rules. Come on, let's get some breakfast."

'Breakfast' seemed to be another word the dog recognised so he barked, leapt off the bed and raced downstairs, all before Sam had got his slippers and dressing gown on.

"Wait for me!"

Sam made the usual toast and cup of tea, having emptied half a 'special choice' salmon and tuna pouch into Hamish's ceramic bowl. Sam smiled as he watched the little tail wagging furiously as every morsel was devoured. He'd enjoy having this new houseguest and hoped Mrs Ellison didn't return too quickly, but then felt guilty for wishing her ill.

"You need to toughen up, Sam. Get a backbone. In just a few hours you're going to bump someone off in true Arnie style… well, less muscles but… and you're concerned about a little old biddy who lives a few doors away who you've probably only spoken half a dozen words to. You're as weak as your tea. You need to start drinking strong black coffee. It'll make a man of you."

Hamish, by this time, had finished his breakfast and was looking up at Sam, as if he were the target of the monologue.

"Would you like some milk?"

Hamish barked.

"Some pizza?"

Hamish barked.

"Some cow dung?"

Hamish barked.

"You'd eat anything, wouldn't you?"

Hamish barked again, his tail still wagging furiously throughout the whole conversation. Sam tipped the remaining droplets of the milk bottle into the beige paw print bowl and Hamish imitated Lewis Hamilton's winning speeds at lapping up the milk. What little there had been now seemed to appear on the hairs on Hamish's chin to the point where he resembled a rather short Santa. All he needed now was the red and white coat, and knowing Mrs Ellison, she probably already had one.

"Do you have a Santa coat, Hamish?"

Hamish wagged his tail again.

"Does it keep you warm?"

The tail action increased.

"Do you want to go for a walk?"

Hamish disappeared into the lounge and brought through his lead, dropping it by Sam's feet.

"Sweet! Let me just have my toast and we'll go, okay?"

Hamish barked then lay on the floor, wagging his tail, looking up at Sam who wolfed down his breakfast and grabbed the lead. His navy trainers were sitting under the radiator in the hall, still warm, his fleece completing the outfit. Sam hadn't collected Hamish's jacket with all his other things but he seemed perfectly happy without it. Sam reckoned him wearing it was more Mrs Ellison's choice than his.

Being a Saturday seven a.m. there was little sign of life; a black BMW was heading out of the close as Sam pulled his door shut. He'd patted his coat pocket to make sure he had his keys before closing the door. He'd locked himself out once before and had to get the spare from the Princes next door and didn't think they'd appreciate it if he had to ask them this early.

Given that Sam wasn't in a hurry, he'd selected an expanding lead and Hamish was already at the length of it by the time Sam had walked down the end of the path. The dog had clearly smelled the plant life around the close so many times before and it no longer held any interest to him. Instinctively, Hamish turned left at the end of the road and headed towards the park. Despite being a village, there weren't many other places of greenery nearby, just a handful of roads and the parade of shops. Either ends of the main road then led into fields, most if not all were private property or virtually inaccessible due to barbed wire to keep the various livestock in. That was another problem with terriers, Sam found out; they would go mad at almost any animal other than dogs, although Sam had known a few over the years that hadn't been too friendly in that direction either… or "overly excitable" as some owners had put it.

The park was almost as quiet. Checking around for distractions, Sam let Hamish off his lead and instead of bolting as Sam imagined he'd do, the dog trotted along by his side. Sam supposed that, like the Greath Close verges, Hamish had seen, and smelled, the area so often before that it was almost too much effort to bother with them.

A tall, thin lady in her fifties approached Sam with a tall, thin Saluki by her side. It was all too weird for Sam as not only did they both have white wispy hair but they also wore the same colour jackets. Sam couldn't help but burst out laughing. The woman stopped, scowled at Sam, put her nose up at Hamish, who by this time had grubby white hair rather than the pristine he'd started with that morning.

"Toffee-nosed wrinkly," Sam said to Hamish, the woman not quite out of earshot. "We don't associate with the likes of her, do we, boy?"

Hamish looked up at his temporary master and, almost smiling, gave a hearty bark. The two boys were having such a good time that Sam decided to carry on past the park and into one of the fields marked 'public footpath'. He spotted some cows so put Hamish back on the lead.

Hamish stopped to sniff a particularly fragrant patch of grass so Sam walked on… and carried on walking until the lead ran out. Sam turned and noticed Hamish eating something. Sam hoped it was some chips or bit of a kebab rather than chicken bones, as he didn't fancy a trip to the vet when it got stuck in his system. So, he headed back, pulling at the lead. Hamish, however, was having none of it. When Sam reached him, he looked down at a not-so-fragrant half-eaten heap and his face screwed up.

"My God, you **do** eat cow dung! That's seriously disgusting, dog."

Hamish just stared back at him, barking and wagging his tail, his 'beard' now a darker shade of brown than his underbelly.

When Sam realised the path was going to lead through endless fields of cows and therefore an endless supply of dung, he returned to the park, taking care to keep the lead as short as possible past the half-eaten pat so Hamish wasn't tempted by seconds.

On re-entering the park, Sam unhooked the lead from Hamish's collar and watched him run off in the direction of a park bench. The Saluki and her owner long gone, had been replaced by a young couple and their Border Collie and a teenage girl with a Westie, slightly bigger and scruffier than Hamish… him on a puddle-avoiding, cow-pat-sidestepping good day. Hamish headed straight for his counterpart, tails wagging furiously as the dogs sniffed each other, spinning around in a 'yin and yang' pattern.

"Morning," Sam greeted the Westie's owner.

"Hiya. Is that Hamish?"

"It is."

"Where's Mrs Ellison. Is she alright?"

"She had a fall at home actually but I think she's okay. Bit of a shock apart from anything. I live a few doors down so I offered to take him in."

"Oh dear. As long as she's going to be all right. This is Heather. Hamish's sister."

"Sweet. I didn't know he had a sister. How old are they?"

"They'll be six at Christmas. Heather's on a diet so she's grumpy. We've had to cut down on her treats, vet's orders, so I'm trying to make it up to her by taking her on more walks, which will also help with her fat."

"Ah, she's not fat," Sam lied.

"Under all that hair is a real porker of a belly. You should see it when she's on her back."

That wasn't a sight Sam particularly relished but he could certainly see who was in charge by the toing and froing the two dogs were doing. It looked as if they were about to have a serious falling out but they ran off to a large section of grass and chased each other round until Heather tired. Hamish, claiming victory, walked back to Sam, head held high.

"Come on, boy, we've got things to do. It was very nice meeting you…"

"Rebecca. Becky."

"Good to meet you, Becky," Sam bent forward, "and you, Heather."

The little dog, in between panting, barked at exactly the same pitch.

"Yes, you're Hamish's sister alright."

Becky said goodbye, called her dog to follow her and they headed off in the direction of the fields. Sam and Hamish went in the opposite direction and out of the park, smiling at the couple and Border Collie as they left.

ooOoo

Chapter 39 – The Smallest Detail

Back in the warmth of Sam's house, Hamish headed straight for his basket and fell asleep. It was still only eight-thirty so Sam decided to pop up the shops and buy a national paper, some dog treats and maybe something naughty for himself. He checked in on Hamish who was asleep so left him to it, closing the door quietly so as not to wake him up. *It's like having a baby*, Sam thought and smiled, *only you don't get social services on your back when you nip out to buy a paper… or get the CSA, or whatever it's called now, involved when you divorce.*

The Co-op was getting busy. It was too early for Emma to be at work so Sam didn't bother looking for her. He recognised an elderly couple and apart from the staff and a man carrying a motorbike helmet, Sam was the only other customer. He took a basket from the rack and headed to the newspaper stand. He usually bought the Mirror but decided to go with a Guardian and the local Echo which he'd been surprised to see as he thought it was usually a lunch-time paper but then he rarely went shopping before mid-day. It actually made a change to be out and about early, seeing a different way of life.

Walking down the first aisle towards the bread, fruit and vegetables, he decided he was okay for bread but could do with eating more healthily so took a selection of fresh produce and headed towards the dried food aisle. Sam had taken enough dog food to last a week or so but there hadn't been any treats in Mrs Ellison's cupboard so picked a selection for small dogs. He felt sure that whatever he presented Hamish with would be greeted with a wagging tail and perhaps if it was particularly tasty, a bark. He decided against getting anything naughty as it would rather defeat the object of the fruit and veg.

Sam paid for his shopping and said "Good morning" to Mr Shah who was behind the cashier, a young girl with a nose stud and lip ring, filling up the cigarette racks behind the counter. Sam didn't ever remember seeing a Mrs Shah but guessed that, if there was one, she spent her time behind the scenes or at home... perhaps looking after some mini-Shahs.

The walk home was pleasant. The sun was out and surprisingly warm for late October. The forecast on that morning's radio had been for showers but there was little sign of clouds and Sam even unzipped his fleece to cool down.

As he approached the house, he remembered that today was going to be no ordinary day, and the normality of the shopping and chatting to Mr Shah were soon forgotten. Hamish, as predicted, loved his treat and skipped back to his bed to munch his way through a rawhide shoe, pulling at the laces before slowly devouring the rest. Sam smiled as he watched the little fellow eat. He would definitely get a dog when the time was right. A little thing like Hamish would be ideal. His companion in the absence of a girlfriend. Then when he had one, the three of them would make a great family. Sam wanted children at some stage but that could wait, he was in no rush.

He glanced down at his watch and was horrified. It was already nearly eleven. How could the morning have gone so quickly? In ten hours he'd be fishing around in the ceiling of The Nutcracker for a gun then two hours later use it, then be back in the Nutcracker tomorrow to put it back. Sunday would be tricky. There'd be families with dads and their sons traipsing backwards and forwards to the loo all day so he'd have to see if there was a lock on the main door when he collected the gun. He doubted he'd be so lucky but it was worth checking. If he was going to be taken seriously then he'd have to have everything covered.

With Hamish happily ensconced, Sam headed up to the 'planning room' to go over the details of the evening. Final searching on the internet for the intended victim, Sam again hit brick walls. He decided Fellini probably wasn't the man's real name anyway so abandoned that trail. He opened up a blank Word document and made a timed plan with mileage and equipment needed. He had everything other than the gun. He'd have to walk Hamish again before he left. Maybe head for the shops to see if he could speak to Emma, no doubt she'd want to chat to Hamish at the very least. Then he could check out the Nutcracker. Not go in, but he could get an idea of how busy it was from the cars in the car park. Parking outside the shops was too limited for anyone there to be a pub customer and as the Co-op and Prime Time didn't shut until late, that was a fairly safe bet.

Sam sighed. The situation with Emma and Libby would probably have to wait a day or two. He might feel differently after tonight. Of course he would. How stupid was that? Even killing ants with a magnifying glass after school was enjoyable at the time but he'd feel sick afterwards. How exactly was he going to feel tonight? Had the reality of it sunk in? Would he be able to go through with it? What if he bottled out? What if he got caught? He shouldn't think like this. It was a job. He had to think he was the good guy and VF was the bad guy and he was doing the world a favour.

With everything planned down to the smallest detail, Sam put all the information to one side of his desk and went downstairs to get a drink. He felt like something stronger than tea but he needed a clear head. But then he didn't feel like tea either. He needed something to wake him up. Coke would do the job. He grabbed a cold can from the fridge and poured it into a glass, cursing as the froth overflowed the top.

"Get a grip, Sam. Don't lose your head." He burst out laughing as it was the head of Coke that was being lost. He shivered but was boiling. The mixture of nervousness and adrenaline was kicking in.

He had eight hours left until Nutcracker time so decided to squeeze in an extra walk, just a couple of blocks. It was too early to go up to the shops and if he went twice and saw Emma both times she'd think he was stalking her.

"You can't make someone love you; all you can do is stalk them until they give in." Now where had he heard that before? He couldn't remember who'd said it, but it made him laugh.

"Right," he said out loud, and Hamish came running into the kitchen.

"Does that mean something to you, boy?"

The dog wagged its tail furiously. Sam reckoned that saying anything in the right kind of voice would mean something, as the earlier reference to cow dung had proven.

That reminded Sam he'd not eaten anything since breakfast but all of a sudden wasn't hungry.

ooOoo

Chapter 40 – A Popular Choice

The shops were busy, which surprised Sam as he thought that people would have gone shopping in the towns like Northampton, Towcester or even Milton Keynes. Hamish wasn't complaining though as he received lots of attention from people who recognised him, prompting an explanation from Sam, and promised he would pass on their best wishes.

With no groceries needed, he went straight past the Co-op and headed for Prime Time. The shop was packed but Emma only had a queue of a couple of people so he picked a case at random and joined it, waiting his turn.

"Hello, Sam. It is Sam today, isn't it?"

He laughed. "Yes, it's Sam today."

"We're not supposed to let dogs in here... so I'm afraid you'll have to stay outside. But Hamish, you're welcome."

Sam laughed again, this time sarcastically, clutching his sides as if they were splitting. "You know Hamish?"

"I'd recognise him anywhere. Blue collar Hamish, pink collar Heather. Are you walking him for Mrs Ellison?"

"He's staying with me actually."

"Really?"

"She had a fall but nothing serious, I'm sure. She seemed more shocked."

"You saw it happen?"

"No, I got to her house as she was being taken into the ambulance."

"That's awful. Did she go to Northampton?"

"I think so. The General, is it?"

"Yes, near the town centre. I'll pop over tomorrow."

"I'm sure she'd love to see you. Would probably be bored rigid. I could take you tomorrow if you like." *Would be something to think about while I'm trying not to think about 'you know what,'* he thought.

"Er, that might be nice."

A man behind Sam coughed impatiently, obviously in a hurry to go home and watch the movie tucked under his left arm.

"Much as I'm bowled over by your enthusiasm, I shall leave you to it. Shall I pick you up from your house or..."

"Here is fine. Say midday… or is that too early for you? Are you a lie in kind of guy? It's just that I don't know what time visiting hours are going to be and I have to be back…"

"No, midday is fine. Not too early, not too late."

The cougher coughed once more.

"Okay pal!" Emma shouted. "I'll be right with you." She then imitated an air stewardess smile and wound up her conversation with Sam.

"Sorry about that." Emma then beckoned Sam to come nearer. She whispered, "He's a regular. If you know what I mean."

Sam didn't have a clue what she meant but winked and smiled anyway. "I'll see you tomorrow. Here at twelve. Look forward to it."

"Indeed. You can't beat the smell of disinfectant on a first date."

"First date?"

"Our real first date didn't exactly go to plan, Sam, did it?"

"Not exactly, Emma."

The man, a white haired chap in his fifties, cleared his throat, presumably figuring it was safer than coughing. This time Sam turned and shot him an icy glare. "Okay, well, I'm going now. Lovely to see you again, Emma. See you tomorrow."

"Bye, Sam. Oh, Sam."

"Yes," Sam said, turning back round.

"The DVD?" She nodded at the case.

"Oh, yeah," he said, handing it over.

"How to raise chickens," she read. "Embracing the country life then, Sam."

He blushed. "You know."

"Yes, I know. Picked at random. I saw you. Don't worry, I'll put it back."

"Thanks. Erm…"

"Bye, Hamish," Emma said looking down at the dog.

Hamish woofed a 'goodbye' and trotted out with Sam by his side. Sam smiled as he heard Emma serving the man saying, just a little too loudly, "'Tina and Jane go wild' a popular choice, sir."

ooOoo

330

Chapter 41 – Head or Heart

It was nearly two o'clock by the time Sam had got home. They'd met up with Becky and Heather again and had chatted small talk while brother and sister wagged and sniffed. Sam stared at the clock, then the kettle, then the clock again. His stomach was telling him he'd better eat but he still wasn't fussed, so decided on a small microwaved lasagne.

He'd forgotten how good real food tasted. Okay, so it didn't count as real food in most people's books but it was as good as it got for Sam, having used up his mother's food. Hamish, however, revelled in the rest of his salmon and tuna pouch accompanied with crunchy mixer. Sam wondered, if he attached Hamish's tail to a miniature wind farm, whether it would produce enough power to run the house.

With less than four hours to go, he wondered whether he was prepared to carry out the events of the evening. Surely he'd have needed more training. He'd been doing this for what, a couple of weeks? James Bond would have had months, years probably. Even the actors who'd played James Bond would have taken longer to prepare for killing their on-screen rivals. This whole thing was just ridiculous. But then why was he so excited? Excited to run around the countryside and blow someone's head off. Actually, he'd not given that any thought. Head or heart? What's the best way to kill someone? Should it be clean and quick or messy? On-screen James would take the clean route so off-screen Josh would do the same. *If it's good enough for…*

Sam was interrupted by the phone ringing. He dropped the fork full of the lasagne into the plastic container which toppled over and hit the kitchen floor. Hamish bolted over to the spillage and lapped it up. Sam had eaten most of it so he wasn't that bothered, being more concerned with it still being too hot for him and getting to the phone before the ringing stopped.

"Hello?"

"Hello, is that Josh?"

"Er, yes."

"Hello, Josh. This is Adam from the rifle range. I'm just checking that you want your two final sessions. You've only had three and you paid for five. Not that you need them in my opinion but we don't want you wasting your money."

"You're working late, aren't you? Do people shoot on a Saturday night?"

"You'd be surprised, Josh. There always seems to be a demand."

"What slots do you have next week?"

"Monday morning or Tuesday and Thursday afternoons, any of those suit you?"

Sam thought for a moment. Libby was off Wednesdays and Thursdays so he certainly didn't want Thursday and if he went for Monday and Tuesday he'd still be reeling from the weekend. "I'll have Monday and Tuesday then please."

"Sure thing. Monday at eleven and Tuesday at three? You could catch Libby before and after lunch then."

"Er, yes, I guess I could. Er, thanks, Adam."

"My pleasure. Always happy to help, Josh."

Sam felt the conversation a bit strange, Adam weird. Maybe jealous over Libby but then Sam didn't think she cared too much for Adam. That she went for the genuine guys. *Like me? Yeah, really genuine.* She'd obviously not told Adam about Sam's double identity but Adam's tone wasn't jealousy. Sam couldn't put his finger on it but now wasn't the time to dwell. He needed to do some research. Adam seemed to be an expert but Sam couldn't call him. Google would no doubt help.

Opening Internet Explorer, Sam surfed the net. Why did they call it surfing? And how do you actually surf a net anyway? Nets have holes so you'd fall through, even on a fine mesh. Sam was digressing again, something he was good at. What he needed to be good at tonight was shooting. Adam had praised Sam's accuracy and that's something that had to be on form tonight, but Sam felt he needed more practice. He had two hours between going to the Nutcracker and the farm so no time to go to the rifle range and barely time to go to

Mark or Danny's for a cuppa let alone getting any practice in. No, he needed to get to the farm early so he'd have to go from one to the other. Check out the lay of the land in both.

In the search bar of Google's home page, he typed in 'quick death'. He didn't think it would be specific enough but it was a start. The page however, proved him wrong. There was only one link that looked promising but that turned out to be an ironic page by someone called Davy King where you die laughing. Not exactly what he was looking for. 'Shoot quick' wasn't much better and 'ways to shoot' was even worse with many photographic links. He then decided a different tactic and tried 'hitman tips' but then was given hundreds of cheating tips for the game 'Hitman', great for relaxing on a Sunday afternoon but not so useful here. He tried the Wikipedia route and put in 'hitman'. Under a 'Hitmen' heading, Arthur Gorsky leapt out at Sam, a Russian responsible for over a hundred murders in the US and Ukraine apparently. Sam got all excited thinking there must have been something he could use but the link to the Russian's name led nowhere. No, not exactly nowhere but to a page saying that there wasn't a page and would Sam like to create one? "No, thank you." He clicked on the back key and returned to the list of names. The one above looked intriguing. The actor Woody Harrelson's father Charles had, apparently, connections to organised crime but was also freelance.

"Now we're talking." Sam heard a thumping noise behind him. He swung his chair round. He'd not noticed Hamish joining him in his 'planning room' and the dog was now wagging his tail on the floorboards. "Good boy," he said, leaning over to give Hamish a pat on the head.

Sam clicked on the Charles Harrelson link and was taken to a page that someone had actually created. "Hoorah!" Charles Voyde Harrelson, Sam read, was sentenced to two life terms for the May 29, 1979, assassination of U.S. District Judge John H. Wood, Junior. Harrelson was hired by drug dealer Jamiel 'Jimmy' Chagra. Judge Wood — nicknamed 'Maximum John' because of his reputation for handing down long sentences for drug offenses — was originally scheduled to have Chagra appear before him on the day of his murder, but the trial had been delayed. It turns out that he didn't actually do it but 'took credit for it so he could score a huge payout from Chagra.'

"*This incident is mentioned in Cormac McCarthy's book No Country for Old Men. In the film of the book Charles Harrelson's son, Woody Harrelson, plays one of the contract killers.*" Sam read. "Good on you, Woody."

It also turned out that Harrelson senior was responsible for many murders so accepting responsibility for that one probably didn't make that much difference. Sam led a relatively solitary life but he couldn't imagine spending the rest of it in prison. He thought he'd rather die. However cushy prisoners' lives were, the one thing they didn't have that Sam treasured was their freedom.

"You're getting too morbid now, Sam. Chins up."

These pages still weren't helping and with a couple of hours to go before 'Nutcracker' time, he had to get organised. But was he really going to find the information he wanted on the internet? Wasn't there some policing for that kind of thing? There were sites that helped people commit suicide, there'd been plenty about that in the papers recently, but that would be simple. A gun to the head, point blank range. Unless Signor Fellini was asleep, Sam wouldn't be able to get close enough to do that. He guessed he'd just have to wing it. Providing he hit him, wasn't seen and didn't get caught then he'd just have to do his best.

Sam felt better after a shower. He didn't know what it was about standing under pumping warm water that just made him feel so much more, well, human. Cleansing on the outside and in, he suspected, although not too much on the inside tonight please. He could do without a conscience tonight. He got dressed into his blue jeans and sweater, leaving his dark clothes until the last minute. He'd have time in between the Nutcracker and the job to come home and get changed but thought it best not to. Hamish hated him going out without him as it was and he couldn't get white hairs on him unless he could help it. No, he would take his time and do the job properly.

He'd still got plenty of time before he got ready so wanting to do something normal, turned to Hamish who was, by now, fast asleep on the futon on the other side of the room, and said "walkies!" Hamish didn't need to be told twice. He was already standing by the front door by the time Sam got to the bottom of the stairs. "Lead," he said and Hamish disappeared into the lounge to his basket. Unable to find the lead, which Sam had decided to hang in the hall for ease, Hamish returned and looked up at Sam and barked. "Don't worry, boy. It's here," Sam said taking the lead off the coat hook and attaching it to Hamish's collar. "Can't be too long, lots to do. Okay." Sam barked as if he knew exactly what he was being told. 'A quick walk, yep, no problem,' his eyes said. Sam clapped and said, "Clever boy", not knowing whether he was a clever boy but figured he'd reward him all the same.

After a quick and uneventful walk around the block, Hamish settled into his basket in the lounge and went back to sleep, leaving Sam to get ready for his night out. He'd written a checklist and made sure he had everything on it. Torch, check. Black clothes, check. Map, check. Instruction card, check. Sam felt like he'd just opened a board game and was making sure that all the contents were there before playing. This was, however, going to be the most important game of his life. No toy money here. If he was successful, he would be paid in real hard cash. Not that he still knew how much that would be but somehow that didn't matter right now. He knew it was a test of some kind but pass it and... who knew where it could lead? Secret service, MI5, SAS... the world could be his oyster (although Sam was more partial to lobster).

ooOoo

Chapter 42 – Getting the Gun

Sam groaned as he pulled into The Nutcracker car park just after a quarter to nine. It was packed. He squeezed into a space near the bottle banks and had to breathe in getting out of the driver's door. The pub being this busy would mean he'd have to choose his moment carefully. He was on his own so it didn't matter how long he stayed in the gents. He'd just have to wait for a few guys to come out to have more of a chance of being alone. He'd memorised the tile he'd have to pull back and had already worked it loose during his earlier visit. Why couldn't they have chosen a tile that was above one of the cubicles? That would have been too easy. As would having a lock on the door to the gents. This was all part of the test, he supposed.

Sam left the plan pack in the glove compartment and headed into the pub. He ordered an orange juice and lemonade. He'd had plenty of tea and Coke, and didn't need any more caffeine. The orange juice would settle his stomach and the lemonade would make it last longer. It wouldn't do him any good to have too much liquid if he was going to spend any time in the car if he got to the farm too early. But then he wanted plenty of time to relax before he walked to the house. On the drive home the previous day, he'd spotted a better parking spot which was much nearer the cottage. He couldn't afford to lose any time after the event either especially if he had a gun to carry.

He found a table near the toilets. It wasn't the closest free spot but he didn't want it to be too obvious when he was missing. He was early so would stay a while and keep an eye on the comings and goings. Discreetly, of course.

Being nearly nine o'clock there weren't many families but mostly couples so it wasn't as busy as he'd thought. Sam also decided the lack of groups was a good thing. Fathers and sons in toilets took forever, whereas boyfriends would want to get back to their tables. Women could take their time, and always it seemed in pairs.

He was nearly at the end of his orange juice and lemonade when he decided to go to the gent's anyway. Apart from the fact that he needed to, the lasagne hadn't done much for padding out his stomach, he just wanted a last dummy run before getting the gun for real. He looked at his watch. A minute to nine. There wasn't a lot of point in doing a dummy run now. The gun would likely be there by now. He'd not been paying attention on who had been going in and out of the gents but the door had been opening and closing almost all night. This wouldn't be as easy as he'd hoped but then, like the odds of a fruit machine, if it had been busy there would have to be a lull. And that lull looked like it might happen now. He waited for a few seconds. He looked around the room pretending to look at the décor but concentrated on the people. They all seemed deep in conversation so it would be now or never. The Elvis Presley song of the same name came over the speakers, making a change from rap which Sam was the right age for but didn't much like. Sam hummed to the music. It was a sign.

As Sam went to push the door it swung open towards him almost hitting his face.

"Sorry, mate."

"Shit. Oh, hi, Adam. You scared me."

"Hi, Josh. You scare easily then, it's only me."

"I guess so. I didn't realise you lived around here."

"I don't. I'm here with my sister and her kids. We go out every couple of weeks. Bit of a treat for them... and me if I'm truthful."

"I thought you'd have swarms of women to go out with. A guy like you."

"Work Adam is different to social Adam. Most of my friends are female but no one special at the moment. Mostly meet men in my line of work."

"At the gun club. Yes, I suppose you would."

"At the gun club," Adam repeated, "indeed."

"Nice to see you again. Don't let me hold you up."

"Thanks. See you Tuesday then."

"Tuesday?"

"Your last but one lesson?"

"Oh, yes. Thanks. I'd... not forgotten but was on weekend mode. You know how it is." Sam laughed unconvincingly.

"Yes, I know how that goes. Although like Liz, we have weekday weekends, when it's less busy."

"Of course… and how is Libby… Liz."

"She's good actually. Can't stop talking about you. Looking forward to Tuesday apparently. She's pretending to still be angry with you over whatever it was, but she's not. She'd definitely got the hots for you, you lucky guy. But don't tell her I told you."

"Oh, wow. Er, okay. Don't worry, Adam, your secret is safe with me."

"Right then. Better get back to the clan. They were waiting to order dessert but no doubt they've gone ahead without me." Adam signalled in the general direction of the far side of the room although Sam couldn't see exactly which table his family was sitting at as he had other things on his mind.

"Thanks, Adam. Till Tuesday then."

"Yeah, goodbye, Josh."

Sam smiled and shook his head. He didn't think he'd ever get used to being called Josh. It was only pure fluke that he'd not been caught out by now. He had been if you counted Emma and Libby but he'd managed to bluff his way out of that one.

A chap behind Sam coughed and Sam turned, holding open the door. It was the same guy who had been behind him in the queue at the movie store earlier. *He must spend all his time coughing*, Sam thought as the guy walked past, not recognising Sam but nodding to say "Thanks."

Sam was now torn between returning to his seat and entering the gent's but staying in there until the man had gone. Seeing Adam had thrown Sam. He decided he'd hovered long enough so went to the bar and bought another drink returning to the table he'd used before. He finished up the first drink and started on the other. He studied the door for ages and eventually the coughing man came out, still coughing. *The poor chap must have a problem,* Sam thought but then wasted no time in going back. If anyone else was in there, he'd decided he would sit in one of the cubicles until they'd left. He checked both stalls and the coast was clear. With little time to waste, he went into the right-hand booth, shut the door and pushed the overhead panel up and to the right so it was out the way. If anyone came in now he'd have to make an excuse of fixing a flickering overhead light. Staff usually had their own toilets so he shouldn't encounter any of them. With the area exposed, and him feeling equally so, he pulled himself up into the ceiling cavity and there, a couple of tiles away was a pistol fitted with a silencer and small box of ammunition.

"Shit!" He hadn't thought of spare ammunition. Surely there were enough bullets in the gun for what he needed to do. Sam supposed they wanted to be sure, just in case he missed and needed to re-load. Sam leant along the top of the tiles, hoping they were strong enough to take his weight. He grabbed the gun, the box and get back down the hole before anyone came in. He pretended that the noise of his shoes hitting the porcelain toilet was the lid falling down but just to be sure he thumped the lid down as if by accident.

"Are you alright in there?" he heard an elderly voice ask.

"Yes, thanks, just slipped." The ceiling tile was still exposed but he'd wait until the other guy had left to put it back in place. Sam hoped he wouldn't notice. After all, who looks up when they're taking a leak? While the chap was in the other cubicle, Sam washed his hands thoroughly. Having tucked the gun into his jeans pocket and box of ammunition into his jacket pocket, which only just fitted, Sam looked like any other ordinary customer. He hummed to Elvis again then stuck his hands under the dryer. The old man flushed the chain and walked straight back into the pub, bypassing the wash basins.

"You dirty old codger," Sam said once the main door was shut. There was no need for not washing your hands however old you were.

Ensuring the zip on his jacket pocket was secure, Sam returned to the cubicle, put the gun on the shelf behind the cistern and stood back on the toilet rim to push the ceiling tile back in place. He put the gun back in his pocket and headed back out of the bar. Adam, his sister and family were nowhere to be seen when Sam re-surfaced. He hadn't realised he'd been so long but then if they had started dessert without them then they hadn't needed to stay much longer.

Sam, continuing the portrayal of an ordinary customer, walked back to his table, finished his drink without sitting back down and left the pub. There was now an empty space to the left of his car so he got in via the passenger's door and climbed over the gear stick before starting the engine and driving off. He looked down at the clock which read nearly ten pm.

"Shit! I've only got an hour. Shit!" Sam knew he had plenty of time. The journey would be twenty minutes tops but he'd wanted to get to the farmhouse earlier than this. The roads were clear, saving him some time, and he pulled into the parking spot near to the farm at just before quarter past ten. He was slightly off the road so no one would see him and he'd not noticed any other traffic as he'd approached the space. He could see the top half of the building from where he was and a feint light on in the side of the house. There were no signs of life until Sam realised that the flickering light was a television. So, there was someone at home. So was Mr Fellini going to be arriving at the house or departing? Surely Sam wasn't supposed to storm the house with all guns... or rather gun, blazing. THP Services must have some inside information as to where Fellini was going to be. It had to be simple for Sam's first job so Signor Fellini would have to be outside the house for Sam to get a clear shot. He'd originally thought about bringing Hamish so he'd have the cover of a dog walker but Hamish loved to bark and that was the last thing Sam needed so he'd left him at home, curled up in his basket, content to wait.

ooOoo

Chapter 43 – The Deed

Just before eleven, Sam got out of his car and walked towards the farmhouse. He had found a concave dip in the hedge near to the entrance; the perfect spot to crouch when Signor Fellini arrived home. After a first false start, a white van, possibly the one from a few days earlier, raced past, squealing its brakes as it turned down the same lane that Sam had parked on that day.

On the dot of eleven, Sam heard another squeal of brakes as a dark saloon car turned into the short driveway to the farmhouse. As it went past him, Sam saw the driver and although it was dark, he knew it was Fellini.

"This is it then," Sam whispered, his heart thumping so loudly in his ears that he wasn't sure if he'd spoken out loud.

The engine was still running so he had a few seconds to approach the car.

In true Sweeney fashion, Sam crouched behind the car then as the man switched off the engine and stepped out.

Sam shouted, "Hey, Fellini!"

Fellini turned to face Sam and instead of being scared, worried or any emotion Sam imagined him to be, he laughed. Naturally, this pissed Sam off. He aimed the gun at Fellini's chest, pulled the trigger, and fell backwards as Fellini fell sideways.

What Sam hadn't heard with the thumping in his ears were the footsteps of a figure on the other side of the van. The figure, Philip Henry Montgomery, a white haired man in his fifties, cleared his throat before aiming his gun at Fellini's head and pulling the trigger just as the Italian turned towards the back of the car cutting short his laugh. As this was his fifty-third hit, Montgomery had only needed one shot and smiled as the Italian thudded to the ground. Montgomery walked round the back of the house, through a gap in the hedge that Sam had missed, and back down the lane to his white van. He drove back home praying that his wife would already be asleep but looking forward to the welcome he'd get from their dog.

Sam walked back to his car, desperate to throw up but instead blew out a series of puffs of air until he felt calmer. Josh Bradley had murdered someone. It seemed easier under this alias. It wasn't Sam Simpson doing the deed but the pseudonym. Now he just had to get the gun smuggled back into the pub along with the ammunition that he hadn't needed. *Just one shot*, Sam thought, shaking his head. He **was** good. The impact of the bullet must have been powerful to floor the guy and make Sam nearly fall over.

The roads were quiet on the drive back which suited Sam just fine. He didn't want any interaction with anyone. He just wanted quiet. Wanted to think. He'd put the gun and ammunition in the glove compartment and it could stay there until he went back to the Nutcracker. Sure, he could walk to the pub but he just wanted a quick entry and exit. In, out, job done. No doubt, ex-girlfriend Michelle would have had some witty remark to make to that.

Parking up outside his house, he checked the gun and ammo were in the glove compartment before leaving the car. "As if they could seriously be anywhere else?" Sam muttered as he flicked the 'lock' button on the remote control.

He'd left the light on in the hall for Hamish more than anything, as well as the radio in the kitchen and all three of them greeted Sam when he walked through the door. He went to the kitchen, poured a large glass of Jack Daniels with two lumps of ice and headed upstairs, switching the radio and light off as he went. He'd just reached the landing when he realised Hamish would need a walk before going to bed so put the tumbler by the bed, his jacket back on and Hamish on his lead.

The streets around Greath Close were deserted. The Nutcracker was the only pub in the village. It was more of a family pub so there was never any trouble at kicking out time. That had been over an hour earlier so people would be home by now. The only life Sam and Hamish encountered was a chap walking a Saluki dog. Sam recognised the dog from the park that morning and the chap as the one with the bad cough. Recalling the woman who had originally accompanied the Saluki, Sam could understand now why the man was such a sullen chap, and why he needed the company of 'Tina' and 'Jane'.

They exchanged smiles as their paths crossed with the dogs ignoring each other.

"Good choice," Sam whispered to Hamish once the other dog had gone on. They then completed the circle of paths back into Greath Close and to the house. Sam, walking past the car, peered at the glove compartment to check it was still shut. He wasn't sure what he'd have done if it hadn't been and should have perhaps taken it with him into the house. It was too late now to worry about it. Although there was no one else in the road, he didn't want to take any risks.

Sam secured the front door, switched off all the downstairs lights and beckoned Hamish to join him upstairs.

"You can lie on the end of the bed, do you hear? No pillow action tonight, right?"

Hamish remained silent but wagged his tail in some kind of understanding. Just to prove the point, Sam tapped the end of the bed then stuck up his thumb. Hamish wagged harder. Sam pointed to the pillow and shook his right index finger from side to side and emitted a long 'no'. Hamish's tail stopped wagging and the dog put its head down.

Sam got into bed and reached for the glass. Hamish leapt on the bed but stayed in the bottom left-hand corner, as far away from Sam's torso to prove a point. Sam cheered "good boy" and Hamish's tail resumed activity.

Sam downed much of the whisky in one go then winced as the liquor seemed to weld itself to the inside of his throat. He shook his head furiously as if the action might help the Jack Daniels reach his stomach quicker.

With his brain cells shaken not stirred, the enormity of the evening's events, helped along by the scotch, slammed back into his head and he flung back the duvet and ran to the bathroom, throwing up into the toilet bowl. He coughed to clear his throat, tore a sheet of paper off the end of a new roll, wiped his mouth, then threw the paper into the bowl and flushed.

Staring at himself in the mirror, Sam shook his head, then splashed cold water on to his face.

Plodding back into the bedroom, with Hamish still in the same position, Sam got back into bed, took a deep breath, and switched out the light.

Lying awake for what seemed like hours, but was in fact forty-two minutes and fifteen seconds, he tried not to think of the events of the evening but replayed the farmhouse scene over and over. He still thought it odd that Fellini had fallen sideways when Sam had hit him in the chest. If anything he'd twist round and land right.

"It doesn't matter, Sam. The result's the same."

With that, he fell asleep.

ooOoo

Chapter 44 – A Heart Grows Fonder

After the events of the night before, Sam treated himself to a lie in and surprisingly, had slept soundly. He collected Emma as arranged outside 'Prime Time' on the dot of midday and he thought she looked stunning. In stark contrast to the dark jeans and navy 'Prime Time' sweater she wore for work, she had on a pretty floral skirt and pink button up cardigan under which she had a simple white top. Not knowing whether she'd dressed up for him or Mrs Ellison, he hoped the former and complimented her on how much the outfit suited her.

Emma then went a darker shade than that of her cardigan and chatted about how much she disliked hospitals, had only been to visit sick friends and relatives since the birth of her brother, and said she'd be very happy if she never stepped inside one until she gave birth.

Sam tried not to look too horrified but failed.

"Oh, God, no," Emma reassured him. "It's not something I've planned for a few years yet. You?"

"Much the same. When I meet the right woman."

"Plenty of time yet," Emma mumbled.

Sam realised his missed opportunity but didn't want to backtrack. "Indeed. Life's too short to worry about... yeah."

The conversation turned to work. Emma explained that she'd taken the job at 'Prime Time' to be near her mum although they lived together. She, Emma, loved movies, so getting paid to watch them seemed the idea role, not that she actually did see a whole one very often. She'd been there for more than five years and had hoped to be manager when the previous one left at Easter. Tom had been transferred from another branch and they got on really well so Emma didn't begrudge him the job but now hoped to take over when Tom retired.

"He's an ex-policeman."

"He is?" Sam felt sick again.

"I don't know why I said that. I just thought it was interesting."

"Yes." Sam's mind raced.

"He comes out with all sorts of information about criminal law and the like. Would be handy for your friend."

"What?"

"The friend you borrowed the DVDs for the other week. The one doing amateur dramatics?"

"Oh," Sam laughed. "Yes."

"Is that the real Josh? Your am dram friend."

"Er… yes, it is."

"You'll have to bring him over some time and grill Tom. I'm sure he'd be delighted to tell him whatever he wants to know. Bring back old times no doubt, over a cup of tea."

The conversation thinned as Sam and Emma approached the town centre. Sam didn't know what else to say but was grateful of the pause as he didn't drive into Northampton town centre all that often and still had the night before on his mind. He'd considered cancelling but had wanted to see Emma again, away from her work, and it would keep him busy.

"Oh, shit!"

"What?"

"Have you got any cash on you, Sam? I brought my wallet but I haven't got any change and the car park is bound to cost something, even on a Sunday."

"You don't need to use the car park. If you drive past the hospital and turn left into Billing Road, you can park along there for free. It's all businesses so no one parks there on a Sunday. Cost you an arm and a leg otherwise."

Sam smiled thinking of the anatomy analogy in relation to a hospital and shook his head at his dark side coming forth once more.

It turned out that others had the same idea and Sam had to drive quite a way down Billing Road before finding a space. They abandoned the car outside one of several solicitors offices, and made the walk towards the hospital. Although it was a cold day, it was dry so a pleasant walk and Sam was enjoying a conversation about their passion for movies.

Sam could feel himself falling for Emma and thus heightening the dilemma of **her** versus Libby. He'd known Emma for longer but she had a serious, if not tempestuous, streak that Libby didn't seem to have. But then every now and then, Emma did something like this. Sam wondered whether she had a grandmother and if she had, how lucky she'd be to have a granddaughter such as her. Maybe his dark side wasn't so dark, perhaps a lighter shade of grey when mixed with his soft side. As many times before, since replying to the advert, Sam wondered whether he was cut out to be a hitman. The previous night had been an experience; one he wasn't taking too seriously as, he decided, it can't have been real.

"Hello? Earth calling Sam."

"Sorry, Emma. Did you say something?"

"No, you'd just gone quiet and looked like you were well away. On another planet."

"Something like that."

"Anything wrong?"

"Oh, no. Just things on my mind."

"We're here. Have you brought your mobile with you?"

"In my pocket, did you want to make a call?"

"No, it's just that you'll probably have to switch it off."

They entered the building and a large blue and white sign just inside the automatic doors indicated that the Brampton Ward was near the entrance.

Sam resumed the conversation. "You know a thing or two about hospitals. Been here much?"

"A few times. Paul, my brother, is very accident prone."

"Oh?"

Emma smiled. "Always falling off something; a bike, a wall, a pavement."

Sam laughed. "How do you fall off a pavement?"

"Easily. Ask Paul. He's just one of these people that if something's going to happen, it'll happen to him, which hopefully means that it's less likely to happen to me, for which I'm not complaining."

"Yeah, I've got a friend like that." Sam thought of Mark. "Almost every time I see him, he's got some part of his anatomy plastered... and usually because he's injured himself on a night out... when plastered."

Emma laughed and Sam smiled. He was having such a lovely time that the chances of getting together with Libby were now looking remote. Quality time was what life was all about and, although the brief time he'd spent with Libby was lovely, there had been something missing.

Emma was glad that Sam seemed happy. Their previous encounters hadn't exactly gone to plan and although a hospital wouldn't have been her choice of locations, she was having a good time. She felt guilty about Libby but they'd both agreed to play it by ear and see what happened, like boy racers promising to stick to the speed limit when going different routes with the same finish line. Emma laughed.

"Something tickling you, Emma?"

"Sorry? No, it's okay. We're here."

Mrs Ellison looked pale but in generally good spirits. Judging by the amount of flowers and fruit she'd received, she'd had a stream of visitors and that pleased Sam. Emma took out a small box of chocolates from her bag which made Sam both feel guilty at not having brought anything but also proud of Emma for being so thoughtful.

"Hello, you two." The little woman's voice was almost squeaking. "My throat's dry, would you mind?" she said, pointing to a plastic jug of water and glass.

Sam was nearest so duly obliged leaving Emma to ask the questions regarding Mrs Ellison's health. Mrs Ellison explained that she'd not broken anything and was due to have final tests the following day, with a view to being released on Tuesday.

"That's great news," Sam said less than half-heartedly as he wasn't in a hurry to give Hamish back.

"And how's my boy? Has he been good for you, Sam?"

"Oh yes. He's been a little angel."

"Are you sure? He can get up to mischief but he may be on his best behaviour for you. He knows I'd be too soft on him."

"We've been on some lovely walks; up the park, into the fields next door. He's been having a great time."

"And have you had enough food for him?"

"Oh, yes. Don't worry about anything. It's all taken care of. He can stay with me as long as he likes. If you don't feel up to having him back when you get home, if you don't feel well enough…"

"Thank you, Sam. You're so kind. I'm feeling much better, a little weak but that's to be expected they say."

"If you want me to take him for walks when he's back with you, you only have to ask."

"Thank you, my dear. And you two, are you courting?"

Sam blushed and Emma laughed, a little too heartily for Sam's liking. Was it an idea that she found absurd? He'd thought she was warming to him.

"Mrs Ellison…" Emma leaned in and whispered just loud enough for Sam to hear. "Watch this space."

The three of them chatted about the goings on around the close and Singleton Parade, and colour seemed to appear in Mrs Ellison's cheeks.

A little while later, a nurse approached the bed and told them visiting hours finished at three so had a few minutes but they were welcome to return again from six.

Emma thanked the nurse then turned to Mrs Ellison. "I have to go anyway."

"Thank you, you two for coming. It's been so lovely to see someone."

Emma and Sam looked at the mass of flowers and fruit on the bedside cabinet, then at each other and smiled.

The drive home was quiet. It was not as if they'd run out of conversation but were so comfortable in each other's company that it didn't matter if they didn't speak. Emma looked over at Sam who was concentrating on turning right on the A43, smiled then looked back at the road.

Moments later, with a straight stretch ahead, Sam looked at Emma and smiled, before turning forwards again.

"About Hamish, I know what you said to Mrs Ellison but how is he really?"

"Good actually. I'd expected him to be missing her but he's settled in quickly. It seems that providing he's warm, made a fuss off, fed and walked he doesn't seem too bothered."

"That's good."

"A worry off her mind, hey. She looked well, didn't she?"

"I suppose with older people they have to be more careful."

"I've reassured her that everything's fine. Hamish is happy. I've checked on the house a couple of times, made sure she'd not left anything on, the windows are all shut and so on."

"That's good of you, you know. Not many guys I know would do that for a neighbour, especially one they hardly know."

"It's been a pleasure. Not for her, but it's been lovely having a dog around again." Sam then told Emma of the border collies he'd had as a child and before long, they were approaching Kemsley. "Did you want to go home first or shall I drop you off at the shop?"

"The shop will be fine, thanks. No time to go home anyway."

"And I'd better get back to Hamish. Take him out for a walk before it gets dark."

"Thanks for taking me, Sam."

"You're welcome. It's been lovely."

"Yes, lovely." Emma planted a kiss on Sam's left cheek and got out of the car.

Sam held his cheek for a moment, smiled, and drove off in the direction of home.

ooOoo

Chapter 45 – Things Change

Emma was running late and skipped breakfast, figuring she could get something from the Co-op for brunch. She hoped Tom wouldn't be too mad that she was a few minutes late so was surprised when she arrived at Singleton Parade just after eleven and the shop was still closed. She always had her shop keys with her as Tom sometimes left early at night and asked her to lock up. She got ready for the first customer of the day thinking that Tom was running late. It was over an hour later that she noticed the answerphone's light flashing. She pressed the play button.

"Hi, Emma. It's Tom."

Silence. Emma lowered her head and raised her eyebrows in anticipation of Tom's next move.

"Listen… I'm sorry about this but I've had to leave. It's been great working with you. You're like a daughter to me. And my leaving is not due to anything you've done. I'm needed back in Italy and it can't wait. It's family, you know."

Emma did know. If there was one thing that Emma was all too familiar with it was how important family was. Since her father had disappeared – she still refused to think he'd died – her family had pulled together and didn't take anything for granted.

"Shit!" There was no time for Emma to do much about it now, it was approaching the lunchtime rush and she'd just have to cope. All she could do was call in Kevin and crack the whip when he sat around doing nothing. For the time being at least, she was in charge. She rang Kevin's mobile, which eventually went through to voicemail and she left a message asking if he was free. Knowing how often he ran out of credit she wouldn't hold her breath to get a return call as he'd probably turn up when he felt like it. They only paid him by the hour so he was very much a free spirit, although for the amount of work he actually did, he was hardly free. Still, it would give Emma the chance to get a sandwich or go to the loo. Maybe if she explained what had happened when he got there, he'd pull his finger out. More chance of pigs flying but she lived in hope.

The phone call to head office wouldn't be much fun. Emma would have to convince them that she and Kevin could cope, and would then have to prove it if she had any chance of becoming manager. If they sent someone to help out, it would no doubt be a Relief Manager who would take over then be replaced by a permanent one. She couldn't leave it too long before she phoned them either in case Tom had already contacted them. She hoped that they didn't send the guy from last time, that tall young chap with the wandering hands. Alex, Adrian… whatever his name was.

She was deep in thought when she heard a knock at the counter. Mr Rogers was back with a couple of cases in his hands. Emma walked though to the shop and exchanged pleasantries with the man, swiping the cases through the system and bidding him a pleasant evening. Candy, Sasha and Desiree keeping him company would no doubt help. Emma smiled and exited Mr Rogers' record.

The door flew open and in walked Kevin.

"Hiya!" he beamed. "So he's done a bunk then, has he? Never liked him anyway. What do you want me to do, boss?"

Emma smiled. Perhaps they would get on just fine.

Sam was about to walk down the stairs of his house when he heard the post-box. He looked at his watch. Eight o'clock. Too early for George, surely?

Pushing on his slippers (after checking they were empty), he unlocked the front door then the post-box. Just one white A5 envelope. With no stamp. Sam looked around but there was no sign of life.

And it just read 'Josh'. Maybe from Libby then but she hadn't known his address, unless Emma had given it to her from Prime Time records but there was Data Protection. As if that mattered given how he'd treated them.

Oh, just open the thing.

Sam unsealed the back flap and pulled out a single sheet of white paper. The header read THP Services, PO Box 3659 Milton Keynes MK9 1BE. Sam read the main content out loud as he walked into the kitchen to fill up the kettle. He'd need a strong cuppa for this.

'Dear Sam. Congratulations on the success of your first project. You have exceeded our expectations and we are now delighted to welcome you on board as a member of our team. Please find enclosed your initial remuneration which will increase in line with your experience with THP Services.'

Sam looked in the envelope and sure enough, there was a cheque folded in half. He pulled it out and slowly opened it, hoping for at least a couple of zeros at the end. He thumped into one of the kitchen chairs as he looked at the figure: 10,000. Ten grand, and that was just a start?

He read on.

'We shall call on you as and when we need you. The enclosed cheque should enable you to live comfortably until future projects are required to be fulfilled. In the meantime, continue to liaise with Adam Warner who will be your staff partner and answer any questions you may have. You will find his phone number at the bottom of this letter, He has yours and will be in touch with your next set of instructions.'

"Shit. So you're in on it, Adam. That's why you were at the pub and in the gents at nine. Clever… unless it was the guy with the cough…"

The final paragraph read: *As you would expect from your first project, your bullets were blanks, and Mr Fellini was disposed of by one of our more experienced agents. There will be reports of Mr Fellini's demise in the newspapers but there will be no connection to yourself so you will not be contacted by the police. You can continue your life as before.*

As if I could, Sam thought. But then he was surprised how calm he felt. Something at the back of his mind had told him all along that this was all a test and that he'd not received enough training for it to be a serious hit.

Sam looked at the header address again. So, THP Services were local. After making the cup of tea and feeding Hamish, Sam went back upstairs and powered up his computer.

Typing the postcode MK9 1BE into Google's search bar brought up a map showing the train station and the area to its

355

right. Scrolling down the page revealed that the postcode belonged to the Bus Station next door.

PO Box number. Do they have post office boxes at stations? Maybe THP was an employee. Sam stared at the cheque. "They have a Barclays account so the bank must think they're legit." He'd have fun paying that in. He wasn't sure how he'd explain it to the taxman but he could call it a family loan until he figured something else out. He'd not have to pay tax on it, or even declare it, if it was from family.

ooOoo

Chapter 46 – The Pieces Fit

Emma picked up one of the newspapers from the rack just inside the Co-op's front door. She read the main headlines of yet another story about gun crime. A familiar voice made her turn round.

"Terrible, isn't it. Never thought something like that would happen near here," Sam said with feigned sincerity, knowing the story to be a lie.

"Hi, Sam." Emma beamed. "It's great actually."

"Eh? Really?"

"He did the world a favour, especially me."

"He? You knew this guy?" Sam coughed. "Whoever it was who did this."

"No. But there's more to it."

Sam tilted his head. "Go on."

"I can't say too much because the police have told me not to. This guy who got shot, Fellini, had been keeping a hostage at the farmhouse."

"A hostage? Who?"

Emma leaned forward and whispered. "My dad."

Sam screwed up his face and whispered back, "What? But I thought your dad had died or left. I didn't know either way but you never mentioned him. So I assumed…"

Emma leaned back. "We'd been told he'd died, 'though we didn't believe it. Just over ten years ago in Toronto. He was supposed to be there on business… well, New York… but turns out he was involved in something he couldn't get out of."

"So he'd been in that house for all that time? No way!"

"Yes, way. I think so anyway. He's not said much yet. I don't think he knows exactly what happened. They got him over here somehow. Whoever it was that bumped off that Italian guy saved my family. My mum can sleep properly, when she recovers from the shock and excitement – she's like a schoolgirl… Emma grinned "…and Paul and I get our dad back. We obviously have a long way to go but at least he's alive and the hospital says that he can come home in a week or so."

Sam gave her a quick hug and was pleased Emma didn't resist. "Wow, that's great."

"It is. He could come and work with me here. It's not too demanding."

"What about your boss… Tom, is it?"

"Done a bunk… as Kevin so eloquently put it. Left a message on the answerphone this morning. Something about having to go back to Italy."

Sam hesitated. "Italy. Why Italy?"

"Turns out that's where he's from. His full name is Tommaso Pallini, a traditional Sicilian name apparently. I've had to call in our assistant – that's the Kevin – who is as useless as raw spaghetti but at least it gives me a break."

Sam smiled wanly. Tommaso Pallini. TP. THP? It was probably a coincidence but there were too many Italian connections for his liking and that name sounded familiar. "So what happened to your father in the intervening years, do you know?"

Emma shook her head. "The thing that gets to him is that he lived so near, not knowing how we were. They–"

"They? There were others involved?"

"Had to be, don't you think? They didn't let him watch TV or read a paper so he didn't have a clue where he was or even what year it was. It's so cruel."

"I'm not a religious man but thank God he's okay. I would imagine the not knowing must be… have been the worst thing."

"It **was** horrible. Bad enough for me but obviously far worse for Mum. She's always said she knew he was alive and tried to be as normal as she could for us but all the time expecting him to walk through the door any minute. Imagine that going through your head for so long."

"That's amazing. You do hear of people turning up years later, with amnesia, but… How could anyone have treated him like that? Worse than animals."

"We'll never know and I'm glad that guy Fellini is dead. I wouldn't want to think of him in a cushy cell while he treated my dad worse."

Sam knew what she meant. "Will he be alright, do you think, your dad? Will he recover fully?"

"The doctors say he needs plenty of fluids and rest. Just lots of tlc, which he'll get of course. I can't wait…"

"If there's anything I can do."

"Thank you. That's kind." Emma smiled and Sam thought his heart was going to burst. "He's sleeping a lot but we'll be visiting tonight."

"Would you like me to–?"

Emma shook her head. "Thanks though."

"Just let me know."

"Will do. I'd better get off. Left boy-wonder in charge at work so there's probably a riot broken out by now."

As Emma walked towards the Co-ops tills with the paper folded in two, Sam laughed at an image of her shop full of medieval warriors.

When he got home, Sam did a Google search on Tommaso Pallini which didn't show much but there was a fair amount on the Pallini name. Sicilian, with strong Mafia connections. Many suspected cases but none proven. Too much corruption and payoffs, Sam guessed.

If nothing else, it would make a good story for a novel. A quick search for tips on the internet showed a novel-in-a-month project NaNoWriMo starting the following Saturday so Sam opened up a Word document and made some notes. The THP 'project' details he'd already made would save him some work. He could do as much preparation as he liked, the NaNo site said, he just couldn't start the novel until November first.

Clicking on the iTunes play button, Sam laughed as Lulu's 'Man with the Golden Gun' started up then he laughed again as Hamish tilted his head to one side.

ooOoo

Chapter 47 – The Love Triangle

Sam was just settling down to a Weight Watchers beef hotpot that evening when the doorbell rang. "Oh, hi. Libby… Becky? How do you two…?" Sam pointed his right index finger side-to-side between the two girls.

"Hi, Sam. Becky's my little sister. How do **you** know each other?"

"We met the other day at the park. I was walking Hamish for Mrs Ellison." Sam looked down. "Hello, Heather. How are you?" The furious wagging of the dog's tail answered his question.

"She's good," Becky answered.

"Sorry. Do come in." Sam shut the front door behind him.

"So how come Becky was walking around the park near here. I thought, when you said you were in Kemsley visiting Emma, that you lived elsewhere?"

"I do, but Becky and my parents live here, overlooking the park actually. Which is why Heather always looks a mess. If she gets out of the front gate, she runs into the fields behind the park, terrorising the cows. She's a devil in disguise, and a devil to keep clean, as you can imagine."

Heather, at this point, looked innocent and Sam couldn't help but laugh at her.

"A devil in angel's clothing, aren't you, Heather? And how are you?" Sam asked Libby.

"I'm a bit pissed off actually," Libby replied. "Adam's done a runner and I'm going to have to postpone all his appointments for this week, including yours."

Tom now Adam? "I don't mind about the lesson, it can wait. Where's Adam gone, do you know?"

"Haven't a clue. Didn't mention anything to anyone. The boss is furious. Adam was a good worker. Knew his stuff."

"How strange. Had he worked there long?"

"No. Only a few weeks. I guess he wasn't settling in, but he could have said goodbye and given some kind of notice. Didn't think he was the spineless type."

Sam frowned. "No, me neither." He then looked more cheerful. "It's kind of you to pop and tell me."

"We did come to tell you about that, but it's Mrs Ellison we're here about." Becky said, looking at Libby as if she had been putting off the subject.

"She's due out of hospital tomorrow, isn't she?" Sam asked.

"'fraid not," Libby continued. "I have some bad news, Sam. Mrs Ellison, she… died last night."

"No! What happened?"

"Heart attack apparently. Just before she was due to have her pre-release check-up. We were supposed to bring her… home."

Sam gulped. "Poor Mrs Ellison. Does she have family?" Sam looked at the dog who had been sniffing Heather's nose as if they were Eskimos. "What about Hamish?"

"I don't think there's anyone. Could you look after him until we know for sure? I think she'd rather you had him anyway."

"Happy to. As long as you like."

"Thanks, Sam. We'd better go. Busy day at work tomorrow. See you soon. When we get a replacement trainer, I suppose."

"Sure."

Sam watched the two women leave then turned back to his house. Unlike watching Emma return to the Co-op just a few hours earlier, Sam's heart didn't skip, didn't yearn, as he thought of Libby.

Then reality dawned on him.

ooOoo

362

Chapter 48 – THP

Sam felt as if he'd been the one shot as he shut the front door.

He sat at the kitchen table for a moment trying to make sense of it all then ran upstairs to get the note from THP Services that had arrived that morning. Ringing the number on it, he wasn't surprised that the line was dead… and the cheque? A dud, no doubt.

"Shit!" He remembered where he'd heard the name Pallini from. He pulled out a box file marked 'House' and dug back through all the paperwork. Near the bottom of the box was a copy of the contract he and the sellers had signed. He looked at the names:

Vendor(s): Tommaso Pallini and Cassandra Pallini of 90 Spinners Lane, Kemsley, Northants NN30 4ZG

Buyer(s): Samuel Simpson of 14 Beckett Park, Market Harborough, Leicestershire LE16 9ZA and Michelle Everett of 29 Queen Street, Aylesbury, Buckinghamshire HP21 9LB

Sam put the Pallini's postcode in the Google maps search and it came back unknown. He went on to the Royal Mail website and into their postcode finder section which showed that Spinners Lane only consisted of just over forty houses.

Sam hadn't thought much of it at the time, that they'd had a different address to the one they were selling. He'd assumed they'd also owned 5 Greath Close. Sam felt sick. What if… No. It was his. It was legal. Everything would be fine. They'd been selling it for someone else, a sibling or child. Tom must have still had keys and been in the house, turning up the heating and messing about with the computer.

"Oh, shit!" Sam said as he slumped down onto his chair, just as the police car pulled outside.

In the meantime, in the skies above Kent, an Air Italia flight was destined for Rome. Its passengers were moving around as the seatbelt sign had been switched off. Two passengers in First Class seats 8A and 8B were chatting.

"Sandra, as you're nearest, would you be a dear and get my book out of my holdall?"

"Si, mi amo Tomi, no c'è problema," she said then winced at her leg, still giving her trouble.

Cassandra Pallini unzipped the holdall, retrieved the signed hardback first edition of Fredrick Forsyth's 'The Day of the Jackal' and handed it to her husband.

Tom stared out the small window to the land below and said 'goodbye' to England. The only thing he'd miss was Emma, and her mum to a certain extent. Their fling all those years earlier had been fun and she'd been special to him at the time, but then she'd married Alan and that had been that.

Yes, the only thing he'd miss about England was Emma Isabella Dale.

Sandra closed the zip on the small black case and pushed it back into the overhead luggage compartment, with its handle pointing outwards, the handle situated just above three metal initials; the initials which read 'THP'.

THE END

About the Author

Morgen Bailey is a writing-related blogger who spotlights authors, agents, editors and publishers. Other content includes guest posts, flash fiction, poetry, and short story and writing guide reviews.

She is also a freelance editor and offers a free 1,000-word sample edit to all new enquirers.

She runs a free monthly 100-word competition and has been a judge for various competitions including the annual H.E. Bates Short Story Competition (2015), NLG Flash Fiction Competition (2013-4), RONE (2015), and BBC Radio 2 500-word Competition (2016).

The author of numerous short stories, novels, articles, she has also dabbled with poetry.

Morgen teaches creative writing across Northamptonshire (and beyond), belongs to three local writing groups, is a charity shop volunteer, a regular cinema visitor, reads (though not as often as she'd like), and in between she writes.

Everything she's involved in is detailed on her blog http://morgenbailey.wordpress.com. She can also be found chatting away about all things literary on Twitter, Facebook, LinkedIn and Tumblr.

To contact her you can also complete her website's 'Contact me' page or email her at morgen@morgenbailey.com.

Discover other titles by Morgen Bailey at
https://morgenbailey.wordpress.com/books-mine.

Cover photographs courtesy of pixabay.com.
Cover design, internal layout etc.
by Morgen Bailey.

Note from the Author

Thank you for purchasing
'After Jessica & Hitman Sam'.

I'd like to take this opportunity to also thank my writing
friends – especially Joy (and other Northants Authors
members), Tony, Jane, and Pat – for their ongoing
support, and my fabulous beta readers: Deborah, Denise,
Irene (who thought Sam should be played by Simon
Pegg!), Janet, Judy, Neil, Paul, Sarah, Sophie, and
William.

I welcome feedback (and am always grateful for honest
reviews) and you can either find me on social media as
morgenwriteruk and / or via email:
morgen@morgenbailey.com.